# GASPAR BROWN

## ADVENTURE 1

# MORE GASPAR BROWN ADVENTURES

*by*

# HUTTON WILKINSON

# GASPAR BROWN

## AND THE

## MYSTERY OF THE

## GASPARILLA SUCCESSION

### ADVENTURE 1

# HUTTON WILKINSON

Book design by Sue Campbell Book Design

ISBN 13: 978-1-7325653-2-6

*For my sidekick*
*Kevin Greer*

# CONTENTS

# AUGUST 15, 1793

El capitan, José Gaspar stood at the bow of a longboat bearing eight blindfolded young freebooters as it cut through the warm waters of the Gulf of Mexico. They were rowing him away from a mighty 2,500-ton galleon, with three, 24-foot wide decks and a battalion of 100 long-range cannons. *Floridablanca* was El Capitan's pride and joy, the most famous and feared ship of the Spanish Main.

The fabled flagship had been the glory of the Spanish fleet, before José Gaspar and his hearty crew so proudly "liberated" her from the Spanish crown. It was only ten years ago, that he and his cut-throat crew, had stolen *Floridablanca*, boldly sailing her from the Port of Seville, down the Rio Guadalquivir and across the Atlantic, to their hideout in the West Indies.

Stealing such a magnificent prize right out from under the nose of the king's naval minister had been the most audacious act of El Capitan, José Gaspar's entire Pirate career. Now *Floridablanca*, under his iron rule, was wreaking less than *noble* havoc against Mother Spain, looting her treasure ships and disrupting the worlds international commerce from Tierra del Fuego to St. Augustine. José Gaspar, who the world had nicknamed *Gasparilla*, was proud that he had never missed an opportunity to take a rich prize, having sacked every passing ship he'd come across.

As the longboat and its scurvy crew rounded the spit of land, which separated the cove that they were entering from the bay where their galleon lay at anchor, El Capitan watched the soft lantern lights of his cherished ship slowly disappear. The rowboat's progress was lighted by a full moon, set high in the cloudless sky. The expedition tonight would be a short one, for on this night an unusually dramatic tide had rolled back the sea, three hundred yards from the sandy-white shore, leaving its glimmering floor bare. El Capitan had anticipated the super tide as he had made this same journey many times over the years.

Finally running out of ocean, the long boat hit bottom allowing him to remove the blindfolds from his men's eyes. Instantly four of the swarthy crew jumped into the shallows and pulled the heavily-laden boat onto what only minutes before had been the ocean floor.

Gasparilla walked briskly between the four remaining *freebooters* and jumped out onto the former sea bed. Four torches had been lighted and stuck into the soft sand close by the grounded boat's bow. Without hesitation El Capitan grabbed all four of the torches in his massive fists and walked straight ahead into what had been a deep inlet, before the low tide had completely drained it.

The eight mates silently unloaded the small craft. Soon, twenty-four *nailed-leather chests* were piled onto the wet sand and one-by-one, in teams of two, the men began sloshing them up into the inlet where a formerly submerged cavern, awaited. The low, narrow opening to the secret cave was only three hundred feet up from where the pink sand beach normally met the shore. El Capitan easily rolled away the large flat stone that covered the cave's entrance and placed one of the torches inside. Now the mouth of the cave glowed yellow its damp walls glistening in the torch light. Following their leader, the men duck-crawled with bent legs and stooped backs while hauling the heavy chests through the low opening into the cavern. Inside, steps had been carved into the coral rock by an ancient people, and these steps led up to a large, naturally domed vault, now lighted by the three remaining torches, which El Capitan carried there. Although the air in the upper grotto was close, the area itself was as dry as a bone. This was the mother lode, where El Capitan had previously placed over several years and many occasions nine stacks of trunks piled high against the rough coral-stone walls. Each of these trunks was elaborately marked with initials, crests, roman numerals and various heraldic devices. These distinctly individual markings clearly designated each pile as the personal property of various people of means.

As the crew brought up the treasure, El Capitan pointed to which existing group each of the newly delivered trunks belonged, so that they could be stacked together accordingly. The work was completed without a word. Even with the presence of the rough men and all their physical exertion the space was as silent as *Davy Jones Locker*, and El Capitan knew that after the tide rolled back in, the booty would once again be safely under the protection of Davy's firm grip.

# AUGUST 15, 1900

Eighteen-year-old Carlos Munoz-Flores y Gaspar guided his forty-foot sloop, *Santa Catalina*, into the protected cove of a tropical isle, off the southern coast of Florida. Now, within reach of his goal, he was confident that fortune would soon present itself.

Carlos' only crew, Moises—a servant and companion of his same age—lowered the sails and dropped anchor at his instruction. Moises had been sent along by Dr. Mendoza y Mendoza, Carlos' patron and protector, to help him and keep him company during the long journey. Together the two young sailors rowed ashore through the still waters of the protected cove, using the small dinghy which had trailed abaft the sloop these past weeks. Although Carlos loved the sea, it had been a grueling effort to sail from the Yucatan to this remote and seemingly forgotten stretch of Florida coastline. Reaching shore, the two adventurers made camp by an inlet before going in search of fresh water and local fruits.

Carlos Munoz-Flores y Gaspar knew that *this was the place*. Over the past three years, he had studied Dr. Mendoza y Mendoza's maps and journals, and all the pirate lore in his patrons extraordinary nautical-library. The eighteen year old was certain his research would prove accurate.

Arriving on this island, Carlos knew that if Gasparilla's treasure did exist, he would surely find it *here*. He also knew that tonight the moon would be full and the tide just right for discovery.

"Why are we here, Señor?" asked the servant, as he lighted the campfire.

"To search for pirate treasure," young Carlos announced enthusiastically. No sooner had the words left his mouth did he wonder if he'd said too much.

"You mean, *money, gold, jewels*?" Moises eyes flashed greedily in the fading light of sunset.

Carlos and Moises had grown close over their journey and his secret had just slipped out. Now Carlos wished that he had kept his mouth shut. *It couldn't hurt to tell him, could it?* he asked himself innocently.

"I don't know how much you know about my history Moises," Carlos back peddled. "Maybe your father told you about me?"

"I have heard many stories about you from many people. In the village they call you, 'The Little Fish Saved from the Sea,' but I would like to hear your story in your own words." Moises sat back in the sand to listen.

"I was a thirteen-year-old orphan, living in Galveston, Texas when I escaped from my Aunt's home in search of adventure, leaving my younger brother behind. He was the favorite and my aunt loved him like a son, I on the other hand was always a thorn in her side." Carlos chuckled. "I sneaked onto a tramp steamer, the *Santa Margarita*, heading from Galveston for the Caribbean. Galveston is an important American port," Carlos explained.

"I would like to see Galveston someday, *Señor*," Moises replied enthusiastically .

"It wasn't long before I was discovered," Carlos admitted. "I begged Captain Suarez to make me his *cabin boy deluxe*, rather than put me off at the next port. He reluctantly agreed, so I made myself indispensable. Captain Suarez is the one who taught me everything I know about ships and the sea.

"You are a very good sailor Señor," Moises complimented his boss.

"I was fifteen-years-old when the first officer foundered the *Santa Margarita* off the coast of Mexico and sank it. I survived by floating away in a giant cooking pot that I'd grabbed from the galley. I was about ninety pounds back then—just a sardine of a kid and I have no idea how many days I was adrift. I was discovered unconscious on Yucatan's tropical shore. When I awoke, I thought I had died and gone to heaven. The village of Celestún, was nearby and Doctor Mendoza y Mendoza took me in and nursed me back to health. He treated me just like a son, but you probably know that."

"My Father told me how sick you were when he found you washed up on the beach and how he brought you to the doctor's house." Moises recounted. "We all know about the copper cauldron in the courtyard at the hacienda. All of the workers call it 'The Liferaft'."

"Well, in case you don't know it, Dr. Mendoza y Mendoza is not only a medical doctor, he is also a scholar of folklore," Carlos went on. "It was he who told me many fantastic tales of treasure and sunken ships. His library is filled with old documents about the Spanish Main, and pirates in particular, many of which I've studied over and over." Carlos leaned in close to his companion. "Moises, if we're lucky and I've done my research correctly, you and I are about to discover the treasure of The Pirate King, José Gaspar, also known as *Gasparilla*. Most historians think the lore of Gasparilla is just that, a legend, but I believe otherwise. I am convinced that his treasure is right here, on this island!"

"We're going to find *pirate treasure*? Here, on this God-forsaken shore?" Moises looked around the deserted beach incredulously.

"Find it and take it back to Doctor Mendoza y Mendoza!" Carlos declared without hesitation.

"Why are you so sure the treasure is here?" Moises seemed to consider the possibility . "Hmm ... Gaspar ... that is *your* name Señor. Maybe this pirate is your relative?"

"Gaspar is a common Spanish name," Carlos said shaking his head. "Gasparilla was a pirate who lived in the 18th century. Not only did he amass a grand treasure, he did so mostly without firing a canon or even wielding a sword. That's not to say that Gasparilla didn't have his fill of skirmishes, his treasure ship was called *Floridablanca*, and it was the greatest ship ever seen in these waters. Although he won all of his battles aboard *Floridablanca*, his greatest wealth came from commerce. Gasparilla made an enormous fortune as a merchant. He sold the swords and grog and provisions to *all* the pirates from his home base on Sanibel Island which shouldn't be too far down the coast from here. Gasaparilla was also a treasure hunter and found the legendary treasures of other pirates, like Black Bart."

"Black Bart? Who was Black Bart?" Moises asked.

"An English pirate. His real name was Bartholomew Roberts. He captured 470 treasure ships and gained a fortune greater than any of his pirate peers. Gasparilla found Bart's treasure and hid it in his own secret lair," Carlos said. "He also found and re-hid the winnings of Samuel Bellamy—*Black Sam*."

"Was he the brother of Black Bart?" Moises asked.

"No," Carlos laughed. "But Black Sam captured at least fifty ships in his one year on the Spanish Main. Gasparilla also hid Black Sam's *loot* … It's got to be around here somewhere."

"If you say so, Señor" Moises was less convinced than ever.

"There are so many stories about this legendary pirate. They say Gasparilla couldn't refuse a challenge, which is what eventually led to his death."

"How did he die?" Moises asked.

"Well, legend has it that he was ready to retire and share his treasure with his mates. He assembled his crew on the beach, probably *this very beach*, and just as he was about to reveal the location of his secret hiding place, he spied a rich prize cruising off the horizon. It was a British merchantman, riding low in the water, a sure sign that it was carrying a lot of loot. Gasparilla couldn't resist one last heist, so he rallied his men back on board *Floridablanca* and attacked the ship. At that moment the merchantman lowered the Union Jack and replaced it with the flag of the United States of America. The ship was the *USS Enterprise*, disguised as a rich decoy to lure the pirate into its web. The ruse worked and *Floridablanca* was sunk with great loss of life.

"And El Capitan?" Moises asked, riveted, "What happened to him?"

"Gasparilla, it is said, wrapped the anchor chain around his body and declared that if he were to die, it would be by his own hand. He jumped into the deep and was never seen again."

"If this is true Señor, and this is the place, then *Floridablanca* must be out there." Moises said pointing to the inky horizon.

"Perhaps, just past the breakwater, I would imagine." Carlos said solemnly as his eyes scanned the sea. His gaze then crossed to the inlet's water, now glittering in the light of the full moon. His eyes widened as he noticed the water begin to pull quickly away. "Moises. Look. The tide!" The two young men leapt up and ran into the shallow bay, staring wide-eyed as the water all around them drained away, rolling far out into the Gulf. The super-tide exposed the shell strewn ocean floor for hundreds of feet in front of them. Then Carlos turned his attention back to the inlet and saw the opening to what had only minutes earlier been an underwater cave.

# CHAPTER 1

# THE PHONE CALL

T HIRTEEN-YEAR-OLD GASPAR BROWN RODE SHOTGUN IN HIS MOM'S NEW SUV AS THEY DROVE DOWN THE freeway with the stereo blasting. Elvira Brown's cell phone rang loudly over the car's Bluetooth system, cutting off the music, much to young Gaspar's annoyance.

Keeping her eyes on the racing traffic, heading north towards the San Fernando Valley, she swerved a bit while pushing the button to answer the call. Gaspar watched the road. He knew his mother had *never had* an accident, but he had a feeling that she'd *probably caused* several.

"Hello," his mother answered loudly and impatiently, speaking in the direction where she thought the microphone was, but where Gaspar knew it wasn't.

Gaspar saw an old red Buick Le Sabre cut left in front of them then swerve across traffic into the fast lane. "Whoa, Mom! Watch out!"

"Jerk!" Mom cried, braking to avoid a collision.

"What?" Boomed a mans voice over the loud speaker. The deep voice was tinged with a heavy southern-twang. "Is this Elvira Munoz-Flores?" Whoever was calling pronounced her name *El-vi-raw*.

"Not you," Gaspar's mom replied, "I didn't call you a jerk, and it's pronounced *El-ver-a*."

Gaspar noted the irritation in her voice.

"This is Peter Cawthorne calling. I'm an attorney, Ma'am, working on Perdido Isle, in Florida. I'm representing an estate comprised of unclaimed assets, in desperate need of an heir."

Elvira rolled her eyes and sighed loudly. "Very funny, what's the punch line."

Gaspar recognized his mother's most sarcastic tone. He could tell that this was going to be a good one and started counting the seconds until his mother hung up.

"I'm serious Ms. Munoz-Flores. It may be well worth your while to cooperate with me."

"Actually, it's Mrs. Brown, Mrs. Franklyn Brown. I'm a widow. Now, what's this all about?" She glanced at Gaspar, who just shrugged his shoulders.

Gaspar hated it when his mother referred to herself as a widow. Since his Dad died last year, he had yet to accept his loss, and although they rarely mentioned him between themselves, hearing his mom refer to his dad's death in any way, always caused him confusion more than sorrow. Since the accident, Gaspar had found nothing but trouble, but he couldn't tell his Mom about his problems, she had enough of her own lately. His big mistake had been getting involved with Jimmy Larsen, the neighbor kid who wanted him to help his pals pull a little caper. When Gaspar figured out it wasn't a practical joke but an actual robbery that they wanted him to participate in, he bowed out, but not without taking a beating from the older boys who promised to really mess him up if he ever squealed on them. He still had the scrapes and what was left of a black eye which he told his Mom he got by falling off his skateboard while performing a major trick off the playground steps. After the gang was arrested and sent to Juvi, Gaspar feared that someday they'd come after him, thinking that he'd tipped off the cops, but that wasn't the case. These fears of retribution from the older boys or their friends, who he'd had nothing to do with, always caused him to break out in a cold sweat. It was times like these when Gaspar missed his dad the most. They had been great friends and he certainly had never held back any secrets from his father. Gaspar prayed his dad's accident wasn't caused because of something he'd done wrong.

"Are you the daughter of Joséph and Anna Calhoun Munoz-Flores?" The caller started a barage of questions.

"Yes."

"Was your father Joséph, the son of Felipe and Argent Munoz-Flores?"

"Yes, but my parents dropped the fancy-hyphenated last name years ago," Elvira replied. "Too pretentious."

"Well, if you are who I think you are, yours is a very distinguished family indeed. Was your grandfather, Felipe, the son of José Luis and Elisa Calhoun Munoz-Flores and your great-grandfather José Luis, the son of Carlos Rudolfo and Elvira Munoz-Flores?"

"Let's not get crazy now Mr. Cawthorne. What could any of this have to do with my great-great grandparents. For heaven's sake, they were alive when Napoleon was on the throne!" Gaspar's mom shouted in the direction of the mysterious phantom microphone.

"Did you know that your great-great-grandfather Carlos Rudolfo owned 500,000 acres in Mexico?"

Gaspar perked up, giving his mother a nudge from the passenger seat.

"Well I hope its part of Texas, or California now," Elvira responded, "but with my luck it's probably in Tijuana," Elvira said, in a tone of voice mixing hope with sarcasm.

*Enough of that Mom, time to get all the information you can.* Gaspar spoke to her via mental telepathy, a form of communication between them, which only he believed in.

"In case you're not aware of it, Mrs. Brown, your family name is actually Munoz-Flores y Gaspar. But it was changed in the mid-19th century to Munoz-Flores and now it's just Munoz.

"Yes, I know all about that." Elvira shot back. "So what kind of an inheritance could this possibly be—a pair of candlesticks? If it's 500,000 acres in Mexico, who's been paying the taxes on it all these years?"

"Did your father ever speak of his Uncle Carlos, also known before his death in 1967 as Charles and more often as Charlie, who had an adopted daughter named Eugenia Floride?"

"Never heard of them," Elvira replied.

"He was a sort of eccentric black sheep. You're *sure* you've never heard of him?"

Gaspar was all ears. Could it be possible that he actually *did* have relatives other than his Mother? And better than that, *rich* relatives? *This is getting good*, he thought.

"I'm quite sure, and I think if my father were alive, he'd be *angry* to learn that he had an uncle out there, and a cousin too," Elvira replied. "My father told me that his father, had been raised by a Great Aunt in Galveston, Texas. Her name was Aunt Henny Calhoun. My mother Anna Calhoun was my father's second cousin, twice removed."

"Yes. Henny was your great-grandmother—Elisa Calhoun Munoz-Flores' sister."

"So what do you really want from me Mr. Cawthorne?" Elvira asked pointedly.

"I want you to believe me, Mrs. Brown. This is not a hoax."

"So what are we talking about, a hundred-million dollars?" Elvira asked facetiously.

"We are talking about an estate in excess of a hundred-million dollars … " the lawyer wasn't playing around and allowed a dramatic pause as envisioned Elvira driving off the road.

"*In excess of one hundred-million dollars?*" Elvira yelped, catching her breath and regaining control of the vehicle while her son pulled his seat belt tighter.

"That's correct Mrs. Brown," the lawyer knew he had her full attention now. "We're talking about a 500,000 acre island off the coast of Florida,Perdido Isle, of which 100,000 acres are divided into ninety-nine year land leases. These leases will be coming due in just a few years. There are also several bank accounts, and a portfolio of blue-chip stocks and bonds valued at around a billion dollars. There is also a house, several houses in fact, and valuable furnishings and other items of personal family interest which I think you might like."

"What's the catch?" Elvira asked suspiciously.

"You are very discerning, Mrs. Brown. In fact there is a catch, a very important one. If I can't locate a legitimate heir or if that heir doesn't agree to accept the inheritance and live in the house for at least ten years after transfer of title, everything will go to the Perdido Isle Historical Society Museum. That was the stipulation in your great uncle's trust and that, I can assure you, is what will happen if you don't cooperate with me," the lawyer finished coldly.

"So how much is all this going to cost me?" Elvira asked point blank.

"Not a dime, Mrs. Brown. My father was Carlos Rudolfo Munoz-Flores y Gaspar's lawyer, and I succeeded him as your cousin, Eugenia Floride's, lawyer. My job is to make sure that this inheritance stays in the family, if there is a family. All I need from you are the names of your siblings, uncles and aunts, cousins, and anyone else who might be a direct descendant of Don Carlos Rudolfo and Elvira Munoz-Flores y Gaspar."

"That's easy, Mr. Cawthorne," Elvira's voice trembled as her heart pounded in her throat. "It's only me and my son Gaspar," she said sticking out her tongue and making a face at the wide-eyed kid sitting next to her, who to his credit, did the same right back at her. "I have no brothers, no sisters, no uncles or aunts, or cousins that I have ever heard of."

"Very well Mrs. Brown. Please give me your mailing address and contact information so that I can inform you in writing after I look into all of this a little further.

Gaspar listened while his mother gave the lawyer the information he requested.

"Thank you Mrs. Brown. I look forward to speaking with you further after I cross-reference what you've told me," the lawyer informed her before saying, "Goodbye."

After the phone clicked off, the radio resumed blaring. "That was weird," Gaspar's mom murmured focusing her full attention on the traffic as she sped the car forward.

"Tell me about it." Gaspar responded while staring blankly out the passenger window watching the heavy traffic. *Was all of this for real?* he wondered. That's when he noticed a white haired man with rosy cheeks and piercing blue eyes gazing up at him from a vintage 1926 Rolls Royce Silver Ghost convertible. The man was wearing a fringed buckskin coat and had a white scarf tied in a bow at his throat. *A country western Santa Claus,* Gaspar thought, giving the old dandy a little wave.

The flamboyant driver smiled and gave a friendly nod to Gaspar while controlling the car with one fringe-gloved hand. The old boy then accelerated his shiny white tank with its white-wall tires, and red painted spokes, pulling forward with the traffic.

A moment later Gaspar realized that they'd missed their off ramp. "Mom, Sherman Way is *way* back there!"

"Oh!" Elvira quickly accelerated to cut through several lanes of traffic to make the next off ramp.

Gaspar looked over his shoulder to make sure the coast was clear and noticed that the old red Buick Le Sabre that had cut them off earlier had fallen behind them and was slicing in and out of lanes. His eyes widened when the Le Sabre cut off a kid in an old Volkswagen Beetle, causing the teenager to spin out of control. Gaspar held his breath for the kid in the Beetle as his mother maneuvered safely off the freeway.

He didn't see that the Buick had followed them off the freeway and right back on again in the opposite direction. The Browns took the Sherman Way exit, then turned right, merging into the flowing street traffic. That's when the red Le Sabre, which had been following them from the next lane, swerved toward them, missing them by inches.

"What's that guy doing?!" Gaspar shouted staring out the passenger's side window as the old red car swerved close again. "Mom!"

"He's trying to run us off the road!" Elvira screamed, "Hold on Gasp!"

The red Le Sabre successfully maneuvered Elvira over the double yellow line, into the oncoming traffic. She slammed on the brakes forcing the menacing Buick to race ahead of her. Reaching the intersection she turned sharply left, in a cacophony of honking horns and squealing tires, onto a side street, out of harm's way.

Gaspar watched over his shoulder as the red car sped down the street. He was surprised to see that the Le Sabre was being chased in hot pursuit by the white-haired Santa in the vintage Silver Ghost. *That's so weird,* Gaspar thought, *Is Santa trying to help us, or is he in cahoots with the guy in the Le Sabre?*

Elvira pulled the SUV to a stop by the curb, breathing heavily. "What was that all about?" she panted, looking back over her shoulder nervously.

"He did it on purpose Mom!" Gaspar blurted, "He tried to kill us!"

"Let's not get dramatic Gasp." Elvira said running a hand through her sandy blond hair, then smoothing out the front of her blouse. "Besides," she said looking into her son's bright blue eyes while mussing-up his curly black locks, "it was probably just an accident. We were just in the wrong place at the wrong time, no big deal."

"Mom he did it on purpose," Gaspar blurted again . "He tried to kill us!"

"No, no. He couldn't have, for what reason? It doesn't make sense." was all Elvira could come up with, as she gripped the steering wheel and started the car in the direction of home.

Gaspar wasn't so sure about that. *He was trying to run us off the road* … he thought, but he couldn't make heads or tails of it either. What he really wanted to know was who Santa with the apple-dumpling cheeks in the Rolls Royce Silver Ghost was and what was his part in all this? His worse fear was that these two crazies were part of the gang who thought he'd sent them up the river. He could kill himself for putting his mother in harm's way like this. He was so confused and nervous his stomach was tied in a knot. He didn't know what to do next or who he could tell.

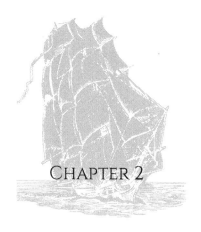

# CHAPTER 2

# A SECRET MEETING

GWENDOLYN CRUMP, PRESIDENT AND EXECUTIVE DIRECTOR OF THE PERDIDO ISLE HISTORICAL Society Museum, drove through Calaluna, the small working class town on Perdido Isle, late for her appointment. Maneuvering her Prius through the less than heavy traffic in town she turned left onto a two-lane road, which was soon flanked by tropical jungle. She was headed east toward the resort town of Llojeta, the only other development on the island. Approaching a pair of carved, coral-stone columns, holding enormous wrought iron gates, she slowed down and glanced to her right at the monumental entranceway.

Satisfied that the gates were chained and padlocked shut, Gwendolyn resumed her drive. A complacent smile crossed her face. She couldn't wait until those gates and the property behind them would be all hers. She smiled even wider at the prospect as she entered the only other town on the island, the resort town of Llojeta, and headed for the yacht basin just past the Grand Hotel Floride.

Gwenolyn walked down the pier to where a high-speed motor launch bobbed in the water. The black-hulled boat and its crew of three black-clad men had been awaiting her arrival. Gwendolyn boarded and took a seat without acknowledging the crews presence but let them know by her demeanor that she was impatient for them to cast off even though it was she who had been keeping them waiting. Once free of the dock the driver opened up the throttle, and skimmed the boat over the whitecaps toward s a big black yacht waiting at anchor just a few miles out. The name of the yacht was *Revenge*, and it had Yucatan registry. Pulling alongside its ominous black hull, the crew helped Gwendolyn disembark. Gingerly, she climbed the ships long exterior staircase. Once topside, she was immediately escorted below decks by another pair of waiting black-T-shirted crew. They led her deep into the belly of the ship where she knew her host, Unzega, the mysterious Yucatecan billionaire awaited.

Unzega—she'd never given the man's name much thought but suddenly she realized, if he had a last name, she didn't know it. Just Unzega, just Garbo, just Madonna, so chic, the silly woman smiled with satisfaction.

Reaching the companionway, she passed two foreign gentlemen being escorted in the opposite direction. The foreigners wore dark business suits and heavy-framed glasses and each man sported an expensive reptile-skin briefcase. The men were laughing and chatting excitedly in their native tongue as they passed her. So wrapped up were they in their sing-song conversation that neither of them even acknowledged her. Gwendolyn figured they were heading back to the deck where she had just come from. She hoped that her business meeting with Unzega would go equally well.

A door creaked ominously open at the end of the passageway and Gwendolyn was unceremoniously guided inside by her rough escorts. She spotted Unzega seated at a massive desk at the far end of the large cabin. He was gazing intently at a closed circuit television screen and like the foreigners in the hall, he too ignored her presence. Gwendolyn wasn't accustomed to such cavalier dismissal as she considered herself *a formidable personage*. Peeking at the TV screen Gwendolyn realized that Unzega was watching the foreigners being escorted top-side. The businessmen were now on deck being hustled by four of his swarthy crew. She watched in horror as the two hapless men cried out while the T-shirted thugs shoved them rudely against the ship's rail. Speechless, she placed her gloved hand over her mouth. Gwendolyn gasped inaudibly as she saw the two victims squirm and kick to get loose. "No! Please!" she heard one shout with a high pitched accent as the cutthroat crew wrapped and padlocked both men together using heavy chains. She covered her eyes when the brutes picked them up bodily and tossed them summarily overboard, briefcases and all, like two sacks of garbage from the galley.

Gwendolyn covered her mouth again and swallowed hard, trying to process what she had just witnessed. Then she looked at Unzega. He seemed so calm … almost bored by the event. Clearly this man wasn't going to be her easy ticket to good fortune. From the glint in his eye and the curl of pleasure on his lips she now realized he was insane!

*I've got to get out of here*, she screamed inside her head.

"Good afternoon." Unzega broke through her panic. "Don't you just hate it when good business deals go bad?" He turned away from the monitor and sat back in his big leather desk chair. "Thank you for coming."

"I-I-it's my pleasure …" she stuttered. *Four men in the room. Four more on deck….*

Unzega summarily dismissed his henchmen with a wave of his hand, and they left the room without a word, shutting the door behind them. "Be seated," Unzega insisted. "I want to know where we stand on our deal. How soon will you deliver?"

That was the problem, Gwendolyn shuddered, since she wasn't sure if she could ever deliver, let alone as quickly as he expected. Her mind raced, thinking of the two hapless foreigners who had by now had surely drowned. She had to stall somehow, but how? *Flirt, that's it Flirt. Men have always found you irresistible,* she told herself. " Unzega, *darling*," Gwendolyn began, pretending not to be the least bit shocked by what she'd just witnessed and hoping that the murderer couldn't tell how terrified of water she was.

"Once I get my hands on it, it will be clear sailing for both of us," she assured him without an ounce of self assurance.

"How soon do you expect the museum to get the inheritance? he asked her.

"Well, there's been a … *development*," Gwendolyn's voice quavered slightly but she convinced herself that Unzega hadn't heard her falter. "You see darling, there suddenly appears to be an heir, ha, ha, ha," she giggled, "and if she's the real thing, I'm afraid she means to occupy the property, ha ha, and start collecting the rents in town too."

"You assured me *that* possibility didn't exist!" Unzega rose to his feet and raised his open hand as if to strike her, making Gwendolyn cringe in her seat. "May I suggest that you persuade this heir to disappear? I don't think after what you've just witnessed that you'd want *our* deal to go bad … *would you*?"

"N-n-no, of course not." Gwendolyn glanced at the exit behind her, which seemed awfully far away. "I'm already on it," she assured him. "But I can't prom …"

"Let me make myself clear." Unzega cut her off. "I *intend* to control Perdido Isle, whether I lease it with an option to buy from the museum or steal it in my own way. One thing I can assure you … you won't like it if I am forced to get my hands dirty."

"But Unzega, *darling*." Gwendolyn trilled, trying to seem casual as she backed away from his desk. "I can promise you, I'll take care of everything."

"You'd better," Unzega replied threateningly, "I've paid you enough in advance to make sure of it. I've already made my plans. It's up to you to deliver the island as promised, or …"

Unzega didn't need to finish his sentence, Gwendolyn knew exactly what would happen. Running from the room all she could envision was herself, bound and gagged, strapped to a chair while one of Unzega's goons carved pretty ribbons of her face while the demon sat by and enjoyed the spectacle. Rather than kill her, the malicious monster would no doubt turn her loose to scare little children and cause people to stare at her in horror. It didn't matter what she had to do to deliver, even if it meant murder, she mustn't fail in her bargain with the devil. Gwendolyn was trapped.

CHAPTER 3

# THE INHERITANCE

I T HAD BEEN ONE WEEK SINCE GASPAR AND HIS MOTHER
HAD RECEIVED MR. CAWTHORNE'S MYSTERIOUS CALL
and a lot of things had happened in the meantime.
Spread out before them on their simple kitchen table
were two official-looking documents and a third less
legitimate looking missive. One was a pink slip from
The Hollywood Mortgage Company, who had employed
Elvira Brown for the past ten years as a loan officer, up
until yesterday afternoon that is, when they had given her
notice. The pink slip had been accompanied by a glowing
letter of recommendation, written on company stationery,
singing her praises as the best loan officer on the planet.

Elvira picked up the letter and laughed. "They *canned*
150 employees and gave everyone the same exact letter,"

17

she said. "I've already put my feelers out for a new job but the word on the street is that everybody's downsizing."

"I can get a job, Mom" Gasper offered. I could teach scuba diving or give sailing lessons to rich kids. Dad always said I was the best sailor in town. You know he taught me everything he knew. I can do it."

Gaspar only wished he could think of some out of town gig to bring in money. At this point he'd do anything to get away, now that he feared the gang wanted his hide after the incident the other day with the red Le Sabre and what had just happened this morning.

"No one can deny you're a mighty fine sailor Gasp but I think you're just a little young for the Navy and although you're a certified diver, I'm not sure you're certified to give lessons.

"Come on Ma, there must be some way I can help?" Gaspar begged. Right this minute for Gaspar, *Running away to sea sounded like a reasonable possibility.*

"Well dear, you're not old enough to work in an office either and the money you make from your paper route just isn't going to go very far compared to the size of our bills. Besides you need to keep what you earn for your own spending money. Don't worry, I'll figure things out," She told her stalwart son, while picking up the other official looking document on the table.

This was also a very formal affair typed out on thick paper with an engraved letterhead, stamped in gold, under the visage of a Spanish galleon announcing Peter

Cawthorne, Attorney at Law, with a glamorous Florida address that screamed of palm trees and hibiscus flowers. The letter read:

*Peter Cawthorne, Esq.*
*Attorney at Law*
*Suite 250, The Vizcaya Block*
Calaluna, Perdido Isle, *Florida*
*petercawthorne@petercawthornelaw.com*
*T. 941 282-5941 F. 241 282-7767*

Dear Mrs. Brown,

Thank you for answering my questions regarding your family lineage. It is my pleasure to inform you that you have proven to be the sole heir of your paternal second cousin Eugenia Floride Munoz-Flores y Gaspar who died last year, intestate. Eugenia Floride Munoz-Flores y Gaspar was the adopted daughter of your father's paternal uncle, Carlos Rudolfo Munoz-Flores y Gaspar, late of Florida.

The estate consists of a furnished house and 500,000 acres situated on Perdido Isle in the Gulf of Mexico off the Florida coast, USA. There are also certain securities including common stocks and tax free bonds valued at approximately $10,000,000.00 and bank accounts totaling approximately,

$5,000,000.00. The inheritance also consists of several, 99 year land leases on approximately 100,000 of the total acreage. Also included in the estate are approximately 300,000 sq ft of leased retail and office space located in the towns of Llojeta and Calaluna, on Perdido Isle as well as a hacienda in the Yucatan which, although fully staffed, brings in no income to the estate whatsoever.

As the executor of the estate, I must tell you that the bequest is subject to an already existing trust set up by your great-uncle, Carlos Rudolfo Munoz-Flores y Gaspar. The Trust states that should his daughter die without heirs (which she did, intestate), that the entire estate will become the property of the Perdido Isle Historical Society Museum. The trust also states a time limit of one year after Eugenia Floride's death, to discover any heirs and if their intentions are to live in the house and take over stewardship of the property. It also stipulates the property including the house and its contents cannot be sold or developed until no less than ten years after title has been recorded.

Please contact me at your earliest convenience, in writing, sent by certified mail as well as by email, regarding your decision to accept or refuse this inheritance. As your second cousin Eugenia Floride died last September, (eight months ago) time is of the essence in making your decision, as there are only four months left before the property transfers automatically to the museum.

Sincerely,
*Peter Cawthorne, Esq.*


The third document was a crumpled piece of paper which Gaspar had smoothed out as flat as possible. Glued to the paper were cut out letters which threatened,

bEWaRE!
dON'T eVEn tHINK oF lEAviNg CalIfORNia
ANy OThEr ClIMAte WoULd
dEFINaTELY
nOT BE sUITABLE tO yOUR
cONTINUED gOOD hEALTH
yOU hAVE bEeN wARNED

The poison pen warning had been wrapped around a heavy stone, secured with a rubber band. It had been hurled through their front window earlier that day while Gaspar and Elvira were eating breakfast. The warning was not signed, but Gaspar was certain, that it had been sent by the neighborhood gang.

When the rock shattered the window, brave, young Gaspar ran over to take a look outside and saw the same red Buick Le Sabre which had tried to run them off the road previously, tear away from the curb and speed down the street. He courageously ran outside to chase the culprit only to see the car turn the next corner and careen out of sight. To his surprise, a brand new Rolls Royce Phantom convertible with a snazzy black and silver paint job sped down the street after the culprit. Gaspar, stood open mouthed on the curb, as the powerful car passed with the same old white haired Santa that he'd seen before behind the wheel, but now the old boy was wearing a bright-red-and-black-plaid tam-o'-shanter. The colorful driver smiled and waved as he sped past. Gaspar, couldn't make heads or tails of the whole incident but now felt more certain than ever that the older boys were out to get him, and that the gang was far more connected with the underworld than he had ever imagined. His stomach filled with butterflies, but lately, it was always that way.

With these three very different documents spread in front of them, downhearted Elvira, looked into the sea-blue eyes of her son Gaspar, who sat across the table from her.

"I don't know what to do." She admitted to her son.

Gaspar felt far more miserable about *his* troubles than his mother did about losing her job. He wanted to protect her from his stupidity and was now more desperate than ever to get far away from what he felt was another beating or worse. He pulled himself together to put on a show of bravado for her.

"Are you serious Mom? There's only one solution, It's obvious. We have to take the inheritance." Gaspar said with all the authority his young years could muster.

"We're being threatened. I would never forgive myself if something happened to you," his mother shot back.

Gaspar was surprised that his mother thought the note referred to Florida. This was a possibility that hadn't occurred to him. Of course, he was sure the threat was local, and he'd do whatever he had to do to get out of town. Taking a deep breath he changed tact. "You're not being scared off by this crazy warning are you?" Gaspar asked dismissively pushing the crumpled paper aside, "At least we should go to Florida and check the place out."

"With all I have to do here, you want to go to Florida?" his mother answered. "Gaspar, I'm scared. That note is ominous!"

"Mom, get real. You've been fired and you've been offered an estate. For someone without a job and no immediate prospects, Florida sounds irresistible ... please don't say no." Gaspar pleaded with her.

"If we can't sell the house or its contents for ten years, then what's the point?" Mom replied. "This letter doesn't say what kind of a house it is. Maybe that attorney is messing with us. That big inheritance may turn out to be some mosquito-infested mobile home with the wheels still on for all we know. Besides, I can't just go sashaying off to Florida on a whim, not now."

"Come-on Mom let's go to Florida. Summer vacation starts in two weeks, and you haven't had a vacation in years. We could drive there and check it out and if we don't like it we can come back home and look for a job then. This is a chance in a million. How will you ever know unless you at least look at it ... just once?"

Mom was silent for a moment. Then sighed. "Okay you little brat. We'll go to Florida," his mother announced with finality with just a hint of trepidation in her voice.

"Cool. All we have to do is put the address in the car's GPS and hit the road!" Gaspar exclaimed. "This is going to be an awesome adventure Mom, you'll see!"

CHAPTER 4

# GASPAR TAKES A TRIP

Two weeks later, with the SUV piled high with bursting suitcases and boxes of provisions, Gaspar and his mom ventured across the country like conquistadors determined to discover a new world.

Although they could have reached their goal in as few as three days, they instead chose to stop along the way to visit every tourist trap and place of historical interest they could find. Finally reaching the Gulf of Mexico, they followed the coastline east through Louisiana, Mississippi, and Alabama before reaching the Florida border. Elated that their destination was near, they sped through Pensacola and finally crossed the Charlotte County line, eventually reaching Charlotte Harbor.

Try as he might, Gaspar couldn't find out much about Perdido Isle. What he did know was that *Perdido* meant *lost* in Spanish so at least he knew that they were on their way to "Lost Island." Soon Gaspar and his mom crossed the bridge, which carried them the short distance over the inland waterway onto Perdido Isle and into Calaluna which was the town nearest to their final destination. With each passing mile the jungle landscape had grown thicker and wilder, but as far as civilization was concerned it seemed desolate to Gaspar, the boy from the big city.

Finally reaching the quaint town of Calaluna, they passed through several streets of houses, some small, tidy and delightfully charming while others were grander, set high up above rolling lawns. Gaspar noted that the town certainly had its share of older, run-down properties whose ramshackle fences were overgrown with flowering vines. Reaching the commercial district they were greeted by an elegant collection of 1920s, Spanish-Revival architecture, mostly two story office buildings with the usual assortment of a bank, a cafe, a hardware store, a large department store, a movie theater, and several small retail establishments offering clothing, housewares, and furniture.

"These must be the buildings Cawthorne told us about," Gaspar suggested to his mother, "the ones we'll be collecting rents on." He enthused at the possibility of becoming a landlord.

At the top of the street sat the City Hall and other civic buildings, and at the bottom of the street sat the imposing palace, which was identified by the bronze letters set into its façade as The Perdido Isle Historical Society Museum.

Not knowing what they might find when they ultimately reached their new house, the two travelers decided to stop at the café to order a quick lunch.

"Hello mates!" the old waitress greeted Gasper and his mom from behind the counter. "I'm Karen, who might you be?"

"I'm Gaspar, and this is my mom, Elvira," Gaspar sang back to the friendly local.

"New in town or just passing through?" Karen asked, good naturedly.

"New in town." Gaspar replied jovially. He noticed that several heads in the café turned to look at them.

"We're headed to a place called La Rinconada, have you heard of it? Elvira asked.

"Who hasn't?" Karen perked up, "We call it the big house around here." She handed them menus. "What can I get you?"

"A hamburger and a coke, please." Gaspar placed his order without even looking at the card. "Lettuce, tomato and onion, no mayo, please."

"WALK A COW PAST THE STOVE FRANK, BURN IT, THEN DRAG IT THROUGH THE GARDEN AND PIN A ROSE ON IT, AND FRANK, HOLD THE MAYO." Karen yelled at the short order cook on the other side of the pass-through. "AND

FRANK … GIMME A SHOOT FROM THE SOUTH … ON THE FLY … GET IT!"

Karen gave Gaspar her friendliest-weariest-smile and then turning to his mother asked, "And for you darlin'?"

"Scrambled eggs and bacon, please." Elvira smiled, "With buttered wheat toast and a cup of coffee."

"WRECK SOME CACKLE FRUIT, FRANK, CREMATE THE DOUGHBOY, AND SMEAR SOME AXLE GREASE ON IT." Karen screamed through the pass through once more, "AND FRANK … DON'T FORGET TO DRAW ONE IN THE DARK FLOWING MISSISSIPPI".

While they waited for their food, a well-dressed couple sidled up to the counter. "Excuse us," the gentleman spoke first, "we couldn't help overhearing that you're new in town."

"Please allow us to welcome you to Perdido Isle," piped up the woman with him. Extending her hand she announced with great pride, "I'm Roberta Turner and this is my husband Gore. We own Turners, the furniture store in town." she said pointing with her thumb, out the window to a large building with red and white striped awnings emblazoned with the name Turner's along their valances. You may have heard of our main store in Chicago?" she added.

"How very nice," Elvira warbled, taking the lady's hand, "We *are* new here. I'm Elvira Brown, and this is my son Gaspar."

"We overheard that you're moving into La Rinconada and we just wanted to say that if you need anything to help make that ugly old house more homey—anything at all—please don't hesitate to call us. My husband's always happy to take trade-ins at the furniture store, you know, your old junk for our new … ha, ha, … and I dabble in interior decorating too, so if you need any help … " She nudged her husband, "Gore, honey, hand the lady your card." Gore Turner promptly did as he was told before being dragged away by his pushy wife.

Elvira glanced at her son. "I don't know whether to be insulted or grateful for the help," she murmured. "The house sounds like a handful."

"Karen pushed a steaming hot cup of coffee in front of Elvira and plopped a large Coke in front of Gaspar. "I see you're already meetin' the natives," she chuckled, "I'm not surprised. Gossip spreads like the wind and we all knew you'd be comin'."

"So I guess you knew my mom's Great Uncle too," Gaspar chimed in.

"Your Great Uncle Charlie was a legend around here." Karen admitted. "After he died, I guess you could say the legend turned more into a folktale."

"He does seem rather mysterious," Elvira had to admit, "

"Oh, he sure kept the local gossips on their toes. Even his death remains a mystery."

"How so?" Elvira asked.

Karen glanced to the left and right before leaning in. "Well … *some* people around here insist that he was … *done-in*," she said, whispering the last two words, "but I don't believe it. Half the stuff people around here believe about *Good Time Charlie*, he made up *himself* and then he let the locals spread the word—at least that's what I've always *heard*."

"*Really?*" Elvira continued, "But he couldn't have spread the word about his own death."

"Don't be so sure," Karen insisted, "knowing him as I did, I wouldn't put it past him."

Just then, three older women slid out of their booth and sidled up to the counter behind Elvira and Gaspar. "Excuse us," a lady with a purplish tinge to her hair cooed, touching Elvira's left shoulder. "We understand you're going to live at La Rinconada, and we just want to say hello. I'm Margaret Mary Montgomery and this is Margaret Mansfield and Margaret Stewart," she added, gesturing to a chubby woman with a gray buzz cut and then to the super-skinny lady with white curls.

"We're the three Margarets," Margaret Mansfield said in a gravelly voice, "and we're pleased to meet you, Mrs. Brown … and this handsome young man must be your son, Gaspar." she added, chucking Gaspar under the chin, to his annoyance.

"I'm the librarian at the Perdido Isle Historical Society Museum," the third Margaret offered. "If there's ever anything I can do to help you get acquainted with our little village, please don't hesitate to look me up." she said handing Elvira an engraved card.

Karen returned with Gaspar and Elvira's order.

"Okay, let's go girls," Margaret Mary Montgomery said to her friends, "Let's leave the Browns in peace to enjoy Frank's cookin'." She waved to Elvira and Gaspar. See you soon!"

"Thanks for the warm welcome," Elvira called after them, "we're delighted to be here."

"Here's your hockey puck, Gaspar." Karen broke up the hen party by pushing Gaspar's burger in front of him. "Do you want some frog sticks too?"

"Frog sticks!" Gaspar barked, "What are they?"

"French fries." Karen seemed dumbfounded by the question.

"Oh, yes please." he told her.

"Here's your cackle fruit, Mrs. Brown," Karen said pushing the scrambled eggs in front of Elvira.

"Those ladies seemed nice," Gaspar commented.

Karen rolled her eyes. "Those old biddies," she snorted, when the triumvirate were barely out the door. "A grander bunch of nosy old Lassie-Lucy's you'll never meet. I would avoid them if I were you," the waitress insisted.

Elvira laughed. "Oh Karen, they seemed harmless."

"I'd believe her if I were you," said the man sitting at the counter only two stools away.

Gaspar smiled to himself. *The drama in this café should go viral*, he thought.

"I'm Floyd Beverwil" the man introduced himself, "I own the hardware store down the street. I've lived here all my life and I could tell you stories about those three women and this town that would make your hair curl. In fact, rumor has it that one of them actually *did in* your Great Uncle. Knocked him on the head with a solid gold candlestick, while he was sleeping on his library sofa. That's what they say, but of course nobody could ever prove it."

Gaspar drank a big bubbly mouthful of Coke, as he exchanged glances with his mom.

"So nobody knows the truth?" Elvira asked. "Not even the police?"

"All gossip and innuendo." Karen put an end to the conversation, giving Beverwil the fish eye. "If there's one thing I *can't* stand, it's a gossip!" she huffed and started wiping down the counter where Beverwil's arms were resting. "You mind?" she asked him pushing her cloth at his elbows.

"Well, it's been nice chatting with you," Beverwil mumbled with embarrassment as he made a quick getaway.

"Such a nice man and so interested in everybody and everything that goes on in this town." Karen scowled. According to him, his news is more accurate than Reuters, and we should hang on every word of it." Karen added acidly. "They say he's actually a blackmailer—honest, I'm not kidding—supposedly he tried blackmailing your Great Uncle Charlie over some scandal to do with the town trollop that happened a million years ago. Anyway, Charlie turned the tables on him and threatened to expose him as a blackmailer if he didn't clear out of town. Charlie would have ousted Beverwil right off the island, if he hadn't died so suddenly."

Why Karen, these are mighty shocking revelations for simple folk like us." Elvira's wide eyed exclamation made Gaspar giggle.

"When you live in a small town like this one," Karen drawled, "people make your business their business. And sometimes they get jealous … Not me, of course, but other people. For instance … "

There was only so much gossip Gaspar could take. He tuned out the hen party and looked around the café. Suddenly he noticed his pal, Santa Claus, the one with the Rolls Royce sleigh, sitting at the corner of the counter just a few seats down from them. The man was wearing a silver gray sharkskin suit with an amethyst tie and he was staring right at him, smiling.

*Where did he come from?* Gaspar wondered. *And where did he get that crazy suit?*

No sooner had they locked eyes than the man got up and walked past the back of Gaspar's stool, heading for the café's rear exit. Gaspar quickly decided to find out what was going on and why this guy was following them?

If he was sent by the gang back in North Hollywood, Gaspar wanted to know it.

"Be right back, Mom," he said, hopping off the stool and heading for the café's back door. As he stepped outside, he saw Santa jump into a coffee and cream colored Rolls Royce Wraith, and take off in hot pursuit of a red Buick Le Sabre, which was just pulling out of the lot.

"I'll be seeing you Gaspar," Santa called out as he gunned the engine and disappeared in a cloud of dust.

*What the heck?* Gaspar tried to process what had just happened. *Every time I see that dude he's driving another fancy car, and now he even knows my name?* It couldn't be a coincidence that those two drivers had followed them all the way from Los Angeles. The question was, why? Were they working together or separately and if so, which one was the good guy and which the bad, and if they were both bad, who were they working for?

"Where have you been?" his mother asked when Gaspar got back to the counter.

"I had to wash my hands" Gaspar lied, not wanting to worry her. He'd do anything to confide in someone about his suspicions. If he could just tell her the truth about the gang back home, but he knew if Mom ever found out about the trouble he almost got into, she might never trust him again. *Would those damned butterflies ever leave his stomach in peace?* Gaspar wondered.

"Hurry and finish your lunch Gasp, it's time we get going." His mother chided him.

"Okay mom, just a few more bites," Gaspar begged, then turning to Karen he complimented her. "Karen, I gotta tell ya, that was the best burger I've had since Barstow."

"I don't know what Barstow is kid, but I'll consider it to be some kind of out of town compliment." Karen chuckled delighted with Gaspar's accolade. "Can I get you anything else? Do you want any more *yellow paint* or how about a little more *hemorrhage* for your *frog sticks?*"

"I'm not sure, Karen. I could use some more mustard and ketchup, but I'm not so sure about the other."

"Gaspar, get with the drill. If you're gonna be patronizing my cafe, you'll need to know the lingo, otherwise a man could starve to death around here. Yellow paint and hemorrhage are mustard and ketchup!"

Having finished off their lunch with two servings of Karen's famous vanilla pudding, which she ordered from Frank by yelling, "TWO SLEIGH RIDE SPECIALS." They paid the bill and said goodbye to their new friend.

Driving on to their destination Gaspar took note of a series of low buildings, looking like an extended Spanish hacienda, which proclaimed themselves as the Andrew Jackson Elementary School, Junior High, and High School, all of which were grouped around a playground built right on the sand, bordering the Gulf of Mexico. This mirage of civilization came and went in a second but it gave Gaspar a look into where he could expect to find himself at the end of summer should they decide to stay on in Florida. On the way out of town the car passed the last of the charming adobe bungalows with their lush tropical gardens and falling-down fences, and headed once again into a jungle of palm trees and vines lining both sides of the two-lane road. Soon Gaspar saw a large stone marker on the right hand side with the words La Rinconada carved onto it.

"This is it." he called from the passenger seat.

It was about thirty minutes later that the jungle opened up on the ocean side, exposing two, carved coral-stone gateposts, supporting two monumental wrought iron gates. Another plaque carved into the posts declared that this was indeed, La Rinconada.

•••

What they didn't notice was the rosy-cheeked old man, standing half-hidden in the bushes across the street. This time the old boy didn't waive or call attention to himself, and his flashy Rolls Royce was nowhere to be seen. From his hiding place, he observed the new comers closely without any sign of emotion. The spy's previously jovial face was now expressionless, absent any sign of familiarity or good cheer. If anyone could see him the suspicious man's demeanor would have betrayed his motives for being there, as something less than friendly. The trespasser's penetrating gaze followed Gaspar and his mom as they pulled up to the gates and got out of the car.

His eyes with their hard, unrelenting glare *meant business*, as mother and son innocently arrived at their destiny.

# CHAPTER 5

# LA RINCONADA

WHEN THEY JUMPED OUT OF THE CAR, THE TRAVELERS FOUND THE GATES LOCKED TIGHT—CHAINED AND padlocked. They could see the crushed seashell driveway through the wrought iron scroll work. It veered off to the right, and disappeared behind a border of tall tropical plantings. Elvira found the whole situation less than inviting, but Gaspar was not one to give up so quickly. With further investigation he discovered a pedestrian gate, just to the left of the carriage entrance, made almost invisible by an overhanging curtain of vines. He pushed on it hard and the narrow gate shrieked open, crying for mercy on its rusted hinges. Having opened it a crack, Gaspar shimmied his way onto the property.

"Come on, Mom." he called. "Let's check it out. Remember, Cawthorne said there's supposed to be a caretaker here named Felix. Let's find him."

Gaspar ran down the driveway ahead of his mother, broken seashells crunching under his sneakers. The driveway curved through the jungle. Birds called and insects chattered accompanied by the rustle of palm fronds which swayed overhead in the tropical breeze. The drive opened into a spacious motor court lined with fancy urns and statuary, in the center of which was a dried out fountain filled with dead leaves, looking to Gaspar as if its trickling waters had stopped playing centuries ago. The massive house filled the right side of the court while what seemed to be an equally large stable or carriage complex mirrored it on the left. The house was shuttered and, by all signs, deserted.

The stables however, and their huge square yard, accessed through a wide archway, appeared more welcoming. Not waiting for his mother, Gaspar sprinted into the stable yard. Reaching the center of the court he stopped short not knowing where to go next. The left side of the courtyard was lined with a two story-high row of pillared arches. The remaining three sides consisted of one story rows of stables set back from a red tile roofed arcade. Most of the rough-hewn stable doors were closed.

"Hello? Anybody home?" Gaspar called out.

A slightly built, darkly-tanned man with curly gray hair appeared from one of the open stalls.

Gaspar smiled but his reception was less than cordial.

"What do you want? This is private property," the man informed Gaspar in thick, Spanish-accented English and a no-nonsense tone of voice. "You must leave immediately!" he said, pointing furiously toward the archway.

"We're the Browns." Elvira announced meekly, as she entered the stable yard.

"We've just arrived from California," Gaspar chimed in almost apologetically

"Then you must be Gas*par*?" the man said, putting emphasis on the last syllables of Gaspar's name while opening his arms wide. "And you of course must be *Dona Elvirita*!" he practically sang in Elvira's direction, a big white toothy smile covering his leathery face. "*I* am Felix, I am your caretaker. Welcome to La Rinconada," the now-smiling man proclaimed. "Forgive me *Mrs*! Of course, Mr. Peter told me to expect you, but that was *weeks* ago. I wasn't sure when you were coming."

"We drove from California," Gaspar explained. "Our car is right outside the gate. The side gate is unlocked. That's how we got in."

"Oh. My son, Alexander, he must have left the side gate open, but for once I am glad he did. I will open the main gate, and bring your car in for you. Please, give me the keys *Señora* and I will take care of everything," he said walking up to Elvira, his hand outstretched. "Alex, ALEJANDRO!" Felix called out.

A screen door slammed shut on the balcony above them where Gaspar spotted a boy about his age hanging over the railing. *"Sí Papa,"* the boy answered in Spanish.

*"Venga hombre, estos son los nuevos patrones, vengas a ayudar me hijo!"* Felix called up to his son.

Gaspar wasn't sure what Felix was saying but it sounded urgent. Without a word, the tall, skinny kid bounded down the stairs and joined his father, who had to reach up in order to put a loving arm around his sons shoulders.

"This is my son Alex. Alex, this is *Señora Munoz-Flores y Gaspar* and this is her son, *Gaspar y Gaspar*—the long lost relatives of Lady Eugenia."

"Actually, our last name is Brown." Elvira corrected him, " I'm Elvira and my son is Juan Gaspar.."

"Call me Gaspar." Gaspar instructed Alex with a smile.

Alex nodded agreement and smiled back.

"Show them around while I bring their car to the front and don't be shy, *hijo*, show them everything. This is *their* house now." Felix instructed his son before darting from the stable yard for the front gates.

"So tell us, Alex," Elvira began her third degree, "how long has your family been at La Rinconada?"

"My grandfather was the first to work here," Alex replied, "then my father." He has worked here since he was sixteen. My mother started working here too after she married my father. I also work here after school, helping my father with his chores. But now with summer vacation, I do all my chores in the morning. We live upstairs ... there." Alex pointed to a row of windows in the central block above the stables.

"Are there any horses?" Gaspar wondered aloud. He didn't know how to ride, but he figured, it might be fun to learn.

"No, no horses, only carriages and old cars too. Want to see?" Without waiting for an answer Alex ran to the first pair of wooden doors under the arcade and swung them open with a swoosh. He then opened another pair and then another.

Gaspar and his mother stepped forward and gazed into the dark interior. After their eyes became accustomed to the shadowed light they could discern in the first stable a magnificent old coach that had definitely seen finer days. They gazed into the next compartment and saw a glamorous Hispano-Suiza touring car sitting up on blocks, unpredictably polished within an inch of its life. In the next shed they found an old Woody station wagon, badly in need of restoration, eight old bicycles in various stages of ruin, and an old Mahogany Riva motor boat up on a frame as if it were being prepared for launching.

Hearing the crunching of tires on broken shells, they walked back through the arch into the motor court. Felix leapt from the driver's seat of the SUV and began unloading everything. When he slammed the SUV's hatch shut Gaspar noticed the word, *Beware*, written across the dusty tail-gate window. He shuddered. Those words were not there when they'd left the café. That meant that someone had to have written them after they'd left the car by the front gate. He scanned the edge of the motor court with its thick screen of wild vegetation. *Was someone out there, watching them now?* He wondered, glancing at his mother. *Should he say something?* He felt such a coward for placing his beloved mother in harms way. What he couldn't figure out was how the gang had actually followed him all the way to Florida and had known their destination well enough in advance to lay in wait for them. He couldn't take much more of these veiled threats and now welcomed a direct confrontation with the enemy.

"Alex will bring your luggage in," Felix announced, more as an aside than as an order to his lanky son. "Come along and let me show you your new home." he motioned them towards the house excitedly.

Together they climbed the few wide steps up to the front door. It was then that Gaspar realized that the steps, in fact the entire façade of the house, was made of giant blocks of coral stone, some of which had been intricately carved.

Felix unlocked the door and stepped aside for Elvira and Gaspar to enter first. Shoulder to shoulder, mother and son crossed the wide threshold. Felix skirted around them to flip a switch and the entrance hall became brightly illuminated by a giant wrought-iron chandelier suspended from the extremely high, beamed ceiling.

"Oh my." Elvira murmured.

"Not exactly your typical double wide trailer, eh mom?" Gaspar murmured under his breath, taking in the rich furniture, paintings, and hangings as well as the stenciled decorations on the ceiling beams. He suddenly realized that the entire inside of the house, like the exterior, was also clad in coral stone.

"Let me show you the *Sala*."

Felix led them through the arch on the left and down two steps into the sunken living room. Stepping to the windows, he pulled back the heavy draperies unleashing a cloud of dust, now back lit by streams of yellow sunlight, reflecting off the Gulf of Mexico.

"Wow," was the understatement Elvira mouthed turning around in a full circle to take in the enormous living room.

The next room Felix unveiled was a vast library. Books covered every wall reaching to just under a suspended balcony, which ran around three sides of the room and was accessed by two matching mahogany spiral staircases. Most extraordinary were the double doors leading into and out of the room, four pair in total, each of which had been paneled with gilded bronze coins.

"This must have been where Uncle Charlie was murdered, " Gaspar said, with a know-it-all tone of authority.

"There was no murder in this house," Felix corrected him quickly.

"We were told by Mr. Beverwil in the village that—" Elvira started.

"Beverwil, he knows better than to talk about murder at La Rinconada, he knows nothing." Felix insisted. "Mr. Charles died of natural causes, Lady Eugenia too. There has been no murder in this house, ever!" Felix was clearly upset.

"I see," said Elvira giving Gaspar a look, eyebrows raised.

"Well, the room is awesome," Gaspar said, smoothing Felix over.

It really was. Every table top was covered with curious objects, scientific instruments, and framed photographs. Interspersed between the hundreds of leather bound books stacked everywhere, were suits of armor and trophies made up of old swords and shields. Wonderful old maps and coats of arms hung over the doorways, along with banners and flags of all nations and time periods.

In all of this what interested Gaspar the most were the intricate models of antique sailing ships which had been placed on shelves, between books whose subjects were written on all manner of sea conquest, oceanography and cartography. Gaspar knew that he would soon be claiming this room as his own special domain.

The tour, which was extensive, and which Felix carried out as expeditiously as possible included an enormous dining room, replete with china cupboards and a silver vault, hidden behind a large tapestry. A cavernous kitchen, which had been updated as recently as fifty years ago and a screened-in service porch with a sink for washing clothes and several wooden rods for drying them on. Gaspar was amused and amazed that there wasn't a single modern, gas or electric powered washer or dryer in sight.

Climbing the grand double staircase that dominated the entrance hall, they reached the second floor where they were shown an enormous upstairs sitting room, off of which eight family bedrooms were accessed. The Master suite had a terrace facing the ocean and was definitely somebody's idea of a French boudoir with its ivory painted and gilded paneling, fancy tasseled curtains, and white and gold painted furniture. There was also the *Sinbad suite*, consisting of a tented bedroom right out of the *Arabian Nights*, as well as a *Marco Polo suite*, which was a nightmare of red lacquer and gilded dragons. Another of the guest rooms was unexpectedly upholstered in black patent leather and hung with now very tattered, ivory satin curtains and matching quilted satin upholstery.

"We call this the *haunted room*," Felix volunteered without divulging any further information.

There was also a blue room, decorated in 32 horrifying shades of blue, and right next door, there was a rose room which Felix inexplicably called *The Room of the Spanish Virgins*. A green room followed these, which like the two previous rooms had been done up with floral chintzes and printed linens to match its predominantly green color scheme. But Felix had saved the best for last.

The Captain's Cabin, *El Quarto de El Capitan*, Felix emphasized in Spanish, as he showed them into an entire suite decorated to look like the captain's cabin on a Spanish Galleon. Gaspar decided, then and there, that the *Captain's Cabin* would be *his* room, no questions asked.

"Gaspar, help Alexander bring up the bags." His mother sprang into action. "I'll take the front room Gasp, you choose whichever of the others you want."

"I'll take the *Captain's Cabin*." Gaspar replied using a voice that he hoped didn't reveal the fact that he was beside himself with joy at the prospect.

CHAPTER 6

# PLAYING HOUSE

"THIS IS MY FAVORITE ROOM IN THE HOUSE TOO," ALEX ANNOUNCED AS HE AND GASPAR DEPOSITED Gaspar's luggage in the captain's cabin. Elvira put away her things in the master suite and had instructed Gaspar to do the same. Felix kindly invited them to dinner and she wanted them both to get a head start on settling in before they went out.

"I can't believe it," Gaspar proclaimed, "this room's like a dream come true for me. My dad and I used to play pirates when I was a kid. We used to watch old pirate movies on TV, all the time. They're really great, full of blood, gore and adventure ... and they all have a captain's cabin, just like this one, only this one's better, fancier, right off the Spanish Main. Hey, is there a TV in the house? Can you get cable and satellite down here?"

"There's a TV in the upstairs hall. I used to watch it with Lady Eugenia when I was little, before she got so sick. We have a TV in our apartment too. We get all three channels but no cable or satellite."

First thing on Gaspar's list was to get cable. "How about Internet?" he asked hopefully.

"At the café in town." Alex replied dubiously.

"Oh," Gaspar lamented, "we'll have to get Internet and cable or at least satellite installed first thing. It's a priority!"

"Tell me about it," Alex agreed. "I've been wanting Internet access for years. Hey, do you want to see the best part of this room?"

"You mean there's *more*?" Gaspar couldn't wait!

Alex grinned and crossed over to a panel on the wall. "Watch this," he said, giving it a tap. Then he stepped back as the panel swung open into the room, revealing a secret passage within the walls.

"No way!" Gaspar squealed.

"This passage leads onto the balcony that circles the library. Go inside, and give the wall in front of you a push." Alex insisted, shoving his new friend into the void, then scrambling in behind him.

Reaching the panel just four-feet in front of them, Gaspar gave it a push and the next thing he knew they were standing on the balcony high above the book and treasure-strewn library. "This is so cool! " Gaspar exclaimed, "Are there *more* secret passages in this house?."

"Plenty, but right now you need to finish unpacking and I need to get back home to help mama with the dinner. Come over at eight, okay?"

"Got it," Gaspar said, "and Al? Can we keep this secret passage thing just between us? Meaning, don't tell my mom, okay?"

"Sure, even my parents don't know about it." Alex laughed, happy to be a conspirator.

"Thanks! The less my Mom knows about my room, *the better.*

"I understand completely. See you later, Gasp."

"Before you go Al, let's exchange cell phone numbers," Gaspar suggested whipping out his iPhone. I want to be able to find you without hollering all over the place.

"Good idea Gasp, "Alex said, taking out his old fashioned flip-phone.

After they'd exchanged contact information, Alex bounded down one of the circular stairs as Gaspar went back through the secret passage, closing the hidden panel behind him. Entering his Captain's Cabin, he secured the second secret panel and turned to face the wall of fan-tail windows on his left.

Peering outside he could see the Gulf of Mexico to the left. Stretched in front of him, directly below his window, lay a once elegant garden. Smack in the middle of the garden sat a huge empty swimming pool. Gaspar was dismayed that the pool only held a flurry of dead leaves at its bottom. Farther out, but not that far away from the end of the pool, a wide canal had been dug from the sea, inland. To his amazement there in the middle of it was a half submerged, white and gold sailing yacht, with three tall masts standing above a weathered mahogany deck.

"It must be a hundred feet long," he commented to himself, suddenly remembering his beloved father and how he would have loved to have sailed in such a vessel. *Oh Dad, how I wish you could be here right now, I really need you right now, more than you can imagine,* he prayed silently to his deceased parent as visions of the neighborhood gang appeared threateningly before him.

Shaking off his fears, he turned his attention back to the yacht. Gaspar deduced that it had to have been built around 1910, a product of the turn of the last century, and had obviously sunk at harbor a long time ago, as water now lapped the deck where it had listed slightly to starboard. Gaspar couldn't believe that such a treasure had been allowed to founder and rot, out of what he could only imagine was sheer neglect. Just to the right of the dead ship's prow were steps leading out of the water, up to an octagon-shaped boat house, which was complete with a widow's walk and a columned porch. Beyond this was jungle, as far as the eye could see.

To his right, partially hidden behind a neglected hedge was a tennis court whose, torn and sagging net, fluttered shamelessly in the gentle trade winds coming off the Gulf.

"What a mess." he mouthed noticing how decrepit the pergolas, pagodas and arbors were with their falling-in roofs, dead vines and broken columns. Gaspar's blood ran suddenly cold and the hair on his arms stood up when he saw a tall man scurry from behind a hedge and lurch toward the octagon-shaped building. The man was wearing a loose fitting black suit covered with a voluminous black shawl and on his black bandanna covered head, a wide brimmed black hat was pulled down low on his forehead. He watched the man look furtively left and right before disappearing around another hedge, out of sight.

Gaspar would like to have opened a window and called out to him, but before he could react the man was gone. There was something unsavory about the specter in black that Gaspar couldn't put his finger on. He knew instantly that it was his nemesis, the enemy, but then he thought wishfully, *maybe he's just another employee, perhaps a gardener?"* he hoped , although the damned butterflies were suddenly back, fluttering around inside his stomach.

Focusing on the gardens he hoped that his mother hadn't yet discovered the extent of the ruin she'd inherited. He decided it was better not to say anything, but let her discover the hopelessness of the situation by daylight, in her own good time. He feared she might make a rash decision and cut and run for California, and he was convinced that it would be a real disaster for all of them considering the threats they'd already received.

# CHAPTER 7

# THE DINNER PARTY

"HURRY UP, MOM, I'M STARVING!" GASPAR CALLED FROM THE BOTTOM OF THE STAIRS. HE WAS waiting for his Mother to come down so they could go next door for dinner.

"Be right down," Elvira called from the landing.

Gaspar had been amusing himself by turning on all the lights he could find. The house was now ablaze with incandescent light. It suddenly looked alive, almost even welcoming, he thought, pleased with what he saw.

Finally his beautiful thirty two year old mom appeared looking like a million dollars in a pretty pink cotton dress printed with white polka dots.

"Mom, you sure clean up good." Gaspar complimented her. "You look more like a twenty-four year-old college girl than a mother of a teenage brat who forced

55

you to drive all the way from California via hells acre to get here." His bouquets for his mother were easy for him to throw, she meant so much to him, now more than ever.

"Thank you Gasp, you know your full of crap but that's why I love you." She beamed, blowing him a kiss then taking his arm as they walked towards the door. "By the way, are those your best party clothes? Somehow I don't think Levi's and a T-shirt are going to cut it around this Palazzo, didn't you pack anything else?"

"Mom, these are my *best* jeans and my *best* T-shirt. When I go out with you, I always wear my *best*." He knew he'd messed up but covered his tracks the way his dad had taught him.

They walked across the motor court and into the stable yard, where the windows of the caretaker's apartment blazed brightly overhead. Gaspar bounded up the exterior Spanish-tiled staircase, two treads at a time, while his mother picked her way in the dim lamplight. Alex threw open the door wide, just as Elvira stepped forward.

"We're here," smiled Gaspar.

"Sorry we're late," Elvira added.

"You're not late, don't worry about it." Alex insisted standing aside to let them pass. "This is my mother, Angela," he introduced his mother with a flourish, "*Mama, esta es la nueva patrona, la Señora Elvira,*" he informed her in *Castellano*.

"I'm very pleased to meet you Mrs. Brown." Angela greeted Elvira, in perfect English.

"It's my pleasure. I'm glad you speak English. My Spanish is awful," Elvira confessed.

"Actually, Spanish is my second language, but Alex and I speak it because my husband, Felix, after thirty-five years living in this country, still refuses to speak English unless he absolutely must. Please promise me that you'll only speak to Felix in English, we need to force him to apply himself. Lady Eugenia only spoke Spanish to him, she only wanted to be a Spanish *Señorita*. She was a wonderful woman, but she lived a fantasy life here at La Rinconada."

"We didn't know her. In fact we had no idea that we had any relatives at all until a few weeks ago. But we look forward to learning more about them and this magical place." Elvira confessed.

"Dinner is served." Felix announced from the arch leading into the small dining room.

Gaspar and his mother crossed the living room with its old overstuffed furniture, and entered the dining room. The caretakers' apartment, like all of the rooms in the main house had obviously not been redecorated since the place had been built, which guessing by the *Sunset Boulevard*, Hispano-Moresque style of the place, Gaspar thought, had to have been in the 1920s. The significance of the date suddenly struck Gaspar. *That would have been almost one-hundred years ago*, he thought.

Felix and Angela had set the dining table with old lace doilies and a collection of mismatched silverware, thick glass goblets and old crockery, as well as a banquette of covered dishes whose cracked and chipped tops allowed steam to escape, filling the room with a delicious aroma.

"Let's eat." Alex insisted, pulling Gaspar by the elbow as everyone took seats.

Grabbing the large covered casserole and a big spoon, Alex offered it first to Elvira and Gaspar then next to his own mother and then to his father. "This is tamale pie," he explained, "It's mama's secret recipe!"

The conversation around the table was lively with Elvira and Gaspar shooting questions at their new friends and retainers about the house and the history of the land, and what role they had personally played in the saga. Their hosts were barely able to get a word in edgewise to ask about California, the movie stars and what it was like to live in a big city like Los Angeles.

After gorging themselves on Angela's fantastic cuisine, Gaspar and Alex got up to clear the table and wash the dishes. While cleaning up, Alex told Gaspar about his friends Mark and Pat and about the great fishing hole they'd found just off the inland waterway, and Gaspar told Alex about his pal, Kevin back in L.A. and the rivalry they had playing video games against each other. Alex told how he and Felix liked to hunt in the swamps around the island for alligators and turtles and how they'd bagged a ten-foot monster one day and dragged it home. Wide eyed at the thought, Gaspar was suitably impressed.

Gaspar told Alex "my dad used to go scuba diving every year near the channel islands off of Santa Barbara. We'd hunt for fish like yellow tail, white sea bass, halibut, calico bass, and if we were lucky we'd even spear mahi mahi." Gaspar enthused. "One time I speared a thirty-six-pound yellowtail and my dad got a fifty-seven-pound sea bass. It was awesome." Gaspar bragged. "I'll never forget that night when we barbecued the yellowtail on the beach for my mom and some of her friends who went with us." Gaspar reminisced. He knew he hadn't one-upped Alex's story of the ten foot gator, but felt that he'd held his own against his new pals hunting prowess.

After drying the last dish, Gaspar twisted the towel into a whip and snapped it at Alex's rear-end. "Al, I'm so lucky to meet you on my first day in Florida. Something tells me we're gonna be new best friends."

"That's just what I was just thinking Gasp, best friends, you got it."

"It's mental telepathy Al. I believe in it."

"Whatever you say buddy, hey come on, I want to show you my room."

Gaspar sat on the floor as Alex shared his personal treasures with his new pal. One by one he showed off amazing sea shells, tortoise shells, coral branches, and perforated rocks, all found on the property, and he also brought out memento's given to him by Eugenia Floride, including a gold stick pin initialed with an "A," and an old tortoise-shell cigar-case monogrammed "TD," as well as a carved crystal eagle head, which Gaspar recognized as a fancy 1920s radiator cap for a car.

"This is the best present Lady Eugenia ever gave me, it's a book on Florida Pirates, If you like, I'll lend it to you … anytime." Alex promised.

To his delight, Gaspar learned that he and Alex were exactly the same age, although Gaspar was a little older having been born in June, while Alex had been born in November. Of the two, Alex was a taller, five-foot four, to Gaspar's minuscule four-feet, eleven-inches. They also discovered that they both wore the same size shoes, and had the same interests in sports. Alex confessed that he wasn't the best student in school, but Gaspar rightly decided that whatever Al lacked in book smarts he no doubt made up for in street smarts. This was going to be an important friendship, and both boys knew it.

"Who's the tall guy who works here?" Gaspar asked his new buddy.

"My dad is the only man who works here," came Alex's quick response.

That wasn't exactly the answer Gaspar wanted to hear, "I saw a man in the garden, from my room. He was dressed all in black, wearing a wide brimmed black hat."

"Sounds like a weirdo. Who knows? People are so curious about this place," Alex replied. "My dad hates trespassers. I'll tell him about this one. Don't worry, dad will take care of him ... unless he's a *ghost*," he added with a mischivous grin.

Gaspar felt the butterflies again but rolled his eyes and laughed. "I hope you're right. What's with you and ghosts anyway?"

"Don't laugh," Alex retorted, "You'll see, there *are* ghosts at La Rinconada."

*Oh great*, Gaspar thought, *more trouble in paradise.*

As the two boys wandered back into the room where the adults were chatting over coffee, Gaspar heard his mother ask. "Tell us about our cousin, Eugenia Floride."

"She was the most wonderful lady in the world." Felix answered reverentially. "My father and mother and I were devoted to her. She was a *lady*, who needed our protection."

"If you would Felix, I'd like to hear your version of the history of this place, in English *por favor*," Elvira insisted sweetly.

"I will be happy to tell you what I know from what I was told by my father, and Lady Eugenia. Alexander, you fill in if I leave anything out or if my English doesn't work *too good*." Felix threw in apologetically. "But rather than hear my memories, you will probably learn so much more by just looking at the old scrap books in the library. There is a lot of information there, everywhere, you will see books and books and books ... I have not looked at them all, only a few. Lady Eugenia had taken them out one day, but she told me that those were only the tip of the *icebox* or something like that."

"It's *iceberg*, dad," Alex corrected his parent.

"Iceburg, icebox, what's the difference? They're both cold, no?" Felix made excuses.

Alex glanced at Gaspar who shrugged and smiled. "He's right." Gaspar got the feeling that Felix almost considered Eugenia Floride to be his true mother. His devotion to her and his recollections of her many kindnesses seemed uppermost in his mind.

"Tell us everything then," Elvira leaned back and made herself comfortable for what she hoped would be a detailed history.

Alexander and Gaspar took seats on the floor near their parents, as Felix began his story.

"I wonder if it will seem to you as recent a history as it seems to me," he began. "You see, we are not really that old, the house, the legend, the myth. There was a man, the father of Lady Eugenia, his name was Carlos, or Charles or Charlie, depending on what part of his life, or who is referring to him. Carlos Rudolfo Munoz-Flores y Gaspar. He was the brother of your grandfather, and the uncle of your father," he said looking directly at Elvira. "There is no mention of a wife, and Lady Eugenia was definitely his adopted daughter, whom he loved. From what I've heard your Uncle Charlie, let's call him that for the sake of argument, never worked a day in his life. He told everyone that he was an orphan and that he was the heir to a Central American fortune. I heard him say it to someone myself." Felix insisted.

"My grandfather, Philip was an orphan. He was raised by his Aunt Henny Calhoun in Galveston, Texas. He was just a child when he went to live with her, and as far as I know he never told my father that he had a brother ... and my father certainly didn't know that he had an Uncle, let alone a rich Uncle." Elvira told what she knew. "My dad would have loved to have known his rich cousin, Lady Eugenia."

"Well, that is unfortunately part of the legend. You see, Lady Eugenia was not rich, not that we know of. But I digress. Let's get back to Mr. Charles. He came out of nowhere, my father told me all of this, and he heard it from local gossip too. He was young in 1900, around eighteen years old, and rich when according to the records, he purchased this 500,000 acre island from the Seminole Indians, for fifteen cents an acre. He began building this house and developing the property around 1915 and called it La Rinconada after his grandfather's old hacienda in Mexico, which had been lost many, many years earlier. Charles established a town at each end of the island around 1920. Calaluna at the western boundary and Llojeta at the eastern boundary. Both towns were named after other haciendas your family used to own in Peru, before the family moved north to Mexico in the nineteenth century. The land is leased to the people living in those towns and is a source of income to your estate, but Mr. Cawthorne will explain all of this to you when you meet with him."

"We are meeting with him the day after tomorrow, it seems he's out of town on an important case in Pensacola," Elvira informed them, "but please go on."

"The first thing he built was the grand canal to anchor his sailing yacht, and the boat house. Have you seen that yet?"

"I saw the yacht from my window," Gaspar piped up, "What a disaster!"

"Then he built the house, the stables and these apartments for his staff. At one time he had twenty people working here, including grooms, gardeners, sailors, maids, cooks, a butler and a major domo, too. A full staff, not just to serve him and his daughter, but also to serve his many house guests. His parties in the 1920s, 30s and 40s were famous. Everyone came here. It was like your Hearst Castle, but in Florida, and where your Mr. Hearst owned a publishing empire, Mr. Charles had no known source of income. Even the tax collectors couldn't discover how he lived and they were never able to tax his income, because except for the rents, he just didn't have any."

"But how could he live like this and build two towns?" Elvira asked. "Where did the money come from?"

"That is the *mystery*, Señora," Felix concluded.

"And Eugenia Floride, did she continue the parties and the extravagant living?" Gaspar asked.

"Oh no, Lady Eugenia, she did not. She had beautiful clothes, but they were old clothes. And she had beautiful jewels, not new jewels, but they were mostly gifts from her father. She traveled all over the world on her yacht, but in the end she became a recluse and would see no one except Mr. Cawthorne. He was a very young lawyer when she first hired him. His father had worked as an attorney for her father, Mr. Charles."

"She must have had some money. The house seems well-cared-for although the gardens look like they may have suffered." Elvira wondered

"Well nobody thought Señorita Eugenia was actually poor. The house and contents were left to her in trust. There didn't seem to be a lot of money, and she was precluded from selling anything or developing the land by the terms of the trust agreement. She also had the income from the land leases, but you will discover that this is not a lot of money considering the value of the property and the heavy Florida taxes. I understand all of this because she spoke to me about it on several occasions, although I was just a laborer in her employ. Toward the end, Angela and Alex and I were all the human contact she had except for Mr. Cawthorne, and he treated her very well and with great dignity. Let me just say, she had me drain the pool because she didn't want to pay for it, even though it cost her nothing. She also planned, *one last trip*, around the world on her yacht. She had us load the boat full of provisions, boxes and boxes, just like in the days when her father was alive. Then just before hiring a crew to man her, she told me to open the seacock's and sink her where she was, at anchor in the canal. She supervised the destruction personally. When Mr. Cawthorne saw the boat foundering in the canal, all he could do was shake his head, but he never said a word to her. It wasn't his place, just like it wasn't ours to ever refuse her anything.

"So that's what happened to the yacht. Gaspar blurted, "How long ago was that—the sinking that is?" he inquired.

"Only five years ago. Every time I look at her with the water lapping at her decks, my heart breaks." Felix moaned, shaking his head..

"Well, this has been a very interesting evening, but I'm afraid it's getting a little late for me and Gaspar." Elvira announced standing up. "Thank you for a very enjoyable dinner and a lovely end to a very long day. Gaspar, I think you and I should get to bed, as something tells me tomorrow will be even more full of surprises than today has been."

Gaspar stood up reluctantly. "Thanks for being so kind to us on our first night at La Rinconada. Dinner was delicious."

"It has been our pleasure my friends." Felix said walking them to the door.

"We'll see you tomorrow," Angela added sweetly, "sleep well."

"I'll walk you back to your house." Alex offered, pushing Gaspar towards the door. "I'll be right back, Mom," Alex called over his shoulder as the two boys scurried past Elvira and ran down the stairs.

"What are you doing tomorrow, Al?" Gaspar asked his new pal.

"I always have my chores in the mornings. Helping my father is important, he has so much to do," Alex explained, "but I can be finished by late morning, and that's when I can play."

"I suppose I should clean up my room in the morning. When you're done, come and get me. Maybe we can go swimming or take a look around the place together." Gaspar suggested.

"Okay. Have a good night, and, hey, don't let the ghosts keep you up." Alex laughed.

"Come on man ... Give me a break with the ghost stuff ," Gaspar rolled his eyes.

"Maybe they're all *friendly* ghosts," Alex laughed again.

"Yeah. I'll let you know," Gaspar replied. "Or maybe I'll just send them over to your room." Gaspar laughed back, but with everything else he had going on inside he couldn't help feeling a little weird about the thought of moving into a haunted house.

CHAPTER 8

# MEET THE FAMILY GHOST

WALKING UPSTAIRS TO HIS ROOM, GASPAR CONTEM-
PLATED WHETHER THERE COULD BE SUCH THINGS
as ghosts. *This old house certainly is filled with other peoples
memories and as such those are definitely ghost-like,* he
thought, *but an actual ghost, a spectral disembodied entity, I'm
not so sure such a thing exists. Then again,* he told himself, *I
do believe in the immortal soul and an afterlife and if someone's
soul decided for whatever reason that it wasn't ready to leave
town, then what the heck, maybe there are ghosts hanging
around on earth.* He finally decided, *if I was a ghost I'd
probably never want to leave La Rinconada, either.* Then he
perked up, *maybe Dad's a ghost and maybe he's watching out
for me right this minute.* Suddenly the butterflies in his
stomach flew away and when he opened his bedroom
door he hadn't a care in the world.

Once inside his lair, Gaspar bolted the door, *just in case* and gave the place the once over. It was then that he realized that the Captain's Cabin alone wouldn't work for him. Opening doors and cupboards crammed full of his dead Uncle's memorabilia he soon found out that as a practical room, the Captain's Cabin was useless, but as a signature space it suited him just fine.

Entering his blue marble bathroom, Gaspar discovered that there was a connecting door to the ugly blue suite next door, which he immediately decided to take over as an office so he could have *more elbow-room* to spread out in. But right now his most pressing need was to pee.

The elaborately appointed bathroom had an alcove set aside for what his mother would have called, *the unmentionables.* There he found to his disbelief, a crazy old blue marble urinal sticking out from the wall, carved to resemble a seashell. Right across from that were two sea shell shaped toilets, one with a seat and one without. Zipping up, he searched for some way to flush the urinal but there was no lever, button or chain in sight. Then he saw it, a simple round blue marble button, set flush into the blue marble wall above the sea shell shaped contraption . He pushed it. *Whoosh*, and wondered … *when it had been used, last?*

Exploring further he found a similar round button placed over the toilet but the seatless model was a different story. This one had two gold plated seashell shaped knobs on each side of a plunger which he discovered, shut the drain like a sink. Standing over it he twisted one of the knobs, *Whoosh!* He was rudely hit in the face by a jet of rusty brown water, which shot up from the center of the bowl.

"Ugh!" He shouted, springing away he grabbed one of the towels hanging above it and dried himself off. "What's s that?"

"*That* … is a *bidet*," a man's voice answer back. "You usually use it to clean your bottom, not your face."

"Who are you?" Gaspar shrieked, scared half out of his wits, as he whirled around and saw Santa Claus sitting on the edge of the blue marble bath tub. Gone was the sharkskin suit of this afternoon. Now the dapper dude was wearing an elegant blue smoking jacket, over black and blue striped silk pajamas. An elegant monogrammed blue velvet carpet slipper covered his right foot while the left slipper dangled precariously from the tip of the very pink toes of the old boy's pointed right foot. The intruder was posed with his right elbow on his crossed leg, holding his chin in his hand, with a bemused smile on his face.

"Why have you been following us and what are you doing, in my bathroom … *d-d-d-dressed like that?* Gaspar slowly inched towards the exit but before he could get there he slipped on a fluffy carpet square and landed on his butt with the burglar looming over him.

"Don't get excited boy." The strangely dressed intruder held up his hands in surrender. "I'm your Uncle Charlie."

"You mean my GREAT, GREAT, UNCLE CHARLIE?" Gaspar hollered, pushing away from the threatening man, crawling backwards towards the door, dragging the scatter rug with him, using his hands and feet to frantically push away while still sprawled on the floor,. "The one who's *dead*?!"

Gaspar jumped up and assumed a threatening stance, holding up his hands, *karate-style*. "If you're a ghost or a phantom … g-g-go into the light or whatever dude. But if you're here to harm me or my Mom, I'm warning you right now, I know Judo!"

He didn't, but Gaspar figured that his inappropriately costumed, would-be-assailant, didn't know that. "These hands are registered with the government as lethal weapons," he warned the thug, "they're classified as weapons of mass destruction." Gaspar had to bite his lip to keep from laughing at the absurdity of his threat.

"Don't tell me that you don't believe in ghosts?"

"Of course I don't. It's not possible." Gaspar blurted without thinking.

"Hmm, if I'm a ghost then I guess I haven't anything to worry about as far as your karate chop goes, so the question is, *am* I dead?" the strange man asked. "Funny, I don't *feel* dead. Do I look dead? How did I die, can you tell me?"

"Are you kidding? If you're a ghost, you tell me. If you're not, then your some kind of a deranged, psycotic, pajama-oriented, fashion victim who has broken in here looking for trouble. If its more fancy clothes you want, there's an entire European wardrobe available to you in the closet right behind you. Take what you want but leave me and my mother alone. Now GO!" He commanded, pointing towards the window before realizing the only real way out was behind him. Gaspar was too scared to worry about what the crazy man thought of him, he wanted him out as he feared the situation might soon deteriorate into violence."

Relax kid. I'm not going to hurt you or your mother," the man replied with a grin.

Gaspar let down his guard and leaned against the bathroom door never taking his eyes off his would be assailant. "Why are you here, what do you want. You have to go back to California and leave us alone." He begged, hoping to be left in peace.

"But Gaspar, I'm not from California, I'm from here, this is my house, I built it. I really am your Uncle Charlie or the ghost of your Uncle Charlie. Please believe me."

Something in his tone made Gaspar believe him. "Then what were you doing in California? Why have you been chasing us?"

"I'm not following you or chasing you. I've been looking out for you! I've been chasing your enemies. Don't ask me who they are, I haven't figured that out yet, but believe me you've got trouble kid. I've been watching over you for a long time, I just never made myself known to you. But after that incident on the freeway with the red Le Sabre, well I realized that I had to take action." Uncle Charlie confessed. "Tell me the truth kid, have you made any enemies back in L.A.? Have you come here to runaway from something? You can trust me Gaspar, tell me everything, it's important."

Gaspar couldn't believe his good fortune, *finally an adult male he could talk to and spill his heart out to* ... but his elation turned to caution, *Could he trust him?* Since his dad died, there wasn't anyone Gaspar could talk to. None of his pals or teachers were good enough friends or mentors, nor were they even on his same wave length. But there was something about Uncle Charlie, his kindly face, the twinkle in his eyes, and he certainly didn't mince words. Most importantly, the old boy seemed sympathetic, and worldly wise, and from his assured demeanor and advanced grand-fatherly age, he certainly must have had a lot of life experiences to draw wisdom from. It was a moment of inner struggle but Gaspar finally surrendered to his inner voice and let down his defenses, deciding to take the old boy into his deepest confidence.

After he'd finished telling Charlie everything, the ghost admitted that he knew about the gang, and claimed he was the one who made sure Gaspar said, "No," by suggesting the right path to the boy while he was sleeping. He assured Gaspar that if it was gang retribution that had sent the red Le Sabre to threaten them, that he would be right there to make sure no harm came to him or his Mother.

"I'm the one who persuaded your mother to come to Florida and accept the inheritance. Let me tell you, she was a tough nut to crack. When I saw that red car following you all the way out here, I thought I should stick close and make sure they didn't try anything. Stick with me kid and nothing can harm you," Charlie promised, "I just thought that since we'll be sharing the same house, now was as good a time as any to introduce myself. Listen kid, I'm a stickler for neatness, cleanliness and order so if we're going to bunk together it's best to get the ground rules behind us so that we can get on with becoming good friends.

"Rules? Like what?" Gaspar *didn't like rules at all*.

"Like ... anything goes! Listen Gasp, I'm young, single and rich and I like to have fun so let's decide right now that we're going to be pals. I've got plenty of laughs left in me, and lots of things you'll need to know if we're going to be able to keep all this going," Charlie spread his arms around in an all-encompassing arc. "You'll see, Good Time Charlie, that's me!"

"But I already have a best pal," Gaspar informed him, "his name's Alex."

"Oh yes. Well there's just one thing, Gaspar. You can't tell anyone about me. Nobody will believe you anyway. I only make myself visible when I choose and to people whom I choose. Right now that person is *you*. Even my daughter, Eugenia Floride only saw me in her dreams. I knew she couln't handle my presence any other way, so that's how I spoke to her."

"What do you want with *me*?" Gaspar asked with a slight quaver in his voice.

"Well Gasp, you're my heir … you're … the *one*. I've got plans I need you to help me fulfill. This place is a wreck. Look at my beautiful yacht, nothing but a *rust bucket*. I tried to get through to Eugenia Floride about fixing this place up, but she just wasn't into it."

"Maybe she couldn't afford to do the work, Felix says she was poor." Gaspar suggested.

"Don't start with me. There's always been plenty of money, Eugenia just didn't want to spend it. Besides, where there's a will, there's a way. Leave the details to me kid and follow orders and you'll see, even your mother will sit up and take notice. You're the man of the house now, Gasp. Just do as I say and you'll be in clover. It's late now and I have work to do. I'll need to suggest a few ideas about this inheritance to your sleeping mother, and you look like you could use some shut-eye too. Take either of the built-in bunks. If you need me, I can usually be found in the library. I know you've found the secret passage. Use it! Time to go now, Goodnight." Without any undo theatrics, flashes of light or even a puff of smoke, Uncle Charlie dematerialized right before Gaspar's disbelieving eyes.

"A *bidet*?" Gaspar said out loud, and turned and walked out of the bathroom as if nothing unusual had happened. Back in the Captain's Cabin, he pulled off his clothes and threw them on the floor. Remembering Uncle Charlie's admonition, on *neatness, cleanliness* and *order*, he folded them into a small stack which he placed, *just so*, on a carved oak side chair.

# SNOOPING AROUND

D*ON'T BE AN IDIOT. THERE'S NO SUCH THINGS AS GHOSTS,* Gaspar thought when he woke up the next morning. Walking over to the bathroom sink Gaspar surprised himself by actually moving his hands over the counter, just in case Uncle Charlie might be sitting there, but nothing happened. Of course not. *Maybe that whole thing with Uncle Charlie last night was just some weird hallucination* … but then again, his uncle did say he only appeared when he wanted to. *Maybe old Charlie was sleeping in … so to speak.*

Rusty brown water spilled into the sink from the mouth of a gilded bronze sea tortoise. He let it run until it turned clear, before brushing his teeth. Then he went down to the kitchen in hopes of finding breakfast.

To Gaspar's surprise, Angela was already there cooking scrambled eggs and bacon. His mother was also present, sitting at the kitchen table with a steaming cup of coffee in her hands while Angela worked the stove.

"Good morning, ladies," Gaspar called out nonchalantly. "Did you sleep well?"

"Like a Goddess," came his mother's surprising reply.

"Me too," added Angela, "I slept like a Goddess too."

"What's a bidet?" Gaspar exploded.

"A bidet, what on earth ... why do you ask, Gaspar?" his mother giggled looking at Angela and shrugging her shoulders.

"Is it like a drinking fountain or something?" Gaspar guessed.

"It's usually found in a bathroom, right next to the toilet," his mother suggested.

"Exactly, but what's it for." Gaspar plowed blithely ahead, not realizing he was heading for the shoals.

"It's used by ladies and gentlemen to clean their bottoms," his mother said putting it as delicately as she could.

"Yikes, you've got to be kidding what the heck ... I have one in my bathroom and it squirted me in the face." Gaspar shouted, "What a nightmare."

"How'd ya know it's called a bidet?" asked his mother innocently, choking back laughter.

"I don't know ... maybe I dreamed it ... I really don't remember." Gaspar tripped all over himself with embarrassment.

"Scrambled eggs and bacon?" Angela broke in changing the subject.

"Cackle fruit. Yes please." Gaspar answered, "Where's Alex?"

"He's doing some chores with his father. He'll be done soon." Angela informed him almost apologetically.

"Oh bummer," Gaspar intoned.

"That will give you plenty of time to put your things away and help me around the house too," his mother suggested. "While Alex does his chores, you and I can get moved in. Then Angela and I plan to go into town to do a little bit of exploring together. If you and Alex want to join us, you're welcome to come along." Elvira said in her friendliest, motherly tone.

"Nah, Ma," Gaspar definitely didn't want to hang out with the girls, "I'll unpack and hang out with Alex around here ... maybe go for a swim."

"Okay, but if you change your mind, you're welcome to join us." Elvira extended her invitation again.

"Cool," Gaspar actually looked forward to meeting the locals and checking out the town, but not today. Deep down inside, he wanted to find Uncle Charlie again, or had that all been a hallucination?

After breakfast, Gaspar raced back upstairs to get organized per his mother's orders. Checking out the closet he realized that he'd first have to clear an area and rearrange some of the drawers in order to make room for his own *important* things.

*It was all Uncle Charlie's stuff*, and what a collection it was. Surveying the contents of the closet and rummaging through the chest of drawers Gaspar discovered amongst all of Uncle Charlie's furnishings what appeared to be, *a solid gold key*. Gaspar placed the large key around his neck using one of the many gold chains he found there. He vowed to discover exactly which lock it would open. Searching further he came upon mountains of custom made, monogrammed shirts with matching boxer shorts, stacks of cashmere socks and sweaters in every color imaginable, paraphernalia for every type of sporting activity including hunting, fishing, swimming, hiking, skiing and tennis, and a vast assortment of dress suits for every occasion from business to dinner and dancing. Seeing all of this Gaspar could only conclude that Uncle Charlie most probably had to have been the best-dressed man in the world.

Finishing with Charlie's extravagant wardrobe, to which Gaspar had added his own two pairs of jeans, two cutoff shorts, twelve pair of underwear, twelve pair of white sox, and six pair of black socks, six polo shirts and twelve T-shirts in every color but white, two pair of sneakers, and one pair of black loafers, and a dark blue suit, two dress shirts, a striped tie, and two belts, most of which his mother had insisted he bring along just in case they had to go to church or something. Conspicuously missing from Gaspar's wardrobe were pajamas which he wholeheartedly had refused to wear since childhood as opposed to the nearly fifty pair of Uncle Charlie's silk pajamas arranged on the shelves.

Next, Gaspar attacked the Captain's Cabin. Throwing open all the built-in cupboards and drawers that he could find. *But what he was really hoping for were some more secret compartments*. Digging around he didn't find any treasure, but instead came across old boxes of pills, dried out creams, hair brushes, combs, toothbrushes, pins, cotton balls, and dozens of matchbooks proclaiming, Cotton Club, Stork Club, Mocambo, Starlight Roof, Top O' the Mark, Coconut Grove—night-spots from coast to coast that meant something to Gaspar who loved the nightclub scenes in old movies. He searched the desk which sat squarely in front of the fantail window, and although it had many drawers, all of them except two seemed to be either locked or stuck. He took the key he'd just found, out of his pocket to see if it would fit, but he knew it wouldn't before he'd even made the effort. The first drawer that he was able to open was completely empty. *That was a bust*, he thought.

The other drawer contained a pair of glasses, an ivory handled magnifying glass, an old checkbook with only stubs left inside and a ruler. There were also several cobalt blue and purple bottles, which had skull and crossbones emblazoned across their labels. Everything he'd found so far had been a haphazard jumble, and looked to Gaspar like it had been rifled through before.

Disappointed, he decided it was time to check out something really important—Uncle Charlie's yacht!

Kicking off his sneakers he bounded downstairs and out the front door. He skirted around the house to the right, dashed across the terrace and took the stairs down to the beach. Reaching the sand he ran between the garden wall and the shore, towards the yacht canal. Reaching the intersection where the garden wall hit the canal wall, he stopped and looked out to sea, following the canal wall which headed straight out into the bay as far as the breakwater. From his position on the sand, he marveled at the two giant alabaster lanterns which stood atop the wall, on each side of the opening to the Gulf. Turning to his right, he climbed another staircase back up to the garden level and found himself standing between the yacht canal and the swimming pool.

The house now loomed on his right and he could see a complete other aspect of it. There jutting out from the center of the second story facade was the back of a Spanish galleon. That was *his* room. It looked as if a giant, had picked up a pirate ship and shoved it right through the wall. The Captain's Cabin, complete with giant lanterns and three theatrical flags made of sheet metal painted with Spanish armorial motifs were hanging in mid-air. Above his room was a balustraded balcony, formed by the protrusion of the cabin, and looking like the poop deck on a Spanish Galleon. He could also see the outline of a concealed door on the building's façade.

*I wonder how I can access that door and get to that balcony*, was the first thought that crossed Gaspar's mind. *There's got to be a secret staircase connecting that door from the Captain's Cabin*, he decided.

Coming back to the goal he'd set for himself, he turned to his left and there she was, the sunken or sinking yacht, he couldn't tell which yet. He could still read her name, which was proudly emblazoned across her stern, *Argente, Merida*.

*That's funny*, Gaspar thought, *Mexican registry*.

He wondered how deep the canal was, and if it had filled up with silt since it was built, and if the boat was lying on the bottom or just listing tragically. He needed to find out all these things. Without another thought, he stripped to his briefs and jumped into the warm water. Gaspar paddled around the wreck, grabbing hold of portholes that were still above water, to look inside. What he saw was heartbreaking. The most beautiful paneled interiors had water lapping lopsidedly almost three feet from the ceiling, doors had opened, exposing more water on the other side of the ship, sloshing against the ceiling beams. He could see the remnants of pretty wallpaper, old light fixtures, some antique furniture, ruined mirrors, framed paintings and prints, all water stained and hanging askew against the peeling walls. There was still detritus floating about, but nothing recognizable like chairs or books, just flat objects like peeling paint or rotting garbage. Gaspar ducked under water but the visibility was nil. He decided he'd have to come back with a mask and some fins.

Paddling down the starboard side, he reached the prow which was lower than the stern due to the boat having taken on more water forward than aft. Gaspar continued his leisurely swim, dipping under now and then hoping to touch bottom, but he couldn't. He wondered how deep of a draft the *Argente* had, to need such a deep canal. Coming up the port side, he was able to grab a toehold on the edge of one of the portholes and pull himself up and over the railing onto the rotting deck. Gaspar didn't fear that the boards wouldn't hold his weight. At four-foot, eleven inches, he weighed a mere 90-pounds, even so, he walked along the deck gingerly just in case. Heading towards the wheelhouse, his bare feet wanted to slip but Gaspar was nothing if not agile and balanced himself on the listing deck with precision. Reaching the wheelhouse, he stepped through the door which was hanging in mid-air over the sloping deck. It was all there—the equipment, the logs, binoculars, pencils, both terrestrial and celestial maps, rulers, telescopes, barometer, wireless transmitter, astrolabe, the works. In a closet he found wet weather gear, and even four sets of dress uniforms for the crew, just rotting on hangers. The whole scene was mind-boggling. Crossing the bridge to the high side of the deck, he proceeded aft towards the saloon, dining room, and poop deck. He had to really heave with all his might to get the door to the saloon open. Pulling as hard as he could, he cracked it open and got a foot in. Using his body like a crow bar, he gave it a final heave, folding the door flat against the exterior wall of the cabin.

How he wished his father could be with him now. An ensign in the Navy, Gaspar's dad had taught him everything he knew about ships and the sea. Some of their best times were spent at yacht and boating shows or pouring over yachting magazines and reading the ads at the back for old used sailboats. More weekends than not they would be walking the docks at the marina pointing out their favorite sloops, and they loved to eat outside at the harbor in San Pedro and watch all the boat traffic passing too and fro. Seeing this forlorn yet beautiful ship made Gaspar sad. *Dad why couldn't you have held on just a little longer,* he prayed, *you would have loved this.*

The list had caused a lot of the furnishing in the saloon to shift to port, and although it reeked of mildew and mold, its faded decor of soft rose, ivory and silver told the story of a more elegant time. The dining saloon had fared no better than the rest. The central table had been bolted to the floor when the yacht was built, but the neo-classical Adam arm chairs had slid across the room along with the tea trolley, and anything else that hadn't been nailed down. What Gaspar couldn't believe was that it was all still there, a silver tea set, a gorgeous silver plateau, and an Edwardian silver epergne were all just lying in a heap. Looking inside the large buffet, he saw that all the silverware was still in the drawers and the china and silver serving pieces still stacked in the cupboard ... all of these just having listed port side along with the rest of the ship.

Stepping out onto the aft deck he found that the wicker furniture, complete with their rotting cushions, had also shifted, port side. The striped canvas awning overhead now hung in tatters but otherwise except for the listing deck, it was ready to receive guests ... *sort of*.

"Ahoy, Gaspar," came a familiar voice from atop the sea wall.

"Ahoy, Alex," Gaspar called back, come on, you've got to see this."

"I'm not wearing any trunks," Alex called back anxiously.

"Neither am I," Gaspar chuckled, holding out the front of his Calvins. "Come on, the water's warm. Besides, I need your help over here."

Gaspar watched as his friend stripped down to his un-Calviny baggy old BVDs and jumped into the water. Alex took the quick way around the stern and swam midway down the port side where the water lapped against the listing deck.

"Welcome aboard *Argente* me hearty," Gaspar called offering Alex his hand to help pull him up. "Have you ever been on board before?"

"Not after she sank it. Lady Eugenia forbade any of us to come on board, *ever*. Hey man, what's that crazy necklace you got on?"

"I found this key in a drawer in my closet, and the chain too. I think its solid gold, but I don't know. Anyway, I'm gonna keep it around my neck till I find out what it opens."

"Cool. So what's up,? If my dad catches me on this boat … he'll kill me. So wha-da-ya wanna do here, Gasp?"

Gaspar ignored his friends fears and dove right into his plan, "There's a lot of valuable stuff on board—furniture, paintings, light fixtures, silver, china. Good stuff," Gaspar explained. "I'll bet we can salvage a lot of it and sell it. Ya-wanna help me?"

"Sure, but how? I don't think we can build a bridge between the deck and the wall of the canal. What's your plan, Gasp?

"Well, we could either swim in and out, but that would be too difficult and some of the stuff isn't even wet yet, so there's no point in ruining it now." Gaspar pondered the situation. "I know! How about the lifeboat, I bet it's still sea worthy, we could load it up and float the treasure over to the boat house."

"We'll need some fins, masks, underwater flashlights and baskets or canvas bags for carrying a lot of small things." Gaspar suggested.

"We can get all that stuff in town, I know just the place." Alex assured him as they walked aft.

"We better get some boy butter to grease the winches just in case and some rope to lower the baskets or bags over the starboard side," Gaspar was nothing if not thorough.

"Boy butter, what's that?" Alex asked.

"That's what they call grease or oil in the Navy. My dad was an ensign in the Navy, he taught me all the best Navy slang." Gaspar informed Alex proudly.

"Cool Gasp, you'll have to teach me the lingo now." Alex suggested as they reached the stern where the lifeboat hung on it's davits. "Okay, let's check it out. Hopefully the winches aren't totally rusted." Alex worried "Let's see if they're still working."

The boys checked out the condition of the davits and the pulleys and decided to wait until they had all the supplies they needed from town before tackling the problem.

"Once we get her launched Al, it might make better sense if we just pull the lifeboat up portside and walk the stuff onto it," Gaspar suggested logically.

"That would work." Alex agreed.

"Okay, let's get to town so we can come back and do it."

# CHAPTER 10

# ANOTHER RAPIER IN THE ROAD

LATER THAT DAY, GASPAR AND ALEX PLANNED TO CATCH A BUS INTO CALALUNA FROM THE RINCONADA STOP JUST outside the house's main gate. Alex informed Gaspar that the buses stopped there every half hour on their route between Calaluna and Llojeta. The two towns were situated exactly an hour away from each other, La Rinconada marking the halfway point between them.

Close on Alex's heels, Gaspar stepped out of the gate, looking left for on coming traffic, then right before catching up with his pal. "There aren't any busses coming in either direction," Gaspar complained.

"Just wait … they'll be here. Lady Eugenia used to say, 'you could set your watch by them … just like Benito,' whoever he was." Alex filled him in.

Just as they began walking across the road a vintage black Oldsmobile Cutlass pulled out from a side lane swerving straight for the two boys who were walking shoulder to shoulder as they crossed the two lane road.

Gaspar turned to his right to inform Alex that the Benito, Lady Eugenia was referring to, could only have been Benito Musselini, who was famous for getting the Italian trains to run on time back in the 1930s. Before Gaspar had a chance to inform his friend he saw an old black car which hadn't been there a moment ago, barreling towards them at high speed.

"LOOK OUT!" Gaspar yelped, pushing Alex across the road while standing directly in the path of the careening vehicle. With less than an inch to spare Gaspar jumped out of the way, falling flat on his back with his legs in the air while Alex watched in horror from his place in the dirt on the other side of the road.

The whole incident was over in less than the blink of an eye and both boys were shaken up.

"What in blazes!" Gaspar shouted, still sprawled on the ground, looking through a cloud of dust at Alex. "That guy was aiming for us! It was an obvious attempt to hit us, he wasn't out of control he was *hellbent* on murder Al."

"That was a close one," Alex called back as he got up and ran back across the road to his prone friend. "Holy hell, are you all right Gasp?"

"That *blistering barnicled budgerigar* should be drawn and quartered." Gaspar sputtered. "Whoever told him he knew how to drive should have their brains examined!" Alex insisted.

"Yeah," Gaspar said, breathing hard, "Where did that guy come from Al? Do you agree that he was deliberately trying to hit us."

"You mean hit *you*." Alex corrected him.

Gaspar wasn't kidding anyone, *He knew he was the target and he was pretty sure that the car had to be a California import brought in for the occasion*. "You didn't see his license plates did ya." Gaspar asked weakly.

"Nah. That's the first time in my life that I've ever had to dodge any traffic around here." Alex insisted.

"That car. It was an Olds Cutlass." Gaspar, a keen antique car aficionado had learned all the models by heart from his father at an early age. "My mother and I had a run in with another rapier-named model in L.A., Al. It was a red Buick LeSabre to be exact. I wonder," Gaspar murmured, staring down the road at the cloud of diminishing dust, "it couldn't just be a coincidence, could it?"

Alex reached down to help his pal up. "We've got to go in and tell your mom or at least my dad," he insisted.

"No way!" Gaspar's word was final. "If my mom finds out that our lives are in any way, in danger, she'll yank me out-a-here faster than you can say *salamugundi*. No way are either of us to speak of this to any of our parents Al.

Maybe the police, but not the parents, not now anyway Al, not until we can figure out what all this hostility is about.

"Okay Gasp, if you say so." Alex didn't sound convinced. Here comes the bus, Gasp," Alex pointed up the road while dusting Gaspar off. "Let's go Buddy."

Jumping on board, they told the driver about their narrow escape but the man was unable to make heads or tails of the incident, nor shed any light on having seen an old black Oldsmobile Cutlass in the vicinity. Unable to put aside their near accident the two boys rode into town in silence. For Gaspar, the butterflies were back, while his head filled with a million scenarios, most of which ended with harm to him or his mother.

Reaching Calaluna, Alex came-to and shook Gaspar out of the constant replaying in his mind of the near disaster and worse.

"Gasp, we need to maximize our time in town, so why don't you go introduce yourself to the police while I hit the hardware store and the dive shop to buy rope, grease, some canvas bags, and the underwater flashlights, fins and masks." Alex reiterated the shopping list. You okay buddy?" Alex asked, concern in his voice. "Are you cool with the plan?"

Gaspar shook his head, in silent agreement.

The bus dropped them at the corner of Main and Center Streets. "The station's right over there," Alex said pointing up the block to the complex of buildings which comprised the Calaluna City Hall, Police Department, and Fire Department. "I'll meet you up there after I get our stuff."

Reaching the station, Gaspar went inside and introduced himself to Sergeant O'Malley, the officer on duty and told him his reason for stopping by.

"Crime around here is rare, Mr. Brown," he told Gaspar. "I think you'd better meet the chief and tell *him* what happened."

Minutes later Gaspar was seated across the desk from Chief Morgan, an older man who listened with a grim expression on his face as Gaspar recounted the recent incidents leading up to his arrival on Perdido Isle, and the recent attempt on his life.

Gaspar was excited and tripped all over himself trying to piece the facts together. He'd seen enough old murder mysteries to know to stick to the facts, and he tried to speak in a calm articulate way, but it was to no avail. No matter how hard Gaspar tried, he felt he might be dramatizing the situation out of proportion although he didn't know how much more could be made of *attempted murder* than what he had just explained to the chief.

"This is a very serious situation, Mr. Brown. From what you've told me of the events in Los Angeles, and now here, the written threats and a second attempt on your life, I'll certainly put out an all-points bulletin for an old black Olds Cutlass and a red Le Sabre too. There can't be too many automobiles around here that fit those descriptions. In the meantime, I'll have a chat with your mother, and please keep me informed if any more threats, actual or even imagined spring up."

"I will," Gaspar promised, "but if you don't mind Chief, I'd rather tell my mother myself. She knows nothing of this incident, was not a witness or anything so there's really nothing she can contribute and I don't want to worry her unnecessarily if I don't have to." He pleaded.

"I understand Gaspar, I think your decision is wise for now. Are you sure you've told me *everything*?" the wise man asked. "You can't think of any reason at all why someone might want to see you or your mother or Alex Mendoza dead?" he asked looking at Gaspar thinking he'd gotten a slight reaction from the kid. "Now be honest son," the chief insisted.

"To be very honest Chief Morgan, I cannot." Gaspar lied. *There was just no way he could tell the chief about his troubles in L.A, without getting his mother involved and that was out of the question at this point.*

"Okay Gaspar, then I guess that sums it up for now. We'll do our work at this end and get back to you."

"Thanks, Chief Morgan, I appreciate your help, and your discretion." Gaspar shook the police chief's hand.

"I'll call you in a day or to and check in, and I'll definitely let you know if I learn any more information regarding the two cars or any other clues that may turn up."

With that the Chief stood up and escorted Gaspar to the door, watching after the new-comer as the boy left the precinct.

"Let's get back to the house," Gaspar exclaimed walking up to Alex who was waiting for him outside the station. "Here comes the bus, let's grab it and get going."

Once on board they rode in silence each lost in their own thoughts which both centered on recreating the near accident in front of La Rinconada.

"You know something, Gasp," Alex finally piped up, trying to lighten the mood, "we're a couple of *breakers*," he announced proudly, as the bus bounced them back home.

"Breakers? What's that?" Gaspar drawled unimpressed.

"Breakers are salvage men. They were all over Florida back in the day. They were pirates who went *legit* and helped the Spanish salvage treasure from galleons that went down in storms. Sometimes they'd move landmarks or guide unsuspecting ships right onto reefs and shoals and then offer their services to do the salvage work. As you can imagine, when the United States took over Florida, they put a stop to the breakers, although from what I've read, several legitimate *breakers* continued doing salvage work under the new US rules and regulations.

"Breakers. Cool!" Gaspar agreed a smile returning to his face.

"Yeah, I read about them in that book on Florida pirates that I showed you the other night in my room, it said that breakers were some of the wealthiest citizens in Florida during the pirate heydays.

"That so," trilled Gaspar, "ya don't say. Did you see Beverwil when you were at the hardware store?" Gaspar asked.

"Yeah, he was there. How do you know him?"

"I met him in the cafe yesterday. What trick was he up to today?" Gaspar smirked.

"He had an assistant there who helped me but Beverwil came in from the back after a few minutes, all sweaty and dusty and out of breath like he'd been running a race or something." Alex recounted.

"He's a kinda nosy guy, don't ya think?" Gaspar kept fishing.

"My dad says he knows more about the people who live in Calaluna than they do themselves. My mama says he's the biggest gossip in town and not to believe a word he says about anyone. He certainly was curious about *you*, the *new boy* in town."

"Wha-da-ya-mean?" Gaspar drawled.

"I was only in his shop a few minutes, but he grilled me like crazy—knew all about you, all about your Mom, where you lived in California and why you're here, and wanted to know what I was going to use the boy butter, rope and canvas bags for too."

"He called it *boy butter*?"

"Yeah, he must have been in the Navy too, like your dad. There's something fishy about that guy," Alex pondered. "Somehow, Beverwil doesn't seem like Navy material to me."

"You didn't tell him anything about me or what we're up to did you?" Gaspar asked anxiously.

"Nah, none of his business. What's eating you Gasp." Alex asked nervously,

"Eating me, wha-da-ya-mean, Al? Nothin's eatin' me."

"Come on Gasp, level with me, what's up?" Now it was Alex's turn to be insistent.

"Okay Al, you're my best friend. I need to tell some-body—somebody alive that is."

"Wha-da-ya-mean, someone alive?" Alex seemed really confused now.

"Oh never mind Al, it's just a turn of phrase. Listen. I almost got in a lot of trouble back in L.A. After my dad died, I was so lonely and so miserable and this neighbor kid, Jimmy Larsen asked me to join him and his pals to do some goofy stuff, and I was impressed cause they were older kids and they wanted me to hang with them, but all they really wanted was a little kid who could break into places and squeeze through tiny windows to open front doors for them. I never did anything illegal Al, you gotta believe me. After I found out what they wanted me to do, I told them no, and in return they beat the crap out of me and told me that if I ever told anyone about their gang and what they were up to, that I'd be sorry. Well, they all got caught robbing an electronics warehouse, and even though I never ratted on them, I think they think

I did. Anyway, ever since they were sent to Juvi, I've had this strange feeling that their friends have been out to get me. I even think they've managed to follow me to Florida, and I'm miserable because I can't tell my mom. If I did, she'd never let me out of her sight again. Even worse, I feel like I've put her in harm's way with that red Le Sabre trying to run us off the road, and now I've almost gone and gotten you killled by that black Olds Cutlass. I don't know what to do. Please Al, please don't mention this to anyone, it's gotta stay between you and me. Maybe together we can get to the bottom of all this and I can make a clean break of it here in my new home."

*There, he'd said it, he now had a compatriot, someone other than an imaginary old ghost, maybe now, with a sidekick like Al, he would be able to set things right.*

"Wow Gasp, that's real cops and robbers stuff you're talking about. Count me in man, I'll be your cover, just tell me what you want me to do." Alex assured him as the bus pulled up to the Rinconada stop.

"Thanks Al, I knew I could count on you, but for now mums the word. Let's go inside and grab something to eat so we can get back to work on the yacht." Gaspar suggested as they jumped off the bus and headed for the gate.

# CHAPTER 11

# RAISING THE *ARGENTE*

RUNNING INTO THE HOUSE GASPAR AND ALEX FOUND THE KITCHEN A BEEHIVE OF ACTIVITY.

"What've you boys been up to?" Elvira asked as they ran into the room.

"We got some fins and masks from town and now we're going to go swimming."

"Not before lunch," Elvira protested, "I've made sandwiches for all of us. Angela has been a Saint helping me sort things out here all morning, so let's sit for a minute and have a little bite together."

"Okay Mom, but just a quick lunch. Al and I have a lot to do still."

Elvira eyed the boys suspiciously. "What are you both so excited about?"

"Yes, Alex, tell us what you two are up to." Angela demanded.

"We're hunting for *pirate treasure*." Gaspar offered, knowing the Moms wouldn't believe the truth. *If he told them what they were really up to, there'd be holy hell to pay. Besides, salvaging treasure from the yacht was the same as finding pirate treasure to him, so he rationalized that it was just a little white lie and of no real consequence.*

"Yeah," Alex backed him up, "*pirate treasure*, millions in gold bullion and *pieces of eight*."

"Oh well, why didn't you say so," Elvira said, giving Angela a wink, "we promise not to keep you away from your hunt too long. What do you say Angela, after they find the treasure, I hope they give us first pick of the spoils. Maybe a ruby necklace for me, and how about emeralds for you." Elvira joked.

"Oh emeralds," Angela whined, "so common, sapphires are the only stones I wear anymore, with diamonds of course to bring out their true color." she simpered.

"But we really *are* looking for treasure," Alex protested before Gaspar elbowed his ribs.

After lunch, the two boys quickly changed into trunks, grabbed some towels and their gear and headed back towards the yacht. Taking just the rope and the boy butter, they dove in and raced around the stern. Gaspar reached the deck first, laughing and snorting, and hauled himself up, and then helped Alex come aboard.

"Let's see if we can get the lifeboat free, even if we have to cut it free. I don't care." Gaspar told Alex.

Together they removed the canvas covering off the lifeboat only to find the remains of several dead rats rotting on the bottom.

"Ew! Gross! Alex gagged.

"Don't puke on me," Gaspar warned him . "If you have to toss your cookies, do so … over the side."

Balancing along the aft rail, with one boy on each side of the lifeboat, they stretched to grease the rusting pulleys and winches and then worked on the davits. Jumping down, they untied the rotting lines, jumping back just in time as the ropes slipped through their greasy hands and the lifeboat splashed hard into the water. The small craft had been set free, and the ends of its lines now floated behind *Argente*, like a couple of *Irish Pennant*s or at least that's how Gaspar's dad would have describe them in Navy lingo.

"Well that was easy," Gaspar joked, "Grab the rope and tie it around the davit and I'll lower myself down into the boat."

"Or you and I could swim abaft and float the boat portside and double it up to the railing, athwartships, right about there," Alex suggested pointing to the railing."

"Huh?" Gaspar said.

"Don't ya know *pirate-talk* when ya hear it?" Alex asked, astonished.

"Pirate-talk? Al, I'm from California, we don't have any pirates out there."

"No problem, by the time I get done with you, you'll be swearing like a pirate." Alex promised.

"Okay, whatever. Now let's get *abaft*, and *double up* the lifeboat *athwartships*, on the double! Jumping over the stern, Gaspar made a mighty cannonball-splash, into the water.

Alex followed, making an even mightier splash. Together the two boys edged the large lifeboat around the stern and over to the yacht's portside rail. This time Alex sprang up on deck first and tied the rope to the ring at the prow of the lifeboat and then to the railing, repeating the process with the ring at the stern of the lifeboat so that the small craft was doubled up right alongside the yacht making it easy to reach over its rail to load the treasure.

Gaspar scrambled on board suggesting, "Let's get the obvious things first from the dining saloon."

They started with the cream and gold Adam style chairs, then the silver tea service and its heavy silver tray. Next came the silver plateau and the epergne and then they grabbed an important looking pair of silver candelabra before looking into the sideboard again for what was hiding there.

"We'll need to get our canvas bags before we can load all this small stuff," Gaspar decided.

"Let's fill the lifeboat as much as possible with the big stuff before heading to the boat house. We can pick up the canvas bags then." Alex suggested.

The boys crossed the rotting carpet of the salon, which was littered with a lot of moldy old books bound in leather stamped in gold. They worked hard, filling the lifeboat with a Louis XVI salon set, a small liquor cabinet in inlaid wood holding a set of fancy bottles and tiny footed glasses. There were also several oil paintings, and mirrors in gilded frames which they threw in for good measure.

Having filled the lifeboat to capacity, the boys dragged it along the portside up to the prow, then slipped into the water to float it the additional thirty feet to the steps in front of the boat house. Tying off near the stairs they began unloading the treasure, lugging it up the stairs where they piled it under the covered porch.

"Let's go back and get some more," Gaspar urged.

"I need a break," Alex insisted. "Let's go for a swim in the surf and then go back and get some more."

"Race ya! " Gaspar jumped up and ran for the beach, with Alex not far behind him.

Hitting the surf, Alex grabbed Gaspar and dragged him into the water, then threw himself on top of him. Laughing and sputtering they began a mighty water fight, flinging waves of water at each other, knocking each other down in front of small waves, and body surfing the bigger waves again and again. Laughing, panting and out of breath they finally dragged themselves to the water's edge and plopped down on the wet sand, faces turned to the sun. Lying there they let the soft waves wash up over their legs and let the hot Florida sun bake their faces and warm their bodies.

Gaspar realized that he was happier than he'd been in a long time, the butterflies had flown away again, at least for now.

"Look at that." Alex said, breaking Gaspar's reverie. He was pointing out to sea at a huge black motor yacht bobbing at anchor, just past the breakwater.

"Is it ours?" Gaspar asked facetiously.

"Nope," Alex replied. "Never seen that one before. Must be a visitor, maybe we can get a better look using binoculars," Alex suggested.

"I saw a pair on the bridge, let's go get-em and check her out." Gaspar insisted.

Dragging themselves off the sand they climbed the steps to the top of the terrace and ran to where they had tied the lifeboat up at the boat house landing. Grabbing their canvas bags, they pushed off using the oars, and rowed back to the side of the sinking yacht.

"I'll get the binoculars," Gaspar shouted, reaching the deck first and running towards the wheelhouse. "Wait for me at the stern."

Returning to where Alex waited for him, Gaspar raised the glasses to his eyes and focused on the shiny black motor yacht.

"She's called, *Revenge* and she's a real beauty." Gaspar reported to his matey. "Take a look," he said passing Alex the binoculars, "Now that's what I'd call a super yacht. It makes this bucket of bilge look like *old-mother-hairnet*," Gaspar noted sadly. "But to be honest I'd keep Argent over her any day of the week, Al. I prefer Argent's classic lines, not those ominous, four dark curvy decks looking like a stack of misshapen black pancakes."

"Do I detect jealousy?" Alex ribbed him.

"Not at all, Al. To me it looks just like a stealth bomber, but on water … and you have to admit, there's definitely something sinister and forbidding about her appearance."

"Two hundred feet long, four decks, shiny black and gunmetal gray superstructure, and a lot of open decks." Alex rattled off her attributes.

"What they call in yachting circles a purposeful and imposing silhouette, sinuous and lithe, created by the lateral rounding and the combined affects of shape and color …" Gaspar parroted what he'd read in some old yachting magazines.

"Good one Gasp." Alex complimented.

"That's what you get from my reading too many "yachts for sale" brochures with my dad." Gaspar chuckled.

"Swheeeee," Alex whistled. "That's some sweet boat, and you have to admit her look is astonishing. I've never seen anything like her around these waters."

"She's even got a big black helicopter on deck!" Gaspar marveled.

"Yeah, that's the first thing I noticed." Alex pretended to be unimpressed.

"Look she's leaving, Al." Gaspar wailed, handing Alex the glasses.

The boys watched *Revenge* pull quickly away from where it had been anchored.

"Must have seen us watching them with our glasses," Gaspar guessed out loud. But to himself he wondered, *Could they have been sent from California to find him?*

Considering the size of that yacht he had no idea that his old neighborhood gang was so highly connected with the mob but apparently they had very long, far reaching fingers. The butterflies were back again.

"Let's get back to business, there's still treasure to unload," Alex reminded.

Starting back in the dining saloon, they filled the bags very carefully with solid silver dishes and salt and pepper shakers, knife and place-card holders, wine coasters, and barrel shaped mustard and jam pots, all made of solid sterling silver. Curiously they found no crystal stemware, only silver goblets, tumblers and highball cups as well as other silver bar ware and serving utensils. Having made two more salvage trips to the boat house, the boys decided to call it a day. Tying up the lifeboat, they started back toward the house.

"You never told me what you had to do this morning?" Gaspar asked.

"Just help my father. Repairs, and painting, odd jobs … stuff like that. It's only a couple of hours a day, we start early and then I get the rest of the day off to *lollygag* around!"

"Lollygag?"

"That's pirate talk for goofing off." Alex informed him.

"Ah." Gaspar nodded. "That's cool.

"What about you, Wha'd you do?"

"Me, I just had to clean my room. I just hope my Mom doesn't get any ideas about giving me chores to do, just cause we're in a new place.

"You're lucky Gasp. I've only known you a couple a days, but I can see that you call the shots in your family. Your Mom just lets you do whatever you want." Alex was jealous.

"Not really, Al." Gaspar explained. "I'm just not interested in giving up my mornings to do chores when we only have three months of vacation to get all this salvage stuff done.

"Salvage stuff? Whad-a-ya talkin' bout? What *else* do you have in mind?"

"Wouldn't it be fun, Al, if you and I could get *Argente* to float again?

"Well I can't say you don't think big, Gasp, then we could really play pirates!"

# UNCLE CHARLIE RETURNS

T HAT NIGHT AFTER DINNER, GASPAR TOLD HIS MOTHER
HE WAS EXHAUSTED BY HIS SEARCH FOR PIRATE TREA-
sure and that he was going straight to bed.

"Take a shower before turning in," his mother said. "I
don't want to hurt your feelings but you stink."

Gaspar took a whiff and had to agree. "Yeah, okay.
By the way, have you *seen* my shower? It's a mechanical
wonder, and the tub is like a small swimming pool."

"Sounds just like my bathroom. Mine's all pink marble.
I've never seen anything like it."

"Mine's all blue marble." Gaspar bragged, "I can't
wait to see what all the taps are for. I'll give you a full
report in the morning.

"The problem with all that pink marble is ... I think
actually I like it." Elvira giggled.

Gaspar joined his Mom in a chuckle. "You'r really starting to like it here aren't you Mom?" he asked hopefully, "I mean, you seem a lot happier since we've arrived here and you look like you're settling in quite well."

"I can't say I've taken to La Rinconada, like a fish to water like you have, but hey, when I look around, I have to admit, it beats North Hollywood any day of the week. The décor may not be my idea of *cozy*, but it's certainly comfortable. I still have financial questions about how we're supposed to pay for this new fancy life, but for now, I'm thinking of this as a vacation, and if it doesn't work out, we can find a smaller place somewhere else or just go home."

That wasn't exactly what Gaspar wanted to hear, but he figured they'd cross that bridge when they got to it.

"Yeah ... well ... I better go take my bath. Goodnight Mom.

"*Night*, Gaspar, love you."

Gaspar decided that, *if he was going to bathe, he may as well do it right.* Turning the taps on the blue marble bathtub he watched the rusty brown water flow out of a gilded dolphin's mouth, as it filled a small blue marble seashell before cascading over into the carved blue shell-shaped tub. As soon as the water started coming out clear, he got down on his knees and inserted the old rubber stopper into the drain. Rummaging around in one of the vanity drawers he came up with an old canister of something called *Dr. Simon's Attar of Roses Curative Bath Salts.*

*What the hey?* he thought to himself, sprinkling a generous amount of bath salts into the water. Taking his clothes off he threw them in a heap, while a massive mountain of foam begin to rise inside the tub. *This will be fun*, he thought. He couldn't believe that the steam actually carried a scent of rose petals and that the glistening foam actually had a pinkish tinge to it.

Grabbing a wash cloth and an old bar of Roger Gallet soap off the sink, he stepped cautiously into the tub. *It is hot!* Being accustomed to only showering back in California, he realized that this was the first bath he'd taken in a long, long time.

Slowly he lowered himself into the steaming bubbles and closed his eyes.

"Tough day?" a voice boomed.

Nearly jumping out of his skin, Gaspar opened his eyes wide and saw Uncle Charlie materialize on the edge of the bath tub. The ghost was wearing turquoise paisley patterned silk pajamas, Gaspar's initial fear quickly evaporated into annoyance.

"Uh, hello? Could I have a little privacy here, or is this the only room in the house you hang out in?" Gaspar asked derisively before closing his eyes again in hopes that Uncle Charlie would just disappear.

Uncle Charlie laughed out loud at Gaspar's discomfort.

Opening his eyes, Gaspar complained, "Still here I see. You really are a ghost aren't you, not just some mix-up in my head?

The old boy nodded in the affirmative.

You can understand how hard this is for me to believe." He closed his eyes again, hoping the apparition would disappear.

"Boo!" Charlie clowned.

"Crap," Gaspar cursed. "I've really lost it. Okay Uncle Charlie, let's get this over with, I'm not accustomed to an audience while in the bath. *Wha-da-ya* want?"

"Listen kid," Uncle Charlie was enthusiastic, "I wanted to talk to you before turning in, and I can only see you when you're alone, so here I am."

"What do you want from me?" Gaspar asked again in a bored drawl. "When I woke up this morning I thought you were just a dream, and now, here you are again."

"Look," Uncle Charlie changed direction, "I like your initiative, salvaging the *Argente*. Good work boy. … Do you really want to raise it?"

"Now how could I, a thirteen and three quarters year-old kid, raise a hundred-foot yacht?"

"A hundred and *fifty* foot yacht. *Easy*! All you need is money, and if you need more … I happen to know where you can get some more."

"You, a dead ghost, have a bank account?"

"Gasp, show some respect. I, a *dead ghost* as you so daintily put it, know where *you* can get *more than a bank account.* Just as much as you need, *to float your boat*, if you'll pardon the expression.

"Tell me what you have in mind," Gaspar asked warily.

"What I have to tell you is important," said Uncle Charlie, "so listen carefully."

When it came to spending money … Gaspar was all ears.

"I found pirate treasure on this island way back in 1900, but not just any ol' pirate treasure. I found the mother lode, the treasure hoard of The Pirate King, José, Gaspar. That's right boy, the seemingly limitless fortune amassed by Gasparilla himself."

Gaspar stood straight up, splashing water everywhere. With soap suds clinging to his glistening body he shouted, "Eureka! Where is it Uncle? When can I see it? Tell me, huh, come on, show me now!" He begged.

"Slow down kid, it's not that easy. First you'll need to *find* the treasure, and believe me, that's going to be more fun for you than spending it." Uncle Charlie informed him.

"How, where? Give me a clue Uncle Charlie, I'll go searching tonight." Gaspar had no idea where to begin as he plopped back down into the tub sending a tidal wave of soap suds Uncle Charlie's way.

"All I'll tell you is that it's hidden somewhere on this property, and don't forget that the 500,000 acres of this island includes a lot of the land surrounding the island, which is underwater.

"Well that's a big help," Gaspar complained. "What are we talking about here, gold, jewels, cash?"

"Yes, gold, and silver and jewels, which you can turn into cash … but understand, this is not some puny little treasure chest buried under the sand. What you're looking for is a vault, a huge secret space, because Gasparilla didn't have just one haul, he had nine. He had his own treasure as well as those of Black Bart, Mary Read, Blackbeard, Calico Jack Rackham, Black Sam, Charles Vane, Black Caesar, and Anne Bonny, too. Some of those hoards he'd found but others had been given to him for safe keeping. His treasure was bigger than any of his peers because besides his own winnings from overcharging pirates like Captain Kidd, John Taylor, Hezekiah Frith, Vincente Gambi, Jean and Pierre Lafitte, Sam Hall Lord, Roberto Cofresi, Charles Gibbs, and El Diabolito for provisions and supplies, he also found time to board and rob a few rich prizes of his own.

Gaspar was a huge pirate buff and listened intently totally fascinated … "But Uncle, why don't you just tell me where the treasure is? Is it cursed or something? Come on, you could make this so easy!" he implored.

"You don't get it Gasp. Anyone can be told where to look for treasure, the fun part is finding it on your own. This isn't about the money, you already have plenty of that, although it may fall short considering how much needs to be done around here." the old ghost mused. This is about adventure. I want you to learn to trust your instincts, don't leave any stone unturned, you'll find it, I promise." The old buccaneer lured the young buccaneer with the romance of pirate lore.

"So tell me your story, and be sure and throw in a lot of clues please," Gaspar said in a tone of voice that belied his growing frustration.

"When I was just fifteen, I ran away from home and stowed away on an old freighter that later shipwrecked off the coast of Yucatan. An old Spanish doctor took me under his roof and nursed me back to health. Dr. Mendoza y Mendoza was a history buff, crazy about pirate lore. It was he who filled my head with tales of treasure and sunken ships. Doctor Mendoza y Mendoza had a major library full of old documents regarding all kinds of history about the Spanish Main and pirates in particular. Let's just say I knew how to read and write and how to put two and two together and I figured out exactly where I thought Gasparilla had hidden his treasure. I told old doctor Mendoza y Mendoza my theory, and that if he would bankroll me a sloop and some supplies, I would find the treasure and bring it back to him and that is exactly what I did. He sent me out to sea with the son of his most trusted servant, Moises who helped me."

"You sure must have had a lot of confidence in your research to set sail for Florida all the way from the Yucatan," Gaspar marveled.

"Let me put it this way Gasp, if you can read and write, there is nothing that can ever hold you back. Knowledge is power. Remember that boy." Uncle Charlie instructed him before continuing. "All of Dr. Mendoza's books are in *your* library downstairs if you want to study them, and the bulk of the treasure is practically in the same place in which I found it over a hundred years ago."

"Seriously?" Gaspar was dubious.

The ghost nodded in the affirmative. "If you read the history books they all say that Gasparilla died at the hands of the US Navy in 1820 in a mighty sea battle between the *USS Enterprise* and the *Floridablanca*, that was the Galleon, Gasparilla stole, right out from under the nose of the Spanish Navy. To this day, people think that Gasparilla's treasure was buried up the Peace River, near Charlotte Harbor, but that was just a rumor that I started myself to throw other treasure hunters off the scent. Everything written about Gasparilla is just a story, *a legend*. I alone discovered the truth which I have kept to myself." Uncle Charlie added cryptically.

"I took a little bit of the gold, cashed it in for dollars and purchased this land from the poor besotted Indians who owned it. Five hundred thousand acres on the coast of Florida at the turn of the century didn't cost very much my boy, fifteen cents an acre if you must know, and that was for the most expensive part of it. Anyway, as soon as I could, I sailed back to the Yucatan and my benefactor, the good Dr. Mendoza y Mendoza, with a sizable portion of the treasure on hand. During the trip back, Moises, my trusted servant, friend and companion turned into *a scurvy bilge rat* who tried to murder me with a machete. Unfortunately for him, I was forced to conk him on the head with a mallet and toss him overboard, down deep into *Davy Jones Locker*."

"You did *murder*?" Gaspar exhaled,

"I did *self protection*, Gaspar. There's a difference." The ghost set him straight.

"If you say so Uncle … " Gaspar wanted to get on with it as the water was getting cold and he was starting to turn into a prune.

"Together with Dr. Mendoza y Mendoza, his pretty wife Lucilla and his only daughter, Eugenia Floride, I traveled the world, first class. Did we ever have fun while it lasted. In 1912, I left the doctor and his wife and little Eugenia Floride in Europe while I went back to America to have a look around New York, Chicago and San Francisco. They'd booked passage back on the Titanic, I guess you know what happened to that ill fated maiden voyage. Well the Doctor and his wife, and several other of my friends died in that terrible tragedy but the baby was saved, having been put in a lifeboat with her nurse. I was named in his will, as his heir and, as his daughter's guardian. His library was the cornerstone of your library downstairs. I held it all, the books and the treasure, in trust for his daughter, Eugenia Floride, who became my adopted daughter. Now it's all *yours* to enjoy. You have to understand Gasp, we're talking about a lot of gold, and jewels, and at this point antiques … more than you or I or poor Eugenia could ever use or spend in a lifetime. For the most part it's all there ... and it's all going to be yours, Gasp. All you need to do is find it."

"So Uncle, give me a clue, where should I start." Gaspar splashed the now tepid water, ready for action.

"Come on Gaspar, anything worth having is worth working for, and if you have to work make sure it's more of a game than a chore. I know you can find it. It's time for you to get out of your own way and start believing in yourself!" The old boy watched Gaspar pondering his last words. When Gaspar gave him one more imploring look, pleading for help, he just looked back at him smiling impishly and shook his head, "no" before dematerializing.

"Damnation! Gaspar exploded tossing the bar of soap with a splash near the corner of the tub where Uncle Charlie had been seated only seconds ago.

CHAPTER 13

# THE LAWYER

T HE NEXT MORNING, GASPAR'S THOUGHTS WERE ALL
ABOUT WHAT UNCLE CHARLIE HAD TOLD HIM. GASPAR
and his mom were sitting in the kitchen, finishing
breakfast before their meeting with Peter Cawthorne.
Although they'd never met Mr. Cawthorne, they already
considered him to be their family lawyer, but neither of
them knew what to expect from him or what he would
expect from them.

"I'll get it," Gaspar called out springing for the
entrance hall when the doorbell rang. "We'll meet you in
the library, Mom. Angela, would you bring in some coffee
or something?" he said over his shoulder. Reaching the
heavy iron and glass door he could see a tall, well-dressed
man waiting on the other side. He opened the door wide
and greeted the visitor.

121

"Mr. Cawthorne? I'm Gaspar Brown."

"Hi, Gaspar," Cawthorne said, taking the boys outstretched hand. "It's a pleasure to finally meet you. I had no idea when you and your mother would get here, and I've just returned from a business trip up the coast near Pensacola.

"I know, your office told us. My mother's in the library." Gaspar led the way.

"Wonderful," Cawthorne replied, "My favorite room in the house."

"Good morning Mr. Cawthorne, we meet at last," Elvira trilled when Gaspar led the lawyer into the library.

"Delighted, Mrs. Brown."

"Please call me Elvira."

"And you both, must call me Peter," the lawyer insisted. "I apologize for not having been here to greet you but I've been away on an urgent case in Pensacola." He explained again.

"No need to apologize Peter, Gaspar and I have spent the last few days settling in, and making ourselves at home." Elvira told him sweetly.

"Sit here, Peter." Gaspar motioned their new friend toward the big chair behind the desk. "Mom and I will sit together here in front." Gaspar helped his mother into her chair and then took the chair next to her so that they were both facing their lawyer, across the library's mahogany desk.

Angela arrived next, carrying a large silver tray holding, coffee, and a dish of biscuits.

"Good morning Angela," Peter greeted the house-keeper cordially, "What have we here?"

"Coffee and your favorite *galletas*, Señor Peter." Angela answered sweetly, before discreetly stepping out of the room.

Elvira did the honors offering coffee, cream and sugar to her guest while Gaspar helped himself to the cookies.

When they were finally settled, Peter Cawthorne took control of the agenda. "We have a lot of business to go over, so if you don't mind, I'll just jump right in," Peter began. "I don't know how much *you* know, but the estate is as simple as it is complex. What we need to discuss is your income. The residents of the two towns pay a land lease or rent on the 100,000 acres where the two towns are built. The rent is $1.00 per acre per month, or $12.00 per year per acre for a total of $1,200,000.00 per year before taxes. Those are all ninety-nine-year leases signed almost ninety-five years ago. When those come due in a few years we'll be able to raise them to market rates but until then there is nothing we can do about them."

"A dollar a month seems like chicken feed. Back in California that kind of rent would be unheard of." Elvira jumped in.

"You have to understand. Considering your Uncle paid only fifteen cents per acre to buy this place, he was making a killing back in the 1920s when he leased this land for a dollar an acre per month, that was more than a 300 percent per month profit on each acre he leased back then. But of course today it seems like peanuts." Peter made his case. "Besides the ninety-nine-year land leases which come due in a few years, there are several parcels of land that Charles Munoz developed for his own use, commercial parcels in town from which we collect rents for the estate. This is a little more complicated, but when you come into town I could show you the real estate and we could discuss how to maximize the income stream. Of course we need to keep in mind that the more income the land generates, the higher the property value becomes, and the higher the property values, the higher the taxes. It's a double-edged sword!" Cawthorne warned them, "but when the time comes, paying the taxes should be the least of our problems..

"Tell us more." Gaspar implored, figuring the lawyer was saving the best for last. "You mentioned a millions of dollars in your letter.

"Those were only some of your liquid assets. They may all seem like a lot, but you'll soon discover, the money around here goes out almost as fast as it comes in. There is a ten million dollars more or less invested on Wall Street in stocks and tax free bonds and mutual funds, all good safe solid investments, nothing spectacular, all with a conservative income stream which is substantial and we still have around five million sitting in the bank in cash too."

"It doesn't sound so insignificant to me." Elvira exhaled, awestruck.

"Then there's the problem of this house and its contents," Cawthorne continued. "Before I discovered you're existence, the museum society moved forward as if they were the rightful beneficiaries, and they had all of the contents of the house listed and appraised. Let me make this clear, the trust document only mentions the house and its furnishings but not anything found in the vaults, closets, attics, stables or outbuildings, like the sunken yacht for example or the boat house or the church."

"The church?" both Gaspar and Elvira exclaimed simultaneously.

"It's a Catholic church on the property," explained the lawyer. "Very beautiful, and very abandoned. It was once used by the locals for worship. Eugenia Floride unlike her father, chose to close up the church and would not allow a priest from the archdiocese to live in the parish house or use it for his parishioners no matter how much we all tried to change her mind. Basically the place has been closed for the last fifty years. I don't need to tell you that closing the church caused a lot of controversy here, and her actions did not endear your cousin to her tenants."

"Our own church, that's extraordinary," Elvira sighed. "We'll have to look into that."

"You need to be aware that the US government is going to assess the value of this property, and the contents of the house, which unfortunately the museum has already inventoried and appraised. Understand, as a tax-deductible non-profit organization the museum doesn't care how much things are worth because they won't be required to pay taxes on any of it, whereas as individuals, you would need to claim the absolute least value you can for everything. The house and stables, the pool house and even the church can all be claimed as old rundown buildings, *tear-downs* if we're lucky. The land is another problem, but right this minute, in this economy I think we can claim a minimum value for the undeveloped 400,000 acres which I'll argue have *no value*, as the conditions of the trust won't allow them to be sold or developed for at least another ten years, after which the new owners, *you*, can do as you please. What we need to do is think ahead at least ten years and maximize your income and your assets so that when the time comes, if you want to, you'll have the funds set aside to develop more of the land. It makes sense that in ten years, the time will be ripe to start developing the land in-between the existing developed parcels. Plans should be made and approvals sought in advance so that when the time comes you'll be prepared to jump.

"Peter," Elvira interrupted the lawyer, "Would it be possible for me to refuse the inheritance in favor of Gaspar?"

"It's funny you should ask. There is an exception in the trust that would allow just that, a parent stepping aside in favor of their child, or children. Old Charlie thought of everything and worried about the problem of double taxation. There's no reason why Gaspar couldn't be the official heir, and you as his guardian, could be his trustee. That way there'll be no tax should you pre-decease him, and if Gaspar should go first he can make you his heir or leave you a life estate, a brilliant way to avoid a maximum of taxation."

"Then let's consider that settled. Please draw up the papers naming Juan Gaspar Brown as the new *laird* of Perdido Isle," she insisted, grabbing Gaspar's hand.

Gaspar couldn't believe it and felt somehow that Uncle Charlie was behind his mom's decision.

"So you're planning to stay on," the lawyer asked looking for concurrence.

"*Absolutely*," mother and son sang out together.

"I feel I should tell you that we haven't exactly received a warm welcome." Elvira interjected.

"What do you mean?" Peter asked, concern in his voice.

"Before we left California, someone threw this through our window. It was wrapped around a rock with a rubber band." Elvira said extracting the threatening note made up of cut out letters from her pocket, "I thought you should see it."

bEWaRE!
dON'T eVEn tHINK oF lEAviNg CalIfORNia

ANy OThEr ClIMAte WoULd
dEFINaTELY
nOT BE sUITABLE tO yOUR
cONTINUED gOOD hEALTH
yOU hAVE bEeN wARNED

"This is very serious," Cawthorne exhaled after reading the threat. "Have you any idea who it's from? What makes you think this has anything to do with not receiving a warm welcome here in Florida?"

Gaspar squirmed in his chair, and felt himself starting to flush red with heat, as cold sweat trickled down the back of his neck. "I saw a *Red Buick Le Sabre* pulling away from the curb right after the rock with that note on it crashed through our window." Gaspar insisted.

"We think it's the same red car that cut us off while we were on the phone with you." Elvira interjected, "We were driving on the freeway when you called us that first time. This old red car cut us off and we had to swerve in order to miss it, then it tailed us home and tried to force us into oncoming traffic. I realize now that it was deliberate. I didn't report the incident to the police or really think anything more about it at the time other than it must have been an accident, but later I started thinking that maybe it was some form of road rage, but after that note was thrown through our window, I didn't know what to think except that the first incident wasn't an accident. I guess I should have called the police, but by then we had already decided to head to Florida." Elvira recounted the incident in a mixed-up rant.

"Yes, but when I called you that first time, I hadn't even confirmed that you were the missing heirs. At that point my investigation was being conducted very privately, very in-house. I doubt that anybody from Florida would have been out to get you, unless of course another party were doing an investigation on their own into missing heirs. Hmmm … there is a possibility at that." Cawthorne mused, rubbing his stubbled chin.

"The note *must* have something to do with Florida Peter, because after we got here, I saw the same car leaving the parking lot of the café in town." Gaspar wanted more than anything to deflect any thoughts that the note had anything to do with his problems in California. "When we finally got here, the gates were padlocked so we left our car outside and walked in through the little side gate, which was open. While we were inside, looking for Felix, someone wrote *beware* on our car's dusty back window," Gaspar relayed. "Then just yesterday, when Alex and I were going to catch the bus into town, a black *Olds Cutlass* almost ran us down. That car came out of nowhere, Peter. Alex told me he thought it was deliberate. If I hadn't seen it coming and pushed Al out of the way, that car would have flattened both of us."

"Gaspar, I can't believe you didn't tell me about that." Elvira cried, "I thought we didn't keep any secrets from each other?"

"I'm sorry Mom, I just didn't want to worry you. You've got so much happening right now. I promise I won't keep you in the dark again." Gaspar assured her, *Especially since the lawyer had her thinking the attacks were possibly Florida-based rather than coming from California, he didn't mind letting her know everything now ... up to a point at least.*

"Did you report the black Cutlass to the police?" Peter asked astonished.

"Yeah, when Al and I got to town, I stopped in and introduced myself to Chief Morgan, and he took down a report. He said he'd look up all the Oldsmobiles registered on the island."

"I'll call the Chief and find out what he's learned. This is really serious." Cawthorne cautioned, "Promise me you'll both watch your steps and report anything at all suspicious you see to me immediately! I certainly won't have you being bullied into leaving town and thereby losing your patrimony." Cawthorne was furious.

Gaspar didn't feel badly leading the Lawyer down the primrose path. He knew that the threats were California based, but if Cawthorne wanted to explain them away to his mom as Florida-based, that was fine with him. He knew the inheritance was safe, but had never thought until seeing Peter's reaction to his story that there may be someone in Florida who didn't want them to stick around either.

"Thank you, Peter," Elvira smiled. "You'll see, Gaspar and I are made of pretty stern stuff. It'll take more than idle threats to send us packing, but I'm concerned if someone out there means us physical harm. Anyway, don't fear, one way or the other, Gaspar and I are here to stay."

"Okay," Cawthorne smiled, shaking his head. Glancing at his papers again, he continued where he'd left off. "There's also a house in the Yucatan, a hacienda really, nobody I know has ever been there, but we pay the taxes and a caretaker to keep it up. It's not a big place or a big property, but there's acreage involved. It's in a little fishing village near Merida called Celestún, and the house is on the beach, if that means anything to you. They call it "The Doctor's House", but it's official name is *Huayrocondo*."

"Do you think it's worth keeping," Elvira asked, "considering our limited cash flow?"

"Definitely," Gaspar was adamant.

Elvira looked at Peter with raised eyebrows, but the lawyer just kept going. "It's just another piece in the puzzle. But you're right to worry about cash since any day now the estate is going to be hit with massive death duties. It's my job to minimize these so that Gaspar can keep this legacy and not be forced to turn it over to the museum. On the other hand, you're also in a good negotiating position to tell the museum you'll give them the house and contents now with the right to live in it for the rest of your lives ... or in exchange for the acreage, or in exchange for a lot of cash, if that's what you want to do."

"That doesn't work for me," Gaspar stood up. He realized the voice was his but the words were Uncle Charlie's. He saw the look of amazement on his mother's face and the look of admiration in Peter's eyes. "This is our house now, and our land." He continued, "with your help Peter, I know mom and I will be fine." He struggled to get Uncle Charlie's thoughts into his own words. "Thanks, Peter, for helping us. I look forward to hearing how few taxes we'll have to pay in order to settle the estate and move forward." *Darn Uncle Charlie, he's putting more words into my mouth*, Gaspar thought. "You're welcome to stay and speak with my mom, but right now I've got some stuff to do with Al. We're searching for pirate treasure and I don't want him to start digging without me. By the way Peter, have you ever heard of any pirate treasure around here?"

"Ever since I can remember, hidden treasure is all people on Perdido Isle talk about.

Pieces of eight, gold bullion by the barrel full," Peter laughed. "I've heard talk of treasure, all my life, but I have yet to see anything shiny or valuable come of it."

"Me and Al have been playing pirates, see. And we're look-in for treasure," Gaspar made excuses. Tell you what, if you get any leads, let me know, cause I'd like to be the one who finds that treasure first, okay?"

Peter Cawthorne came around the desk and shook Gaspar's hand. "You bet I will, Gaspar, and when I know more about the settlement of the estate, I'll ask you and Elvira to come down to my office. We, no doubt, have some documents that will require your trustee's signature."

Already late and eager for adventure, Gaspar grabbed his trunks and a towel and ran for the boat house. When he got there, Alex was just pulling himself out of the water.

"Sorry, Al, my mom and I had a meeting with Peter Cawthorne. Do ya know him?" Gaspar asked as he stripped off his shirt exposing the sparkling gold key hanging from the chain around his neck.

"Yeah, he used to come around all the time, before Lady Eugenia died."

"He's our lawyer now. When we first heard from him back in L.A. we thought he'd be a jerk," Gaspar explained while he quickly changed out of his jeans and into his swim trunks, "but he's actually an okay guy."

Without further discussion, they put on their fins and masks and grabbed their flashlights. "Let's look through the portholes first," Alex suggested, before they splashed into the yacht canal.

Together they took turns peering through the portholes using their lights to pierce the murky gloom of the submerged cabins. The eerie interior of the ship was more than spooky as the flickering light caught phantasmic shapes floating through the murky water. There were bed sheets, and ragged table cloths entwined around broken chairs, old lamps bobbed on table tops held down by their wire cords and sheets of thin wallpaper floated off the walls where old paintings long since unrecognizable held them in place. Even in all the spectral chaos Gaspar thought he saw a lot of interesting stuff that could be salvaged. Having moved around to the port side of the ship, Gaspar climbed on board.

"Let's go down the main stairs into the water and see what's there," he suggested.

"I'm not so sure that's the best idea," Alex warned him, "We shouldn't go into a closed space without air tanks."

Gaspar had to admit that his friend's fears made sense. "Better safe than sorry", his mother was always reminding him. "You're right," he said. "Can you scuba?"

Alex shook his head. "No. I wish my dad would let me but he's got a thing about water. If he even knew we were messing around on this boat he'd have my hide. How bout you?"

"Actually, my dad taught me. He used to dive for the Navy. I'm still certified, but I only brought my wetsuit … I don't have tanks here."

"You can get anything you need at the dive shop in town," Alex informed him.

"Sounds good," Gaspar mumbled, he really wanted to explore the interior of the yacht right this minute. As a hiding place for hidden treasure it was ideal and he was disappointed at having to wait.

"Let's swim over and explore the boathouse instead." Gaspar suggested changing tack. "I'll race ya!" Diving off the ship, he swam like crazy with Alex in hot pursuit towards the steps leading up to the porch of the pillared structure.

Laughing and coughing they hauled themselves up out of the water, each claiming victory. "How do we get in?" Gaspar asked.

"Follow me." Alex commanded, leading his friend around the octagon-shaped building to a huge bronze door on the side opposite the yacht channel.

Gaspar tried the door but it was locked. "Do you know where the key is," he asked Alex. " Have you ever been inside?"

"No, but my father might have the key. I'll go ask him."

"Wait a sec, Al, I have a key," Gaspar said taking the chain from around his neck. "Let's try it before you run back to the house. You never know," he said as he thrust it into the lock. To the amazement of both boys, It turned, *Click!* "It works!" Gaspar whispered in disbelief.

The boys entered the buildings dark interior, which was dimly illuminated by streams of sunlight filtered through thinly sliced octagon shaped panels of onyx, inset high up on the walls near the cornice.

The minute his eyes adjusted to the gloom, Gaspar knew he'd found the treasure or at least its hiding place. There was a lump in his throat and his heart started beating harder and faster. To his amazement, what he saw were eight carved onyx sarcophagi arranged two by two, fanning out from four alternating sides of a central, eight sided column. Standing like sentries, (between the pairs of tombs) on the other four sides of the column, were four tall, cast-bronze candelabra. The walls, facing the tombs, alternately held the octagon shaped windows which were flanked by colorful banners or large armorial tapestries. The only exception to this symmetrical arrangement was the wall holding the bronze entry door. Here, instead of banners, the door was surmounted by an octagon-shaped window, and like the others, it was also made of onyx.

"This isn't a boathouse." Gaspar whispered.

"What?" Alex croaked.

"Look! Eight crypts. It's a tomb ... and the lamps are electric," Gaspar pointed out optimistically, "find the switch Al."

"Right here." Alex said, pushing the button on the wall by the door.

Blazing incandescent light flooded the space. Gaspar could now see that this one-room, octagon-shaped tomb, was entirely constructed of coral stone blocks including the floor, which had been stained in pink, black and white to form a starburst-shaped compass emanating from the eight sides of the central column. The words, North, South, East and West had been inlaid into the stone floor in bronze. In contrast to the roughness of the building materials, the sarcophagi themselves were made of carved and polished, translucent onyx.

Each of the tombs was designated as the final resting place of one of the famous *Bretheren of the Coast*, by an engraved marble plaque set into the column above it. The first two sarcophagi sitting directly in front of the door were those of José Gaspar, (Gasparilla) and Captain Henry Morgan. Following around the column clockwise, the next pair were those of Bartholomew (Black Bart) Roberts, Mary Read, then came those of Anne Bonny, the most famous lady pirate who had been placed alongside her husband, Calico Jack Rackham. Next in line, was Edward (Blackbeard) Teach, and Captain Kidd. The tops of each of these amazing sarcophagi were composed of the prone, carved-marble effigies of whomever's tomb it was. Gaspar appreciated that these beautifully carved effigies were dressed in the most amazing regalia including carved onyx jewels, hats, lace ruffles and furbelows as well as, exquisite swords, fancy boots and beautiful emblazoned buttons, all of which he pointed out to Alex in detail. What Gaspar loved best was that José Gaspar had a dressed monkey playing with a large jeweled cross seated in the crook of his arm, while Blackbeard had a jungle parrot perched on the pillow under his head, and Anne Bonny had a little spaniel dog curled up at her feet.

In contrast, Blackbeard and Captain Kidd each had a pair of feral cats by their sides.

"Al, I wonder if this is the first, last and only time that these famous Brethren of the Coast have ever been together in the same room?" Gaspar chuckled. He was beside himself with excitement but couldn't let on to Alex. He smelled treasure. *It has to be right under my feet, why else would Uncle Charlie go to the trouble to construct such an elaborate stage set?*

In the blazing lamp light, Gaspar and Alex could better admire the intricate designs embroidered and appliquéd onto the giant banners hanging on the four walls opposite the crypts. They could see clearly that these were armorial banners with coats of arms made out of rich velvets, satins and brocades. Gaspar knew, because of what Uncle Charlie had told him, that these banners and armorial tapestries hung on the walls between the windows symbolized other pirates that Gasparilla had done business with, or whose treasures he had discovered. Without divulging the source of his knowledge, he explained to Alex that it was Hezekiah Frith's coat of arms they saw embroidered in lilac silks, and that the brothers Jean and Pierre Lafitte were well represented by their crest emblazoned with *fleur-de-lys*, lions rampant and ermine tails of France.

"Look Al, Sam Hall Lord and Roberto Cofresi are sharing a wall together, and over here are the arms of Charles Gibbs and El Diabolito. Look, the little devil's banner is flourished with flames and crossed pitchforks as its heraldic devices." Gaspar chuckled. "Uncle Charlie certainly had some fun building this place." Gaspar spoke out loud, smiling to himself at the absurdity of it all.

"Let's load in the loot and get out of here" Alex pleaded, "This place gives me the creeps."

"Oh, Al, there aren't any dead bodies here, these aren't real tombs, it's not possible. This is just Uncle Charlie's tribute to his favorite pirates," he assured his friend while furtively looking for a secret doorway or trap door or someway to access the treasure.

"What are ya messing around for Gasp?" Alex insisted, "Let's load our salvaged stuff in here and get out, I don't like this place!"

*What if instead of dead bodies, the treasure was distributed inside the sarcophagi, or better yet, what if there was a secret staircase, hidden inside the column or inside one of the tombs, leading to an underground vault where Uncle Charlie had hidden the loot? Now all I have to do is figure out a way to have the place all to myself long enough to get to the bottom of this theory.*

Moving their loot inside was easy. The entire time they were stacking it up, nice and neat against the walls, Gaspar continued looking for a chink in the wall or the column or the floor that might lead to a secret passage to the treasure, but his search was to no avail.

When they were done loading in the salvaged stuff from *Argente*, Gaspar turned off the lights and locked the door. He placed the key back around his neck and pushing Alex forward announced. "Let's hit the waves, Al."

"Can you imagine what it would be like, finding a *real treasure*, not just dishes and picture frames and candlesticks?" Alex asked as they headed to the beach.

"I know what you mean," Gaspar said, "But for now our junky old treasure is a pretty good start, don't ya think?"

"It's cool, for now I guess, but maybe someday we'll find something really cool … like an HDTV or an Xbox!"

"Yeah," Gaspar agreed with him, while thinking, *If Alex only knew … if he only knew … but I promised Uncle Charlie, and no matter how badly I want to tell Alex everything, I understand that this secret has to be my own … forever.*

# THE CHURCH

A FTER THEIR SWIM ALEX LED GASPAR DOWN THE BEACH TO A WELL WORN FOOT PATH THAT THEY USED TO trudge through the jungle.

"Where are you taking me?" Gaspar asked.

"You'll see," Alex replied. "You did say you wanted an adventure, right?"

Following the path for what seemed like miles, it suddenly opened up onto the beach again then up a little hill and back into the thick jungle now dark with intermittent shafts of sunlight breaking through the heavy canopy. Following an inlet, they suddenly turned left and crossed a rivulet of water via a log bridge. Shoulder to shoulder they trudged down the narrow trail until there was a break in the jungle and the foot path suddenly opened on to a sunny field.

"Whoa," Gaspar breathed. Standing before him, right there in the middle of *nowhere* was a *huge* church with two bell towers and massive carved doors.

Following the building around to the back they came to a walled garden. Rising above the wall they could see the second floor and roof line of a charming house. The rectory or parish house was attached to the church at a right angle and protruded into the walled garden, in a romantic, storybook, kind of way.

As they headed toward the rectory, Gaspar stopped, and quickly pulled Alex behind some bushes, squatting low, and putting a finger to his lips to warn his friend to keep quiet. He'd spotted three muscular men dressed all in black, covered in dirt and grime rambling out of the garden gate. A tall thin man dressed all in black wearing a wide brimmed black hat over a black bandanna with a voluminous black shawl wrapped around his shoulders followed behind them. Unlike his companions, the man in black didn't have a spot of dirt on him.

"That's the guy I saw in the garden near the tennis court the other night." Gaspar informed Alex, whispering excitedly. "Do you know who he is? Are they supposed to be here?"

"I don't think so," Alex replied as they watched the men exit the garden and disappear out of sight. "I hope they didn't take anything."

No one in the departing group had observed the two boys in hiding. Something was up, but Gaspar couldn't put his finger on it. When the coast was clear, he pushed Al's shoulder saying, "Come on. Let's check it out,"

The boys crossed what remained of the field and headed for the garden's open gate. Once inside they were surrounded by blooming wild roses, and hibiscus flowers, all tangled together with night-blooming jasmine, and shaded by swaying palm fronds and giant bird of paradise leaves. Gazing towards the far end of the garden, Gaspar could see through a decorative wrought iron grill, inserted into the garden wall like a window, that a vista had been cleared through the jungle creating an unobstructed view of the shimmering gulf. At that moment he heard the roar of a motorboat down by the beach. "Hear that, Al?"

"Yeah. They're probably leaving the way they came." Alex said.

"I wonder what they were up to?"

Gaspar stepped up to the front door of the Rectory, which was cracked open. He could see that the lock had been jimmied as the wood around it was scratched and cracked. He entered the small house and was amazed that it was fully furnished, with every surface covered in a sheet of thick dust. He also noticed a trail of dirty grit that the shabby group had clearly left in their wake, as they passed through the rooms. Gaspar and Alex followed the trail of dirt down a hallway which led onto the monumental alter of the church. The interior glittered with

143

carved and gilded moldings, holding painted depictions of the stations of the cross.

"Peter Cawthorne said there was a church, but he didn't say it was a *cathedral*." Gaspar could barely speak, so magnificent was the structure. "Well, it doesn't look like they stole anything, wha-da-ya think, Al?"

"I wonder what they were doing here," Alex added, gazing up at the stained glass windows.

Gaspar followed his friends gaze. What he saw astounded him. The stained glass windows featured scenes peopled with angels and saints, mermaids, Tritons, seashells and sea creatures, who were holding up armorials and coats of arms emblazoned with family names. Also depicted in each and every panel was the Gulf of Mexico with a horizon line and various sailing ships, all of them magnificent, with their names emblazoned on floating ribbons beneath them. Names like José de Gaspar's glorious galleon, *Floridablanca*, William Kidd's merciless merchantman, *Adventure Galley*, John Taylor's beautiful brigantine, *Cassandra*, Edmond Condent's fabulous French man-of-war, *Flying Dragon*, Bartholomew Robert's sleek-sloop, *Sea King*, Charles Vane's fancy frigate, *Ranger*, Edward Teach's sensational schooner. *Queen Anne's Revenge*, Sam Bellamy's sorry slaver, *Whydah*, Dirk Chiver's brawny barque, *Soldado*, William Moody's delightful Dutch fluyt, *Rising Sun*, Sir Richard Grenville's incomparable corvette, *Tiger* and the greatest pirate ship of them all, Sir Francis Drake's golden galleon,

*The Golden Hind.* Turning around Gaspar admired the altar, a twisting, surging, storm at sea motif, of carved marble, gilded sunbursts and painted cloud formations. Suddenly it struck him, *I wonder if the treasure is buried under there? Maybe Uncle Charlie hid the treasure in a secret crypt or catacomb! If nothing else, this church could certainly provide a hiding place!*

Gaspar could practically smell the treasure so sure was he that it was right under his feet. He wished he could talk to Alex about it, but Uncle Charlie had been clear. Gaspar had to do this on his own. He glanced at Alex who was still admiring the stained glass. Then he gazed around the alter for some sort of clue. That's when he saw the discarded shovel, the pile of broken stones, and a mound of newly-dug dirt on the floor near the far side of the altar.

*Those guys were digging for something,* Gaspar realized. *Were they looking for Uncle Charlie's treasure too? Am I too late?*

Gaspar wanted to jump into the hole and check it out right then and there, but he couldn't. Not with Alex present. "Let's get out of here and hit the beach Al." he suggested.

"Sure," Alex started out but Gaspar didn't move. "You coming?"

"I'll be right behind you. I have to find a bathroom," he lied.

The minute Alex was out the door, Gaspar retraced his steps in order to examine the fresh excavation near the altar. It was a big hole, and it led down into a very big cavern. Fortunately the guys who'd done the digging, had left their ladder in place. Taking his iPhone out of his pocket he headed down into the hole using it as a flashlight. It came as no surprise to him, when he reached the bottom, that he was indeed inside a large crypt.

Gaspar shivered when he realized that the ancient tombs had been ripped apart. Lids had been torn off of sarcophagi, and the human remains had been removed and dishonorably disarranged. If there was a treasure hidden there, they certainly hadn't found it since they weren't carrying anything out with them when they left. Gaspar held his breath and looked around a little longer, just in case the intruders had missed something. Satisfied, he climbed back up the ladder and joined Alex on the beach, not knowing what to make of the situation. *Were those men really treasure hunters or were they trying to loot an abandoned church?* Gaspar wasn't sure.

"What took ya?" Alex asked, stepping out of the surf. "Look , there goes that big black yacht again." He pointed out to sea, where *Revenge*, could be seen cruising toward the harbor at Llojeta. "You don't think they're the ones who were snooping around the church, do you?"

Gaspar had a bad feeling about that ship. "Maybe," he replied absent-mindedly. "I don't know."

*One thing is certain. Whoever those men are, they are dangerous. If they could tear apart sacred graves hoping to find something valuable, imagine what they might do to me if I get in their way, or if I find the treasure before they do?* Gaspar shivered at the thought.

# CHAPTER 15

# ANOTHER TUTORIAL

G ASPAR WAS A MAN ON A MISSION WHEN HE KISSED HIS MOTHER GOODNIGHT AND HEADED TO THE library. Uncle Charlie had told him, "the way to the treasure was through the library" and Gaspar was determined to find it. He barred the door and closed the curtains, before starting his search, purposefully beginning with the low hanging fruit. This turned out to be a series of fifty-seven bound albums numbered by years between 1910 through 1967.

Starting with 1910, he saw photo after sepia-toned photo, depicting young, Uncle Charlie, tanned and athletic, standing barefoot in the sand, pants and shirt sleeves rolled up, with rumpled black hair and jungle all around him. He usually had a buddy with him, also casually dressed, possibly a native or a Latino. Other pictures showed an old Spanish house, one story, and low slung, peeking out from behind jungle-like foliage on a beach. The word *Yucatan* was scribbled in the margin near the snapshot. That had to be the hacienda, that Peter had told them about. There were also pictures of Charlie with a distinguished, mustachioed gentleman wearing a loose-fitting white linen suit and a big Panama hat. Doctor Mendoza y Mendoza was scribbled near the bottom of the snapshot. These were followed by many photos taken at garden parties filled with well-dressed ladies and gentlemen, but Gaspar figured they weren't city slickers, just well-to-do country folk. There were several photographs of a pretty young mother holding an infant, and several pictures of the newborn in its little brass cradle decked out with lace curtains and big satin bows. *Eugenia Floride*, scribbled to the side of one of these identified the infant. There were also many pictures of farms, and plantations, and lots of photos of Uncle Charlie and his native pals horsing around on the beach. The whole album reeked of a carefree, well-to-do, existence in Yucatan as so many of the photos had been annotated.

The albums dated 1911 and 1912 showed a different story entirely. Uncle Charlie and the mustachioed gent, were pictured with the pretty young mother and her baby, but now they were all decked out. The men were wearing tailored suits and felt-fedoras had replaced their old Panamas. The ladies looked different too, wearing wide brimmed hats, jewels, furs and feathers, a different ensemble in every shot. The locations were all cities, not country farms. Paris, London, Rome were recognizable backdrops for Gaspar who had studied the European capitals in school. Other iconic places were also chron-icled—the Parthenon, the leaning tower of Pisa, the Doges' Palace and Rialto Bridge, the Matterhorn, and on and on. Also snapped were fancy motor cars with liveried chauffeurs standing at attention. It was a very glamorous chronicle of a moment in time, which Uncle Charlie had lovingly bound in gold stamped Morocco leather. The album dated 1911 contained mostly photos of Charlie on shipboard, some annotated with the name, Captain Smith. Gaspar surmised correctly the Captain Smith in question was the ill fated Captain of the White Star luxury liners, Olympic and Titanic. *I didn't read the story of the sinking of the Titanic*, A Night To Remember, *by Walter Lord, fourteen times for nothing*, he smiled to himself. There were also lots of snapshots of unidentified, well-dressed couples on shipboard which Gaspar thought looked *right out of the movies.* "On the *Olympic*," was annotated in the margin. More pictures depicting city life, taken in America, followed. New York, Chicago, and San Francisco. In these, the old mustachioed gent was out of the pictures, and so was the pretty lady and her baby, too.

*This is when Dr. and Mrs. Mendoza decided to stay in Europe when Charlie went back to America.* Gaspar remem-bered what he'd been told.

Stuck-in, here and there, were newspaper clippings in various languages with photographs of glamorous couples or even actresses. In all of them Carlos Munoz-Flores y Gaspar was listed sometimes as, *of Merida, Yucatan* while in others they referred to him as, *Man about town, boulevardier*, or *well-known millionaire. Scion of a noble and illustrious South American family*, was one of the most often repeated descriptions. These mentions always ended with, *whose fortune is legendary.*

In the album dated 1912, there were several clippings regarding the *Titanic* disaster and several pasted in cable replies from the White Star Line offices regarding Uncle Charlie's request for information on certain passengers, including Dr. and Mrs. Mendoza y Mendoza and their infant daughter as well as a Mr. and Mrs. Diego Saenz de Tejada and a Señor Walter Mendez, all of Merida, Yucatan. The cable confirmed that all had been lost in the sinking except for the baby, Eugenia Floride, whose father had put her and her nurse, Isabel, into a lifeboat alone, when her mother had refused to get off the immense *unsinkable* ship. Gaspar was saddened by the reality of the clippings even though he had heard the story first hand from Uncle Charlie himself. ,

In the volume dated 1913 there were photos of young Uncle Charlie with a three-year-old toddler. The baby was back in the picture and she was Eugenia Floride. Compared to the adult men who Charlie was hanging out with, she was beautifully dressed in white lace with rows and rows of tiny coral branch beads and a huge satin bow in her hair sitting on top of a barrel with a finger up her nose. These photographs were all taken on the beach with jungle all around, it was La Rinconada.

In 1914, the subject of the albums changed. These photographs were taken in a boatyard. A huge yacht was under construction. It was *Argente*, but to Gaspar's amazement, one of the shots showed the yachts fantail and the name written there was very clearly *Floridablanca*.

*I'll have to ask Uncle Charlie when he changed the name and why*, Gaspar thought.

1915 must have been the year Uncle Charlie inaugurated his yacht and taken it and a lot of friends around South America. *With the war on in Europe, the choice of destinations made sense*, Gaspar thought. There were photos of elegant ladies and gentleman sipping champagne on board, and always the little girl. One of the snapshots showed Eugenia Floride wearing a white satin sailor suit with what looked to Gaspar like enormous mink buttons. There were plenty of photos of foreign cities some of which were annotated in the margins as, Mexico City, Buenos Aires, Monte Video and Rio. Gaspar wasn't at all sure about a lot of the photos without scribbled notes next to them, *but the buildings, the cars and carriages and the ladies hats definitely signaled someplace other than Perdido Isle to him.*

The album dated 1916 held more of the same, but no jungle scenes. *Charlie must have taken his yacht out to see the world but with war raging in Europe*, he thought, *it's not surprising that the photographs showed more South American capitals, as well as Caribbean ports, and places of interest in the United States like, the Grand Canyon, Yellowstone, and Sequoia National Park.*

The 1916 album, held a row of photos showing the boathouse or *The Tombs* as Gaspar now thought of it, under construction. There it stood, new, pristine, gleaming in a clearing, but there was no sight of the canal. In one of the photos, a man stood on the roof of The Tombs waving. It looked like Uncle Charlie. *Ah ha!* thought Gaspar, *There IS a secret staircase inside that column, and if it leads up to the roof maybe it also leads down, underground to a secret vault where the treasure is hidden!* Gaspar couldn't wait to find out if his assumption was correct.

The album marked 1917, showed construction cranes, tractors, and bulldozers all surrounded by jungle. La Rinconada, was just being built. There was the grand canal, complete with *Floridablanca* docked in front of The Tombs. *The perfect construction shack*, Gaspar thought. Several photo's showed the foundations for the house and the terrace. Another group showed the swimming pool being dug, and another with showed the tennis court completed. There were many more shots as the house grew, and walls rose up and finally a roof and windows and doors installed. Gaspar loved seeing the house being built in these old black and white photographs.

And so the albums continued—fifty-seven years of living, through party shots, garden shots, or shots of outbuildings being erected. Yachting parties, European capitals, pictures of Charlie with handsome men and beautiful women who looked like old-time movie stars. *Wow. Uncle Charlie sure got around*, Gaspar thought. *But what does any of this have to do with Gasparilla's treasure?*

"Find anything interesting yet?" a voice asked.

"Uncle Charlie!" Gaspar jumped. *Would he ever get used to Charlie popping up out of nowhere*, he wondered. There he stood, cheerful as ever with that ever-present twinkle in his eye. He was wearing an open-necked ivory colored silk shirt, a chocolate brown sweater vest and a geometrically patterned silk cravat. His sleeves were rolled up (just like in the old photographs taken on a golf course) and his beautiful gold watch and bracelet sparkled in the low light. He had argyle socks pulled way up to his knees and wore brown and ivory colored saddle shoes with beige suede laces.

"Looks like you had a great life," Gaspar said. "I was just wondering …"

"Yes?" Charlie, pretended to sink a put with an invisible golf club.

Why did you rename *Floridablanca … Argente*?"

"I didn't. That was Eugenia's idea. How could I stop her, I was already dead."

"Another mystery." Gaspar sighed.

"Another *part* of the mystery" Charlie corrected him. "But it's not important right now. Concentrate on finding the treasure. Those albums are full of clues. Look at the pictures carefully, and then look at them again, and think about them. They are a timeline."

"I'm *trying* Uncle Charlie," Gaspar sighed. "But I'm lost. I need a clue. Just one. Can't you help me even a little?"

"Trust your instincts, Gasp."

Gaspar rolled his eyes. "Seriously? That's it?"

"Well, you were right about my gold key, weren't you?" Uncle Charlie reminded him.

"I know. I figured out which door it opens," Gaspar said, fingering the gold key through his shirt and feeling good about it.

"Just because it opens one door doesn't mean it can't open dozens of doors around here. Don't lose it," Uncle Charlie warned. "Make sure it's always in a safe place."

Gaspar gulped and made a mental note to never take if from around his neck.

"And then there's the church," Uncle Charlie went on.

"You were there?" Gaspar asked, surprised.

Charlie nodded. "I told you kid, I'm looking out for you. You knew to search for a crypt and you knew not to share what you found with Alex. Again, good instincts. Keep using them. The less your friend knows about the treasure, the less chance he has to betray you. I know. It happened to me. And my *friend* did not *live* to regret it …."

Gaspar barely heard what the ghost was saying. He trembled at the memory of those disturbed bodies in the crypt flashed before his eyes. "Uncle, what about those men who dug the hole? I don't think I want to mess with them," he shuddered. "Are they looking for the treasure too? What about that boat, *Revenge*?"

Silence.

"Uncle? Are you still there?" Gaspar glanced around the room. But the ghost was gone. Apparently his golf game couldn't wait another second. *I guess I'll have to get those answers later.* Gaspar made a mental note.

Once more, he poured through the albums starting at the beginning. Once again the photograph of the man standing on the roof of the tombs, waiving at the camera caught his attention. Once again the name *Floridablanca* written across the stern of the newly built "*Argente*" peeked his curiosity. He studied the photographs of Uncle Charlie and took note of one man in particular who could be found by Charlie's side, repeatedly. There was only one note in the margins which read *Runckle*. *Gaspar* wondered if Runckle was the betrayer that Charlie had mentioned.

In later albums, the photographs of Eugenia Floride as a débutante and as a young lady, were also worthy of additional observation, especially because her jewels, which seemed important, never repeated from one photo to the next. Runckle kept turning up over and over again in each album, sometimes by Charlie's side, sometimes with Eugenia, and often standing on one side of Eugenia while Charlie stood smiling on the other.

Were these real clues? He wondered.

After putting the albums back where he found them, he checked to make sure his iPhone was still in his cargo shorts and sneaked out the french doors to the terrace. From there he ran directly over to The Tombs and let himself in.

Turning on the lights he began to trace every inch of the central column using his flashlight to help highlight any possible chinks in the stonework. One by one he fiddled with the arms of each of the bronze candelabra but none of them worked as a secret lever like he'd seen in old movies and besides, he could find no discernible opening into the column anyway. Finally out of weariness he sat on the edge of Gasparilla's sarcophagi which was directly opposite the door into the building and pondered what to do next. As he leaned back his arm brushed the jeweled cross in the carved monkeys hand. The cross tilted sideways and so did the entire sarcophagi taking a good portion of the floor as well as part of the column behind, with it. The secret staircase revealed itself and it not only went up, but it also went down. Gaspar knew that up … led to the roof, but what he was looking for … must surely be *down*. The stairs going up were a spiral, but the stairs leading down started where the head of the sarcophagi had been, and headed down in one straight run.

Without a thought Gaspar plunged down the stairs knowing that the treasure was now within his grasp. The stairs led to a corridor and the corridor led to a big bronze door. Surprise, surprise, his gold key worked the lock like a charm. The heavy door opened into a large square room, which was as bare as Old Mother Hubbard's cupboard. Finding a light switch he pushed it on, and could see that there was yet another door directly across from the one he had just entered. His gold key opened that lock, too. What came next was less exciting. Another staircase leading up, and up, and up, at the end of which was another door and yes, the gold key worked it's magic on that lock too. Gaspar nearly fell over when he opened the door and discovered he was right back where he'd started, inside the library of the house, the door was one of the double doors to the right side of the fireplace, right under one of the spiral staircases leading up to the balcony.

"What the hell?" Gaspar wanted to spit. *What kind of a game was Uncle Charlie playing with him?* All he could do was retrace his steps locking each of the doors behind him and pushing the jeweled cross back into position and watch as the column and sarcophagi rolled back into position. It was past two in the morning before Gaspar finally got to bed.

# EUGENIA'S JEWELS

WHEN GASPAR WOKE UP, HE'D HAD A REVELATION, OR HAD UNCLE CHARLIE BEEN AT WORK MESSING WITH his mind, while he was dreaming. Jumping out of bed, he dressed quickly, and ran downstairs. Popping into the kitchen to say good morning to his mother, he told her he was going to skip breakfast and do some research. Grabbing a piece of buttered toast from the table he headed to the library.

When he got there, he bolted the door, and made for the shelf labeled, *Gemology*. Pulling books from the shelves he found volumes on gems and jewelry, dedicated to various stones, featuring watercolors of each—rubies, diamonds, emeralds, sapphires and more. There were numerous volumes dealing with royal jewels and national treasures amassed by royalty, clerics, and even captains of industry. One particularly interesting book discussed legendary stones, and another featured biblical stones while yet another centered only on apocalyptic stones. Looking through these rare and colorful volumes was mesmerizing.

*What the heck are Apocalyptic stones?* he wondered as he grabbed a book entitled *The Queen's Necklace*.

Leafing through the pages, he discovered the story of the famous diamond necklace created for the French queen, Marie Antoinette. According to the story the necklace was never ordered or purchased by the ill-fated queen, but was stolen by clever thieves who managed to muddy the queen's good name in the process. The scandal of the diamond necklace was one of several incidents that led to the French Revolution which ultimately cost the French king and queen their thrones, as well as their heads.

Gaspar turned the pages, perusing the story and the sketches until suddenly, there were no more pages to turn. Instead there was a large gaping square, where the pages had been cut out and within that square lay an extraordinary diamond necklace, *the diamond necklace*, the one featured on the cover. Gaspar couldn't believe his eyes. He'd *found* the treasure or part of it at least. *So this is what had become of the famous diamond necklace of Marie Antoinette!* Gaspar was beyond himself with excitement, holding up the dazzling jeweled collar, watching it sparkle in the streaming sunlight. *I hope this isn't a fake*, he thought.

Setting the book aside, he looked for similar distinctive titles. The first one that caught his eye was titled, *The Rubies of the Marquesa de Haro*. Once again, the pages of the book became a box, inside of which, lay an extraordinary set of ruby jewels, including a matching necklace earrings, ring, bracelet and tiara. Again he hoped that it was *the real thing* and not one of Uncle Charlie's practical jokes.

Carefully selecting his next title, he decided on, *The Mystery of the Maharaja's Turban Ornament*. Once again, there it was, a magnificent paisley-shaped creation holding a diamond and pearl egret feather.

*That was almost too easy*, Gaspar thought.

The morning sped by and it was time for Gaspar to start getting ready to meet Alex. He was going to go for a scuba dive and Alex was going to tag along. He'd promised to meet Alex at the bus in a half hour. Gaspar replaced the empty book-boxes on their shelves and raced upstairs to hide his new found treasure in one of the Captain's Cabin's secret compartments.

# CHAPTER 17

# UNDER THE SEA

As he was leaving the house in his swim trunks and t-shirt with a towel around his neck his mother stopped him in the hall.

"Wait a sec," Elvira said, "I have news for you. We've been invited to a dinner party by someone named Gwendolyn Crump. Believe it or not, she's the head of the museum!"

"Are we going?" Gaspar asked.

"Why not?" his Mom said. "She seemed nice. Maybe it's a peace offering. Plus it may be fun to see who our neighbors are."

Okay, I guess it would to be cool to meet some new people."

"It's at eight tonight. Don't forget."

"I won't," Gaspar said. Before he ran out the door, he gathered up his wetsuit, fins, and mask and made a dash down the driveway to meet Alex.

Their destination was Calaluna where they planned to pick up tanks and the motorboat that his mom had rented for them. Once onboard, Alex fired up the motor and headed the craft toward the barrier reef that formed the breakwater off of La Rinconada. It had been a while since Gaspar had dived and he thought it would be a good idea to do a test run before he tried searching the tight underwater cabins of *Argente*. As the boat headed out towards the breakwater, Gaspar instinctively guided Alex who was at the wheel.

"Take her left Al, that's it … keep heading west … southwest … that's it." Gaspar played skipper.

"Are we out far enough, Admiral?" Alex joked his bossy pal.

"Not yet Al, another thousand feet, and a little more to the left, over there, where that fisherman's drifting." Gaspar had no idea where or why he was guiding Alex but something deep inside was telling him to go out further just past the breakwater. "Right here Al. This will do."

Alex turned off the engine and let the boat drift.

"I hope you won't find it too boring while I'm underwater, Al." Gaspar asked, struggling into his wetsuit. "I really appreciate your coming along and looking out for me."

"My pleasure," Alex said. "I've got my fishing rod and some comic books and my bacon and peanut butter sandwich. I'm happy to hang out while you dive."

"Bacon and peanut butter! Yuck!" Gaspar pretended to gag as he strapped on his tanks.

"I brought one for you bro … you'll like it … promise."

"Look over there Al," Gaspar pointed.

Looking around Alex could see the shiny black motor launch bobbing in the distance about a hundred yards away with the lone fisherman inside but about three hundred yards beyond that was what Gaspar was pointing at. It was the big black yacht *Revenge*, floating motionless at anchor.

It wasn't long before Gaspar tumbled backward over the side of the boat, leaving Alex alone to fish.

Down, he swam, into the clear water which became darker, the deeper he descended. Kicking his legs briskly, Gaspar could just make out a shadowy shape ahead of him. As he swam closer it became evident that he was about to dive on a sunken ship, not just any old ship, it was a Spanish galleon … *a treasure ship.* Uncle Charlie … it dawned on him. *That's why he'd given Alex such specific directions of where drive the motorboat. Uncle Charlie sent me here to dive on this wreck on purpose!* Gaspar couldn't wait to get back and let him know that he was on to his little mind games.

With a pounding heart, Gaspar put Uncle Charlie out of his mind as he swam forward and downward with growing excitement. Entering the ship he looked with awe at the gun ports where cannon once stood. He swam through passage ways, and down staircases and right into the holds. Then he swam out and up onto the quarter deck, which was raised just above the orlop deck, and just behind the main mast. Gaspar knew from his study of various types of old ships that the quarter deck was where the captain commanded his vessel and where the ships colors were kept.

From the quarter deck he entered what was left of the captain's cabin, which looked very much like his room at home. Swimming back outside, he swam up to the poop deck, which was the highest deck on the ship. From this vantage, Gaspar observed that the masts, which had once been tall, were now mere stubs, having broken off years ago.

Gaspar couldn't help thinking how much he hated diving alone, and how much his Dad would have loved discovering this ship with him. He couldn't get his Dad back, but maybe he could teach his new best friend, Alex to dive. Then at least he would have someone to share the adventure with, and besides there was so much more safety in numbers.

Swimming off the ship, he circled the wreck and admired its aft elevation. The carved frames of the fantail windows were now just mushy unidentifiable blobs but Gaspar could easily imagine the mermaids and sea creatures, dragons and angels, that had once been carved and gilded there. The glass of the windows and most of the frames were nonexistent, and the three giant lanterns which must have hung there were long since lost or removed to some museum. The name plaque of the ship was also gone, removed no doubt by a treasure hunter. Swimming around and along the starboard side and then over to the prow he saw a rotting figure head depicting a mermaid, and on each side of the prow, the carved name, *Floridablanca* was still legible.

Gaspar nearly wet his wetsuit. *Floridablanca!* Gasparilla's treasure ship! Of all the places to explore on his first dive off the island, he had chosen this one. He couldn't believe his good fortune! Next he swam to the ocean floor to search the sand for anything of value that others may have missed. About ten yards from the ships keel, Gaspar found a large pewter spoon in perfect condition and stuck it in his zippered pocket. Thinking he'd found a rich site he searched further until he heard a strange swooshing noise.

Gaspar hadn't noticed the other diver tailing him.

He turned in time to see the spear launched from a gun—and see the arrow speeding toward his head. Gaspar kicked his legs frantically, hoping to break free from it's deadly path. He felt a piercing pain. Then darkness.

"Wake up! Wake up, Gasp!" Gaspar heard Alex shout. He opened his eyes and focused on his friend's worried face.

It took a minute before Gaspar realized he was laying on the bottom of the dive boat. "I'm okay," he murmured and slowly sat up.

"I saw you surface," Alex said his clothes dripping wet. "You were passed out. I pulled you into the boat. What happened down there?"

"I think someone shot me with a spear gun," Gaspar said, feeling his head for a wound before he realized from the sharp pain that his shoulder had been grazed. He was lucky. It had barely torn his wetsuit.

Let me look at your shoulder," Alex insisted gently unzipping the wetsuit and pulling it down off of Gaspar's arms to his waist. "You're cut, Gasp, but it doesn't look too deep. I doubt if you'll need any stitches."

"That's a relief," Gaspar sighed.

"That had to be an accident, right?" Alex asked, incredulously.

Gaspar shrugged. "I don't know, I totally panicked. Maybe that's why I passed out."

"I'm taking you back to shore," Alex said.

Looking around they could see *Revenge* in the distance chugging off in the direction of Llojeta, while the motor boat with the lone fisherman inside, raced away in the opposite direction.

*That motorboat's riding awfully low in the water*, Gaspar thought. *Could it be towing the diver who tried to spear me?"* he wondered. The butterflies were back.

When they returned to the dock, Alex wanted to run Gaspar to the emergency room to be checked out, but Gaspar had applied a bandage from the boat's first aid kit and told him not to worry. Both boys were still shaken up but Gaspar knew he would be fine.

"I guess we really have to report the incident to the Coast Guard." Gaspar sighed.

"Their station is right next to the dock," Alex said pointing it out.

Once inside they told the sailor at the desk the purpose of their visit and he directed them to Lieutenant Carl Jacobson who took down a report. Gaspar handed over his sliced wetsuit and showed the Lieutenant where the spear had grazed his now bandaged shoulder. Now all that was left to do was to tell his Mom, and he really didn't want to since all that would accomplish would be to upset her.

"Let's catch the bus and head for home he told Alex, lugging the rented tanks to the end of the pier."

On the bus ride back Alex made a huge confession. "I don't know how to tell you this Gasp, but I told my father that we're planning to salvage the *Argente*, and he went crazy. He says that it's a death trap and forbids me to go anywhere near it. I'm such an idiot to have told him anything. Please don't get mad at me." Alex was truly remorseful.

*What else could go wrong?* Gaspar thought, *Another attempted murder and now he was losing his salvage buddy.*

"Don't worry about it," Gaspar soothed him, "I guess I better tell my mom before Felix does. Adults," he drawled derisively, "they're always getting in our way." *Salvaging the Argente seems silly in light of the afternoon's events, but something tells me there might be clues on board that will help point us towards the treasure.*

"What shall we do tomorrow, Gasp." Alex hoped his pal would still want to hang out.

"I'm too worn out to think about it, Al. Let's have an adventure. Skip your chores if you have to, but let's have some fun, with no adults telling us what to do."

"Where shall we go, how shall we do it?"

"Who knows, who cares, we have 500,000 acres to explore, and all the time in the world, you give it some thought, and surprise me." Gaspar insisted feeling dejected.

"So what are ya doin' tonight, Gasp? Ya wanna come over and play games at my house? Alex wanted to cheer up his pal as best he could.

"I'd like to do that Al, but I gotta go with my mom. We're invited to dinner tonight in town at someone named Gwendolyn Crump's house. Do'ya know her?

# CHAPTER 18

# DINNER AT EIGHT

G WENDOLYN CRUMP, SAILED THROUGH HER LIVING ROOM LIKE A FRIGATE IN FULL REGALIA, DECKED OUT in pink ruffles and pink crystal jewelry.

"Elvie, hi I'm Gwendolyn," said their hostess who Gaspar thought kind of resembled an over-upholstered love seat. "And this young man must be your son Gaspasian."

"Uh, Gaspar," he corrected her. "Hi."

"We're pleased to meet you." Elvira oozed all sweetness and light but Gaspar knew she hated anyone calling her Elvie.

Gwendolyn smiled. "Please call me Gwenie, Elvie," she purred, "and Gaston, you may call me, Mrs. Crump."

"Okay," Gaspar responded numbly, *now she thinks my name's Gaston?*

"Come and meet your neighbors." Mrs. Crump swooshed around the room, ruffles rustling.

"This is Mr. and Mrs. Turner, from Chicago. They own the furniture store in town and an even bigger one in Chicago. I told them that you'll probably be wanting to get rid of a lot of that old *junk* around La Rinconada, Elvie *Darling*."

"Nice to see you again, Mrs. Brown. We met the other day at the café." Roberta Turner reminded Elvira.

"Of course we did, and you were right about La Rinconada, what a collection of old used junk." Elvira laid it on thick, as Gaspar cringed.

He wondered *if his mom was serious or just funning?* Whatever had gotten into her, she seemed to be enjoying herself immensely.

"Say hello to Asmar and Amelia Hopkin's *children*. Asmar conducts our symphony orchestra and Amelia is one of our most famous, or should I say our *only* famous soprano, at least on this island." Crump steamrolled forward. "You know I considered a career in opera once, but with all the important things I have to do in town I just couldn't find the time," she blathered on idiotically. "Do you know Peter Cawthorne? I'm told by people who claim to know about these things that he's actually one of our better attorneys, as hard as that may be for you to believe just by looking at him." She stage whispered. "Say hello to Elvie and Gaston, Peter, you three should get to know each other."

"We already know Peter, he's *our* attorney, Gwenie." Elvira's remark went unheard and her discomfort in front of Cawthorne, unnoticed by the horrible hostess.

"He's supposed to be one of our most eligible bachelors too, Elvie. I know it's hard to believe, by the looks of him. By the way, I hear your a widow woman, so go on, take a good look. Go ahead, don't be shy."

Gaspar wanted to slap the biddy,

"Here are our three Margarets. This is Margaret Stewart, she's the librarian over at the historical society. Margie say hello to the Browns. And this is Margaret Mary Montgomery, from Montgomery Manor in Monroe, Louisiana. You've certainly heard of the *Monroe* Montgomery's? Mary is our town's only *true* blueblood," Gwendolyn said in a tone that Gaspar thought belied the fact that she herself hadn't heard of the Monroe Montgomery's until someone told her she'd better brush up on her Daughters of Dixie, even if it meant just going on a guided tour through their historic house one Saturday.

"Well no, I'm sorry, but we haven't, you see we've come from Los Angeles. It's a bit removed from Louisiana." Elvira explained sheepishly.

"No, no, mother," Gaspar stepped in, now in the mood to have some fun. "*Montgomery Manor*. She's talking about Montgomery Manor in Monroe, Louisiana. That's the place our silver tea set, *back home*, came from.

Remember the one great grandpa Grant brought west after the Civil War." Gaspar nearly choked on his lie.

"*Oh yes*," his mother stuttered looking befuddled.

"Here in the South, we still refer to *that unfortunate affair* as The War Of Northern Aggression," Margaret Mary Montgomery informed them coldly. "My great grandmother Magnolia Merriweather Montgomery always said, she'd call it the *Civil War*, after the Yankees returned the silver!"

"Oh," was all Elvira could come up with, while shooting Gaspar her dirtiest look, which he shrugged off by smiling broadly back at her.

"And this is our third Margaret, Margaret Mansfield." Gwendolyn plowed through her party guests blithely, "Margaret is our resident treasure hunter an expert on all things regarding *pirates*, shipwrecks and legendary characters of the Spanish Main. Margaret, meet the Browns, Carlos Munoz-Flores y Gaspar's *only living relatives*," she informed her friend conspiratorially.

"I'm delighted to meet you again. Welcome to the neighborhood. I was one of your Great Uncle's *best friends*," she growled, tugging at her necktie, and straightening her double-breasted blazer. "I can assure you, Charlie was one of Perdido Isle's most vivid characters," the mannish Margaret chortled in her deep-throated baritone. I could tell you tales about Charlie, that would positively make you blush young man," she finished up staring soulfully into Gaspar's wide blue eyes.

Without catching a breath, Crump continued maneuvering them around the room. "I can't vouch for any of Margaret's stories," she told them, referring to the treasure hunter. "I suggest you take anything she has to say with a grain of salt. As far as treasure hunting goes, I'm sure she's never, found even a doubloon. I do know that she's as afraid of water as one of my Siamese, but to give the old girl credit, she has visited Mel Fisher's museum twice, and to do that she had to go all the way to Key West at least once." Mrs. Crump confided all of this to them in a conspiratorial whisper as she lead them away from the three gaunt Margaret's. "I love the way Margaret Mansfield goes on about your relative as if Charles would have given her the time of day. Your Uncle Charlie *was* a lady's man, everyone in town who knew him, and a lot who didn't, have told me that if Charlie were alive, *I'd be the one person he'd want to dine with*."

Gaspar couldn't wait to run that bit of information past Uncle Charlie.

"Considering the others present," the woman continued. "I'm really the only person in the room that Charles would ever have considered *an equal*. Don't let the rest of them with their *self-important* airs fool you. Take Margaret Mary Montgomery, for example. I've been to Montgomery Manor and believe me it makes my house look like Versailles, not that I've ever been to Versailles, but it is on my list of places to visit when I'm not so busy doing all my *important work* here. I have friends in Monroe, you know, *the right sort*, and they told me that the Montgomery's were considered a new family, not an old or distinguished family at all. They said that the Montgomerys had only been in Monroe since 1743! Talk about *nouveau!*"

Gaspar and Elvira exchanged horrified glances.

"Well that takes care of the introductions, children," Mrs. Crump prattled on like a school marm to no one in particular. "How about a cocktail?" She asked, grabbing something pink and deadly off a silver tray without waiting for an answer. "Here you are Elvie." She announced, as if proclaiming some royal favor, placing the poison along with a tiny laced edged napkin into Elvira's hand.

Much to Gaspar's dismay the Crump, next pressed a glass of lukewarm water without ice, into his hand. "And this is for you *little Gaston*."

Gaspar could puke, *Now he was little Gaston?*

Do you play bridge, Elvie. We really must get together at *your house* and play, I'll help you make a foursome.

"Oh golly," Elvira stuttered, "I'm not sure about that. You know it's Gaspar's house now, not mine. I'll have to ask his permission if we can play bridge at his house," she informed Crump, sweetly. "He told me the other night in no uncertain terms, that I have to ask his permission before inviting anyone over. He's a very strange boy, almost a recluse. You have no idea what a difficult time

I had getting him to come out of the house tonight," she confessed.

Gaspar loved hearing his mother lie to the pushy woman, while looking her straight in the eye. He wanted to hug her but decided to wait until they got home.

From a corner of the room, a tall, thin, swarthy man dressed all in black, with a black bandanna tied around his head, topped by a wide brimmed black hat, stepped forward. To finish off his weird look the stranger had dramatically wrapped a very long, extra wide black cashmere shawl around his bony shoulders.

Gaspar couldn't believe his eyes. *That's the dude I saw outside the house and again at the church. What was he doing here?*

"Allow me to introduce myself," the weirdo spoke in a deep, Spanish accented voice, "I am Unzega."

"Oh dear," Gwendolyn Crump squirmed, "of course you are. Unzega, may I present Elvie Brown."

"*Encantado,*" he oozed in Spanish, bending over, but not touching Elvira's hand. Turning toward Gaspar, he nodded, then snarled, "*Mucho gusto,*" without accepting Gaspar's outstretched hand and as his thick lips took on a twisted smile. Then without a word he motioned Elvira over to a sofa where he sat down next to her and immersed her in deep conversation, leaving Gwendolyn and Gaspar to fend for themselves.

Gaspar couldn't believe it. His mother seemed transfixed by the mysterious man.

"Unzega invited himself to the party. He won't be joining us for dinner," Crump mumbled to no one in particular. "Elvie should enjoy her time with him while she can," she swallowed her words as she spoke.

Gaspar could tell that *La Crump* wasn't pleased that Unzega was monopolizing her guest of honor. Turning her annoyance on Gaspar, she dismissed him summarily. "I'd better make sure that dinner is served sooner than later," she scowled a tone of apprehension now evident in her quavering falsetto.

*Free at last*, Gaspar sought out Peter Cawthorne, his only friend besides his mother, in the room.

"Peter, give me the lowdown on this crew? Gaspar begged.

"Welcome to Calaluna society, Gaspar. I'm afraid your seeing only part of a very select clique. I am not usually invited to these inside affairs, but Gwendolyn's no fool. Having the family lawyer on hand is probably not a bad idea considering the lawsuit.

"The lawsuit? Gaspar asked, alarmed.

"The *proposed* lawsuit, the one Gwendolyn, Margaret Monroe and Gore Turner and Asmar Hopkins, basically the board of directors of the museum, have been threatening to launch against *you* if they could.

"What do you mean, *if they could*?"

"They've already tried to retain five lawyers on contingency, two from right here in town and three from

Pensacola but none will take the case, because they don't have one. But that small fact hasn't stopped them yet."

"I had no idea so many people were out to get us." Gaspar sighed.

"Don't worry about it, it's not going to happen. But were they to sue, and were they to get the estate away from you, the trust would be broken and they would not have to wait ten years to sell the land, or sell the possessions. They'd just do it and get a lot of money for the historical society and vote themselves huge pay raises and pensions, among other things. That's how it's done."

"And we can't do any of that for ten years. It doesn't seem right," Gaspar pondered the situation for the first time. "Peter, we'll need to talk more. I want to know as much about all of this inheritance business as possible. I want you to work with me very closely. I already have things I want to do around here, so I'll really need your guidance. Would you come to the house for dinner tomorrow so we can talk business."

"Sure, Gaspar," he paused. "Hey, by the way … I heard you had some excitement today."

"How'd you hear about it."

"From Beverwil down at the hardware store of course."

"I reported it to the Coast Guard. How'd he hear about it?"

"The man has his ways. Always has his ear to the ground. He's a veritable coast to coast hook-up. Tell me what happened."

"I guess you could call it another attempted murder." Gaspar said dramatically. When he saw Peter's horrified expression he modified his story. "Actually, I got grazed by a spear, accidentally shot from a spear gun. No big deal. Don't tell Mom, Peter. If she hears about this she'll never let me back in the water."

"So it was another … accident?" Peter asked.

"I guess so." Gaspar wanted to tell Peter the truth. But then again would he really believe that a neighborhood gang from California with powerful mob connections were out to get him because they thought he'd squealed to the police about them? It was about as plausible as someone trying to kill him to prevent him from finding pirate treasure hidden on his own property. Or maybe it wasn't about any of that at all. Maybe it was about the inheritance. All of a sudden Gaspar realized that practically everyone in this room would probably like to see him and his mom out, and the museum in. Things were starting to look differently than they had just a week ago.

"I see your mother has met Unzega." Peter said, looking past Gaspar to where Elvira and the latin lover held court.

"Yeah, who is he?"

"I'm not exactly sure. He's a mysterious guy. I don't know what he does but apparently he lives like a king in the Yucatan. He and his yacht, *Revenge*, showed up in these waters not long after Eugenia Floride died. It seems he's especially close to Gwendolyn Crump for whatever reason. The rumors are that whatever business he's involved in it's probably not exactly legal. Time will tell Gaspar."

"Well I saw him lurking around La Rinconada the first night we got there and other day I saw him leaving the church with three really shady characters. By the way Peter, I think we should get the church locked up tight as soon as possible. Could you help me with that?"

Peter nodded. "Sure."

"Now that I know he owns *Revenge*, it makes me wonder. That yacht's been anchored off La Rinconada, a *lot* lately. And it was off in the distance along with a black motorboat with a fisherman in it, when I got hit with the speargun today. I wouldn't be surprised if he was driving the car that almost hit me and Alex." Gaspar shuddered. "That guy's trying to kill me and now he's over there flirting with my mom!" Gaspar leapt out of his seat but Peter grabbed him and pulled him back.

"Hold on Gaspar. What you're saying is very serious," Peter warned, "but it's only circumstantial at this point. I can't allow you to make wild accusations, especially not tonight, not here. You'll have to get some real proof and present it to the police first, you can't go off half cocked accusing total strangers of attempted murder without evidence." Peter reasoned with his young client.

Every time Gaspar felt safe, the damn butterflies would come back. *What next?*

•••

Gaspar, Elvira, and Peter left the party together, and it wasn't a minute too soon … as far as Gaspar was concerned.

"Peter, would you like a lift?" Elvira asked.

"Sure, I only live a few blocks away, but I'd love to ride with you."

"Hop in," Gaspar commanded, opening the passenger door for him, before jumping into the back seat. "Mom, before we go home, let's go to Karen's and get some real food. I'm starving."

"It was a *hopeless* dinner." Peter agreed with him.

"The café it is then. I'm starved too," Elvira laughed.

Once seated in a corner booth, Gaspar blurted out. "Peter tell Mom what you told me that party was all about?

"Now what's he going on about, Peter," Elvira chuckled.

"That party was all about controlling the largest single land holding in Florida." Peter said matter-of-factly. "If you were this close to getting your hands on it, don't you think you'd do everything in your power to make sure no one else got in your way."

Gaspar wondered, *If that included murder too*, but wasn't going to voice his question knowing full well what the answer would be.

"You see Elvira. The Perdido Isle Historical Society has always felt the land was rightfully theirs. The board of directors personally control the Historical Society. Put two and two together. If the people at the party tonight could just get their hands on it, the trust would be broken, setting them free to sell the land to themselves at bargain basement prices and then they could sell or re-lease the parcels to the existing tenants at enormously inflated prices. But that's just one of several crooked but perfectly legal and highly possible scenarios that come to mind."

"I wouldn't put it past any of them," Gaspar agreed, "and what about that creep, Unzega?" he said, giving his mother the eye, "something tells me he has an interest in this scheme too."

"Definitely a slime ball," Elvira stated, "remember what your father always used to say Gasp, 'keep your friends close and your enemies even closer'."

"I'm glad to see that you both have a good grasp of the situation," Peter piped up. "Those people tonight will stop at nothing to drive you away from Perdido Isle, so they can grab your land and reap the rewards. By the way, I don't want you to think that you shouldn't raise the rents when the leases come due in a few years. You can still bring in plenty of income without gaging your tenants. They're expecting as much. But if we let those *money-grubbing, grave robbing, board members* control the property, I assure you Gaspar, they'll buy up the land from the Historical Society using a series of shell companies that are probably already in place and *bingo*, a few people will become very rich at the expense of many, *including you and your mother*, and the Historical Society will ultimately collapse from lack of funding."

"Yeah, but it sounds to me like we might collapse too from lack of funding unless we can find something to cash in too." Gaspar voiced his mounting concern without divulging his continuing search for treasure.

"Well you're not without assets Gaspar, we can cross that bridge when we get to it." Peter assured him, "There are many ways we could monetize the estate, leave that to me."*

"Peter, we've got a lot to learn about, *money*-grubbing, grave robbing board members, and monetizing estates." Elvira exclaimed, overwhelmed by the possible scenario's he'd laid out.

"That's *just* the real estate part of the deal. Wait till all those *fat-cats* start pawing over your Uncle Charles pretty swag, the silver, and china, the works of art and rare books. They'll sell those to each other or just have them conveniently disappear. Gaspar, imagine Gwendolyn Crump decked out in Eugenia Floride's sparklers, if we can ever find them."

"Over my dead body," Gaspar replied then quickly wished he could take it back.

# ALEX'S BIG SURPRISE

"HAPPY BIRTHDAY, GASPAR!" ALEX HOLLERED WHEN GASPAR OPENED THE FRONT DOOR. HE STOOD next to a shiny red bike, all tricked out with playing cards clipped to the fenders so that they would clickety-clack between the super shiny spokes.

"Wow!" Gaspar whooped, his smile stretching from ear to ear. "I can't believe it Al! What a pal." Gaspar was truly touched. "Nobody has ever done anything like this for me before."

It was an exaggeration, he knew, but he didn't think his Dad would mind if he threw Alex a bone. He'd been so jumpy and preoccupied with fear lately that he'd completely forgotten his own birthday. He was fourteen years old today, and the butterflies were as busy as ever, not in a nervous way, but in a kinda sad way. Every birthday had brought some kind of a special surprise from his Dad and seeing this shiny red bike made Gaspar miss him more than ever.

"It's a real doozy." Gaspar exclaimed with glee, admiring his beautiful new present.

"This is what I've been working on, ever since you told me when your birthday was, that first night. It's one of the old bikes from the stable, but I've fixed it up for you. Hop on," Alex urged, "we've got places to go and people to see."

"Where are we going?" Gaspar asked jumping onto the bike.

"On a pirate adventure, of course." Alex smiled motioning for Gaspar to follow him.

"*Cool!*" Gaspar hated holding off exploring the sunken part of *Argente* but he couldn't let his friend down, not this morning. He pumped the pedals on his new red flyer and caught up with Alex as he sped his own, beat up old bike, through the arch into the stable yard and out the other side into the jungle. They pedaled furiously down a narrow path, skirting the beach, then picked up a trail leading back into the jungle. With each passing palm tree, Gaspar relaxed, leaving the cares of the past few days behind him. The boys powered through an area overgrown with palm and banana trees until it suddenly opened up. They slowed as they approached a tall, coral-stone tower, seemingly appearing like magic, in the middle of nowhere. Right in front was its door.

About twenty feet above that, Gaspar could see another door with a tiny balcony in front of it. The balcony connected with a sweeping exterior staircase which followed the curving block wall up, to the crenelated ramparts on the roof.

"A Crusaders Tower!" Gaspar exhaled in awe.

"Well almost, let me show you," Alex urged. "Now don't get too excited. I don't want you to be disappointed on your birthday."

"Disappointed, you're handing me a crusaders tower? What more could I ask for?"

"You'll see!" Alex pushed the heavy wood planked door open and pulled out his phone to light the way. Gaspar followed suit whipping out his phone to use it as a flashlight. "This is kind-a-spooky but worth it," Alex warned, leading the way.

Together they climbed up the shadowed curving staircase until they reached a high-ceilinged circular room. Light poured in from five tall French doors which each opened on to tiny iron balconies. The French doors were topped by six round window openings. Colorful graffiti covered the exposed stone walls and there wasn't a single pane of glass in the place that hadn't been shattered by vandals. The sixth opening held a heavy door with another round window above it. The big solid door stood ajar and led to the outside staircase he'd observed from the exterior.

Gaspar heard cooing birds nesting in the rafters. "What is this place?" he asked.

"It's where the high school kids hang out. They use it like a club house." Alex explained.

"Cool," Gaspar said. Stepping out onto the stone balcony he started climbing the curved exterior staircase up to the roof with Alex on his heels, right behind him. "This is so weird." Gaspar proclaimed, "is it a watch tower, or a light house, or was it meant to be a water tower? I don't get it."

"Let me show you something," Alex guided his friend to the crenelated parapet. "That direction is west. The house is that way," he said, pointing in the direction they'd just come from. "Over here, to the south is the gulf," he said stepping to his left while pointing over the wall. "Behind us is north. The road is over ther … a long way over there." Then stepping one more time to his left, Alex announced, "This is what I brought you here to see."

Alex stood by the parapet wall, pointing due east and Gaspar stepped to his friend's side and looked over the wall in the direction Alex was pointing.

"Oh my God." was all he could utter.

There, fifty feet below him cut out of the jungle in a straight line, was a landing strip. *This*, he now surmised correctly, *must have been the control tower*. At the very opposite end of the weed-choked runway, just off to the left, Gaspar saw the remains of a corrugated metal hangar. If his eyes weren't deceiving him, it held something shiny inside.

"Do I see a *plane*, Al?" Gaspar all but screamed.

"Yup. That's a plane!" Alex replied.

Before Alex could get in gear, Gaspar was down the stairs, through the door and bounding down to the ground. Alex caught up with him halfway across the tarmac. Laughing like madmen, they raced each other to the hangar.

Stepping into the hangar they found an oil drum conveniently placed so that they could climb up and reach the door of the single engine plane. Pulling the door open, Gaspar saw that the cockpit was pretty much intact, although it was clear that the high school kids had also found it an inviting place to hang out. It was a mess of ripped up magazines, with a large paper bag sitting in the pilot's seat.

"What's this?" Gaspar asked.

Alex pushed forward on the barrel. " Get in and have a seat, it's our lunch," he said. "I'm starved."

The boys ripped open the bag and chowed down on peanut butter, jelly and bacon sandwiches as they sat in the front seats of the plane and talked about learning to fly and traveling the world.

"Al, this is so great. I can't believe you made this lunch and hauled it out here before bringing me over. You're the best! Can you imagine what it must have been like to live here when this place was new?" Gaspar mused. "I really want to fix it up one day—the whole property—I can't see letting it rot away a minute longer."

"You know what? I think you'll do it too," Alex said. "You seem like the kind of guy who always figures out a way to get what you want."

Gaspar smiled. *I like Alex. It's hard to believe that only hours ago I was fretting about my enemies, doing me in, and now here I am, the owner of a Crusaders Tower and hanging out with my new best friend.* "What about you, Al?" Gaspar asked. "What do you want."

Alex grinned. "I want to go swimming. Race you to the bikes!"

Riding along the narrow trail as fast as they could, Gaspar followed close behind Alex mimicking his every move. After twenty minutes, Alex pulled off the path and got off his bike. Gaspar did the same. Together they pushed their bikes in the direction of the Gulf until they heard shouts and calls and laughter nearby.

"Hey guys, we're here," Alex called to a gang of kids splashing in a large round pool which was fed by incoming waves from the Gulf.

"Hey, Al, come on in … the water's warm." Called a sandy-haired boy, whose head was the only part of him visible on top of the water.

Several other boys jumped out of the water chasing each other around and throwing each other back in, making gigantic splashes. Two other guys climbed up the trunk of an overhanging tree and did cannonballs into the pool.

"Let's go," Alex said pulling off his t-shirt. Gaspar did the same and they joined the others in the swimming hole. Alex introduced Gaspar to everybody. "Today's his birthday," he added.

"Happy Birthday, man," a guy named Kevin greeted him.

"Thanks," Gaspar replied.

"Let's play water polo," Kevin shouted. "Mark, bring the ball. The inlet will be one goal, and the bank opposite will be the other goal. Okay, cause it's Gaspar's birthday he can be the captain of that team," Kevin proclaimed, pointing towards the bank opposite the inlet. "And I'll be the captain of this team," he announced, catching the red ball Mark had tossed over to him. "Alex you're on my team, Mark you go on Gaspar's team and the rest of you split up even-steven."

*That was easy*, Gaspar thought. He liked the way Kevin asserted himself and took control, what his Scout Master in L.A. would have called *a natural-born leader*. He deduced that all the kids present were about his own age, ready to go into eighth or ninth grade in September. Kevin threw the ball without so much as a one, two, three, and the game was on. Gaspar saw that Mark was a strong swimmer like Alex, and that two of the other guys on his team were pretty fast too, but the other four were kind of lame ducks. The other team seemed to have six strong players and only two that weren't great.

"You four guys," Gaspar pointed to the four lame ducks, "you guys hang back here, spread out and don't let that ball get past you. You, what's your name?"

"Pat."

"Okay, Pat, you're in charge of these other three. If *they* screw up, *you've* screwed up. So whatever you do, don't let *them* screw up. *Now spread out.*" Gaspar said as he dove away from them, into the fray.

Alex got the first goal past Pat and his crew and Kevin's team went wild with enthusiasm over their easy win. But Gaspar wasn't going to lose on his birthday and he got together with Mark and the other two, whose names he learned were Lou and Sancho. Together they formed a plan to make a goal, with Gaspar swimming underwater, behind Kevin's lines to intercept the ball when Mark threw it. What followed was a terrific water battle with a lot of splashing and major pushing and shoving. Gaspar was pleased to learn that the pool wasn't more than five feet deep for the most part, so he was able to hit bottom and push his way up and out of the water in order to intercept a throw or push out an opposing player. Mark made the sign to Gaspar, who disappeared underwater while his teammates distracted the others. Slipping past the guards, he jumped up and out of the water behind them just in time for Mark to throw him the ball, which he intercepted and threw backwards over his head into the inlet. "GOAL!"

The game continued for another hour until, completely exhausted, both teams claimed a tie and dragged themselves to the water's edge where they all sprawled out in the sun on the sandy embankment. Names were exchanged, ages, tales of what they had been doing so far that summer, gossip about other guys and some girls they knew from junior high. These were followed by questions to Gaspar about what he was interested in and how he liked living in Florida instead of California. Stuff like that. Not one of the boys asked Gaspar how he liked being rich or owning 500,000 acres of Florida waterfront property. He didn't know if Alex hadn't told them or if they just didn't care. That was fine with him. Just the way he liked it.

## CHAPTER 20

# A FANCY DRESS AFFAIR

B Y THE TIME THEY GOT HOME GASPAR AND ALEX WERE EXHAUSTED. RUNNING INTO THE KITCHEN TO GRAB A snack, they found Elvira and Angela hard at work.

"Where have you guys been?" Elvira asked. "We thought you'd never get here."

"What's up?" Gaspar asked grabbing a handful of cookies from the cookie jar and handing several to Al.

"Don't eat the cookies," Elvira scolded, "You'll spoil your dinner. Now run upstairs and get ready." She exhorted. "You boys don't want to be late for the big birthday party do you?"

Gaspar had no idea that his mom had planned a party. "A birthday party. For *me*! Who's coming?"

"Just the family, Felix and Angela and Alex of course and Peter called and told me you had invited him over for tonight, so I told him it was your birthday too."

Gaspar was surprised and pleased, "Okay Mom, I'll get moving."

"Come on Alex, we better get going too. We'll be back in an hour Elvira," Angela said, hustling Alex out of the kitchen.

Before going upstairs, Gaspar grabbed his bike from out in front and brought it inside, posing it on its kick stand under the entrance hall chandelier. After a quick shower and a change of clothes, he was energized and ready to party.

"Hey, Uncle Charlie, are you around?" Gaspar called out loud, doing a flying leap onto his bed.

Charlie materialized wearing a big Napoleonic hat and a great coat sporting huge gold epaulets.

Gaspar squinted at the outfit, confused. "Uh, what's the deal with the costume, Admiral?"

"It's a party, isn't it?"

"Well of course but ..."

"No *buts*. All *important* parties at La Rinconada, have always been *fancy dress affairs*! I see no reason why tonights soirée should be an exception."

"Fancy dress? You mean a costume party? I don't think so," Gaspar protested.

"I insist! We have plenty of costumes, let me show you where we keep them."

Gaspar followed Uncle Charlie down the hall and into the first guest room near the top of the stairs, *the green bedroom*. The closet door was open and inside Uncle Charlie showed him two large wicker hampers which held a topsy-turvy collection of mismatched but very theatrical articles of clothing including capes, hats, fans, swords and other creative props.

"Just drag these down to the entrance hall and when your guests arrive insist that it's a Fancy Dress Party and that they *must* choose their own costumes." Uncle Charlie ordered.

Gaspar did as he was told and dragged the first and then the second costume basket down the stairs. He placed them across from each other in the space between the double stairs. Rummaging around he started laying out attractive costumes across some of the chairs scattered here and there against the walls. Soon he came across a very tight-fitting toreador's suit of lights, and put the tiny pink sequined jacket on over his orange polo. Next he found the toreador's two-eared, curly lamb hat and put that on his head at a jaunty angle. Last but certainly not least, came a huge pink cape spangled with sequins, and lined in imperial yellow satin. This he draped over one shoulder. Admiring the complimentary colors of his costume in the mirror, Gaspar thought he made a mighty fine *matador*. Now he was really ready to party.

"Fantastic!" Uncle Charlie approved. "I couldn't have chosen a more perfect costume for the guest of honor. Now pose here by your new bike and greet your guests." The ghost instructed his protégé.

"Elvira started down the stairs and stopped. "What on earth," she exhaled, seeing *Gaspar the Toreador* standing by his new red bike. "Where'd you get the bike, and what's with the crazy costume?"

"Isn't it great mom. Alex made it for me from one of the old bikes in the stables and by the way ... tonight's a *fancy dress affair*," Gaspar announced. "Didn't you get the invitation? All the *important* parties at La Rinconada were always fancy dress affairs," he parroted Uncle Charlie. "I'll have to show you some of the pictures from the albums in the library. Come on, I found the old costume baskets and brought them down. Look at all this great stuff. Mom , don't be shy, come on ... choose something!"

"Okay, it's your party." Elvira rummaged around and finally came up with a 1920s opera cape, a black velvet headband with a huge egret feather attached to its front by a very large diamond brooch and strands and strands of pearls to wrap around her throat, completing her glamorous flapper costume.

"Mom, you look awesome," Gaspar complimented her. "Look, here come the Mendoza's."

Gaspar ran to the glass and iron front door and threw it open calling "Happy Birthday, Everyone! We're having a costume party. Go choose your costumes," Gaspar said, leading Angela by the hand across the entrance hall.

Alex had already high-tailed it to the hampers and soon found a tricorn hat decorated with rich ostrich plumes, an eighteenth-century style frock coat which was slightly too big for him, but exceedingly beautiful with its gold braid, pearl buttons and lace ruffles at the sleeves. He also found a lace jabot which he tied around the collar of his sport shirt to great effect.

Felix settled on a pair of six shooters which he strapped around the waist of his best pair of jeans, an old leather vest that fit just fine and a calico bandanna which he tied around his neck. He topped off the look with a way too big, artistically bashed up, white Stetson hat, which everyone got a good laugh out of.

Angela tied a black satin Spanish shawl around her waist. It was embroidered with enormous red roses and acid green leaves and edged with a heavy silk fringe. She placed a beautiful carved tortoise shell comb in her thick, black hair, then threw a delicate lace mantilla over this which trailed almost to the floor. Rummaging further she chose a huge red silk rose, which she tucked behind her left ear, and a black lace fan which she unfurled to flirt behind.

"What's going on?" Peter laughed from the open doorway.

"Peter", Gaspar called. "Happy Birthday, come on in. Look at the cool new bike Alex made for me. It's a fancy dress party, and we're all choosing our costumes."

Gaspar grabbed Peter's elbow and steered him over to the costume baskets. "Choose one!"

To everyone's amusement Peter chose a pink velvet ringmaster's coat with black velvet collar and cuffs and a red flannel vest with big gold buttons. He found a white silk cravat which he tied inside his open necked shirt and placed a tall black top hat on his head. "How's this?" he asked the assembled friends, hoping for approval.

"Perfect," Elvira gave her opinion, while the rest all clapped and laughed theirs.

"Let's have dinner." Gaspar shouted.

"Let's have *cocktails*," Elvira corrected him. "Peter, will you do the honors. I've set the bar up in the living room. Gasp, I have sodas for you and Alex."

Everyone found seats while Peter, with Gaspar and Alex's help, fixed drinks all around. Elvira went to the kitchen and came back rolling a tea cart, piled high with platters and bowls of chips and dip, as well as cheese and crackers and olives and crudités. The boys began devouring the chips, while the adults nibbled at the sharp-tasting cheese. Gaspar and Alex recounted their day telling the adults only as much as they needed to know about the Crusaders Tower, The Airstrip and the swimming hole.

"Tonight I've cooked *Yucateco* style, just for *you*, Gaspar." Angela announced proudly.

"Let's eat!" Gaspar cried.

The boys jumped up, ran across the entrance hall, and into the dining room while the adults followed them at a slightly slower pace.

Dinner was a success. The festive atmosphere, bolstered by Uncle Charlie's creative costuming was awesome. When everyone was stuffed with second helpings, Elvira dowsed the lights and brought out the birthday cake, lighted with fourteen candles. Everyone sang *Happy Birthday*, at the top of their lungs, including Gaspar after which Alex stood by in case he needed help blowing them all out. When Gaspar made his wish, it was *for peace of mind*, that's all he wanted going forward.

Gaspar served the cake while Alex, still standing beside him, served the ice cream. At Elvira's insistence, Peter got up and poured everyone, including Gaspar and Alex, a saucer of champagne and then made a toast.

"To Gaspar, a new friend to most of us, and a great guy. May this year bring you all the happiness in the world and may all your days be no less joyous than today has been."

Everyone applauded and sipped their bubbly. Everyone but Gaspar and Alex, who gulped theirs and nearly coughed it out yelling, "*Eeew!*" before breaking into squeals of uncontrolled laughter.

Back in the living room, Elvira offered coffee, but Felix and Angela begged off saying they should really be getting home.

"Alex, it's time to go now, *vamanos, hijo*," Felix called, moving to the entrance hall.

They removed the six shooters, and the Spanish shawl, and the tricorn hat and all their other finery, folding it neatly and placing it carefully back into the costume baskets. Stripped of all their fancy accessories, Felix put his arm around his son's shoulder and led him toward the front door.

"See you tomorrow, Al. Thanks again for a great day and for my fantastic present", he called. "*It's amazing.*"

After the Mendoza's had gone, they moved into the library where Elvira poured coffee for herself and Peter.

Gaspar took a seat in a big chair near the sofa where his mother and Peter sat together. He looked at them now as if for the first time and realized, *They look kind of good together.* Gaspar figured. *Peter is probably a little older than Mother. He's, tall and fit and very nice. A gentleman*, was Gaspar's final opinion. *Mom looks beautiful in her flapper get up*, and Gaspar noticed that when she sat with Peter her demeanor seemed somehow different. More relaxed and carefree. Without the weight of the world on her shoulders. Maybe since his father had died, she needed someone to be there for her as she always was for Gaspar. Why did he feel as if his eyes were just being opened. It seemed like every day since they'd arrived on

Perdido Isle had brought him new revelations about life and how it worked.

"It sounds as if you had a great day with Alex showing you around your domain." Peter enthused.

"It sure was, and he sure did, Peter. I had no idea when we left L.A. that Florida was going to be like this," Gaspar exclaimed.

"It's a nice set up, but it's not all fun and games. It has to be managed in order to keep it running smoothly," Peter suggested.

"I know. I see a lot of things around here that I'd like to do and I want you to help me figure out how to get them done. I want to salvage *Argente*, and secure the church like we talked about. Felix needs helpers … more staff is a priority. And one day, I'd like to bring this whole place back to where it once was … if we can."

"Okay. Let's talk about all that in my office tomorrow," Peter said.

"Any objections if I come along? I'd like to get a handle on all of this business too," Elvira chimed in.

"Sure, Mom. Can we meet at Peter's office at ten? Then we can all go to lunch together at the café."

"Sounds like a plan," Peter stood up. "I think it's time for me to go home and give you people some peace. By the way … I brought you a present, Gaspar." He took a small wrapped box out of his pants pocket and handed it to the birthday boy. "Go on … open it."

Gaspar tore off the ribbon and the wrapping, exposing a small leather box stamped in gold. Inside were a set of fancy fishing flies. "These are great" Gaspar proclaimed. "Have you ever tried them, Peter?"

"I have a similar set. One of these days when you're not so busy going out on adventures, maybe we can go fishing."

"I'd love that, Peter," Gaspar told him, "anytime."

"What a lovely present, Peter," Elvira said touching his arm. "Thank you."

"Yeah. Thanks, Peter." Gaspar beamed at the invitation and his new collection of fancy flies. "Let's go try them out next week if you can, okay?"

"You got it, kid. Get some sleep now, and thanks for including me in the festivities," he said taking off his coat, vest, hat and cravat and leaving them in the costume basket in the hall. "I had fun."

After Peter had gone and they were alone, Gaspar and Elvira also took off their costumes and placed them back in the hampers before climbing up the stairs. "I have a birthday present for you too, darling," Elvira spoke softly.

"Really? You're the best, Mom! That great party and a present too. What is it?"

"I sent for Daddy's collection of Navy memorabilia, his medals, and photographs, and all the books he collected on the history of the United States Navy that the two of you used to pour over back home. They're all upstairs in the blue suite, or your office or whatever your calling that room these days."

"Mom. You're the best. I've missed having Dad's memories around me."

"I know Darling, I miss him too. It's been really hard for me since he left us, but this change has done me good." She said, tearfully, giving Gaspar a kiss and a big hug.

## CHAPTER 21

# TROUBLE

WHEN GASPAR LEFT THE HOUSE THE NEXT MORNING, HE RAN SMACK INTO UNZEGA IN HIS SIGNATURE, sinister black attire, as the mysterious man rounded the side of the house and strolled jauntily up to Gaspar on the terrace.

"Buenos dias, Don Gaspar. You have a surprise visitor, and it is I, Unzega!" The swarthy Mexican gushed in his most oily Spanish-accented English.

"I see," Gaspar greeted the intruder coldly, not offering him his hand.

"I was in the neighborhood, heading to Calaluna, when I saw your gates were open, and thought, I'd stop by and visit my friends, the Browns." The Mexican oozed charm.

"Friends? We're not accustomed to receiving *uninvited* visitors, especially so early in the day." Gaspar informed Unzega cooly.

"Your mother was kind enough to invite me to visit … *anytime*, the night of dear Gwendolyn's party," the trickster informed him. "I apologize for not phoning ahead, but I'm an *impromptu man*—the type who makes *spur of the moment* decisions. People who know me well, say I'm nothing if not spontaneous," Unzega chuckled suavely, still piling on the charm.

"What is it you want?" Gaspar cut to the chase.

"I've been spending the Summer here, on my yacht, *Revenge*."

"I've seen it anchored out in front of my house *a lot* lately." Gaspar cut in.

"*Revenge* is moored at the Llojeta Yacht Club, I would like to invite you and Dona Elvirita to dine with me there one day." Unzega smarmed.

"I know the club. I *own* it." Gaspar deadpanned.

Unzega ignored him. "I'm looking for a place to live around here, an important property, along the coast, preferably with a house, *like this one*." Unzega made himself clear, throwing out his arms in an all encompassing arc as he quickly took in the surroundings.

"I doubt that you'll find anything around here for sale or for rent even *remotely* like La Rinconada," Gaspar assured him. "In all the world, I doubt if you will ever find another property as unique as *this one*. Maybe you should try looking over on the mainland."

"Gwendolyn mentioned the other night that you've decided not to stay on. She told me that, the climate on Perdido Isle didn't agree with you. Therefore, I thought you would consider selling La Rinconada to me, lock, stock and barrel. I'm willing to pay you a handsome sum … in cash." His charm was wearing thin.

"Over my dead body!" Gaspar practically shouted.

"Yes, I see your point," Unzega hissed patronizingly. "But you haven't heard my offer yet. If you won't sell the house perhaps you'd sell me the land, all of it. You understand, I am offering *cash*!"

"Señor, the property is entailed. We could not sell it to you even if we wanted to, which we don't. I don't know what kind of game Miss Crump is playing, but we have never expressed any intention other than to live here, *for the rest of our lives*. Besides, if we leave before ten years pass, the property goes directly and entirely to the Perdido Isle Historical Society Museum, which of course would please nobody more than Miss Crump. Let me just say, *it'll be a cold day in Hades* before that scenario ever plays out." Gaspar informed the slime-bag in no uncertain terms.

"I see." Unzega snarled sardonically. "You've made your position very clear, "I'd hoped we could reach a *friendly* agreement about this, but I can see that you are intractable. There is something you need to understand *boy*," Unzega, changed the tenor of his voice and moved in closer, invading Gaspars space, hissing with clenched teeth only an inch from Gaspar's face. "I want this property and I'll get it, by *hook* or by *crook*. Mark my words boy, it's only a matter of time before you see me, Unzega, in full possession of your beloved Rinconada!" The awful man made his threat before turning away.

Just then, Elvira stepped out onto the terrace. "Señor Unzega," she greeted the monster cordially, "what a pleasant surprise."

"Encantado, Señora," Unzega did an about face and oozed his Latin charm again, bending over her hand without touching it.

"Gaspar, have you invited Señor Unzega inside?" Elvira asked, not waiting for an answer before motioning the evil man through the French doors into the library. "I don't believe that Señor Unzega has ever been to La Rinconada before." Elvira told her son inocently.

"Why should he have?" Gaspar questioned standing his ground. "This is a private house, and unless Señor Unzega was a friend of Uncle Charlie's or Cousin Eugenia's, I see no reason why he ever should have come here."

"In fact, I *have* been here before, many, many years ago." Unzega ingratiated himself, "It has changed a lot here since that first visit. I would be enchanted dear lady if you would personally show me your house." He waltzed through the French doors turning his back on Gaspar.

"Follow me," Elvira smiled graciously.

Gaspar was beside himself with rage that the greasy Mexican was actually making a play for his mother, having realized that dealing directly with her son was hopeless. Rather than say anything, Gaspar decided not to engage further, and continued across the terrace and over to the stables to find Alex.

"What's wrong, Gasp?" Alex greeted his friend. "You don't look very happy this morning."

"Plenty's wrong," Gaspar groaned. "That snake, Unzega, has invited himself onto our property and he's made it clear that he wants to buy it, or better yet steal it from us. I told him we weren't interested, under any circumstances. He says he's willing to do whatever he has to do to get it. Now he's working on my poor unsuspecting mother, no doubt hoping to wriggle the property out of her."

"Yikes," Alex blurted out, "from what you've told me about that creep … we've got to stop him."

"Yeah, but how? He's rich and powerful, and full of Latin charm. For the first time, Al … I'm really afraid."

"Wha-da-ya-mean?" Alex mumbled.

"Picture this. He woos my mother, marries her, kills me, she inherits the property, and he takes it over as his own. Then maybe he kills her too … just for good measure."

"You've been watching too many murder mysteries, Gasp. You should watch cartoons like I do … they're so more civilized."

"Give me a break, Al. Was almost getting run over the other day or getting grazed by that spear caused by watching too many murder mysteries? I'm telling you, there's more here than meets the eye and it ain't pretty." Gaspar was angry.

"I'm sorry Gasp. I understand. You've got enemies, but just let them try and hurt you or your mom, cause I'll be right there to protect you." Alex showed his support in the only way he knew could.

"Thanks Al, I'm sorry I yelled at you, but all this intrigue is getting on my nerves. I don't want to think about Unzega anymore, not today anyway. I need to keep my eye on the prize, and the prize is *Argente*."

*The prize is really finding the treasure, but I can't tell Alex that, so I'll keep our work on Argente front and center as a diversion.* When he was alone, Gaspar spent every spare moment searching through books, albums, and folders, looking for clues, wanting to find that treasure. Uncle Charlie was with him all the way, but the stubborn old ghost wouldn't give him even a hint as to where the best place to start looking was. *Argente* was low lying fruit, and he meant to pick it.

# CHAPTER 22

# ARGENTE

Fitted out in his wetsuit and tanks, Gaspar dove into the canal where *Argente* silently awaited him. He paddled along the sunken port side of the ship with Alex stuck on land (due to Felix's refusal to let him help on board the ship) watching from the side of the canal wall. He climbed up on deck and into the Main Saloon and then climbed down the stairs into the lower gangway.

The water was soon up over his head so Gaspar turned on his flash light and started swimming from state room to state room. One by one he searched each space. One by one he moved furniture and clothing, old books and boxes, opening each box to see what might be inside. So far so bad, there was nothing of real value and no incredible secret compartments to hide treasure in either. He pulled out the drawers of the chests, they were all empty. He found a few crystal perfume bottles with silver stoppers, and a mirrored tray with silver fittings and placed them in his dive bag, but for all his efforts, the first stateroom was a bust. The same was true of the second, third and fourth staterooms that he searched. Finally he found what promised to be the owner's suite, which in the dim light he thought was painted pink. The usual crystal bottles filled his bag and a couple of interesting picture frames. Pulling out drawers from the chest he found a box full of jewels, nothing amazing, a few rings and a brooch but jewels none the less. Well that at least was something for his trouble as long as they didn't turn out to be fake. The next principal cabin he came upon was even grander than the first as it had its very own fireplace. That was *cool*, Gaspar thought but he hadn't found any treasure. In one of the drawers in the bathroom he found a man's gold watch. He knew without checking that it was ruined as far as ever keeping time, but at least it was something ... *in gold*. Meager pickings in hand, he swam back up the staircase and climbed back up on deck, and waived to Alex.

"Not exactly a billion dollars in gold, Al. Now I'm going to go down into the hold and look around down there."

Walking forward Gaspar opened the hatch that lead to the hold and using the metal ladder attached there, lowered himself into the murky water. The yacht was

150 feet long and Gaspar figured that it probably had at least five compartments below. The first one held cases and cases of canned goods, boxes of dried milk and other provisions long since spoiled.

He swam to the second hold, which was lined on both sides of the hull with stacks and stacks of matching opaque plastic boxes sealed tightly shut. Peering closely into these he discovered silver dishes, silver platters, silver soup tureens and silver tea sets, silver candlesticks, silver beakers, silver goblets and silver flatware all tossed in a pile. It was a neatly stacked but jumbled up mountain of silver which he decided would be easy to take up and out to the Tombs. When he entered the third fourth and fifth holds, he found similar storage boxes filled with silver items. Then he had one of his more brilliant ideas. Looking around he found the seacocks which had been deliberately opened at Eugenia's order to sink the ship. Using a crescent hammer he'd seen lying on the floor of the first compartment he turned the ball valves closed. Returning to the deck he waived at Alex and disappeared into the Saloon again. Heading back below decks he checked each of the cabins to make sure the portholes were all closed tight before heading topside.

He was correct in assuming that their were five holds. There was certainly plenty of room down there to hold a lot of treasure, but unfortunately that's not where Uncle Charlie was hiding it. Re-emerging on deck he called to

Alex, "there's not much here but a lot of old silver table stuff, but the good news is … I think we can refloat her."

"Are you crazy? Really? How?" Alex sat stunned, mouth agog.

Gaspar swam over to the steps leading to The Tombs, and Alex ran over to help him out. "Listen Al, we're going to need is an electric submersible pump. I closed the seacocks and checked the portholes so if we can just pump the water out … I think she should float." Gaspar told his friend in all seriousness.

Gaspar ran over to the sea wall and grabbed his cell phone which he'd left there along with his other gear. He made a quick phone call to Peter who without knowing exactly what his young client had in min … connected him with a contractor named Mike Fitzpatrick. Gaspar immediately ordered two submersible pumps to be delivered to the house from Mr. Fitzpatrick … as soon as possible.

•••

The next morning, Gaspar woke up bright and early and looked out the fantail windows of his room. Fitzpatrick's foreman had brought over the submersible pumps yesterday afternoon, set them up, and turned them on. What he saw in the light of dawn, made Gaspar's heart skip a beat. *Argente* was now bobbing on the surface of the canal! He couldn't believe his eyes. Throwing on his swim trunks and a T-shirt he grabbed his cell phone, and ran out of the house and down to the canal. He had to work fast and called Alex, who picked up on the first ring.

"*Shake a leg*, mate, are you dressed?" Not waiting for an answer Gaspar continued, "Go and find your Dad and bring him to *Argente*, rapido!" Without further explanation, Gaspar pressed off and continued running.

Before he could say *Jack Robinson*, Alex was there followed by Felix who was looking anxious.

"Good morning," Gaspar greeted the astonished father and son. "Look, she floats, *she floats*!" Gaspar cried, giddy with laughter.

Not waiting for a reply or even inviting discussion, he continued very seriously. "This is what I need you Mates to do. Felix, you and Al, bring some heavy rope, a lot of it. We need to *double her up* here," he said pointing to the two heavy bronze bollards attached to the coral-stone seawalls of the canal. "We need to tie her down before she floats out into the Gulf with the low tide. I'm going on board to tie the ropes off up there." He pointed. You throw me the lines once they get here."

Gaspar had no idea how he was going to climb up onto the deck now that it floated ten feet above the water. Then he remembered the Irish pennants, dangling aft, from where the lifeboat had previously hung. He hoped they'd hold his weight. He dove in and swam to the stern where the rotted lines hung from the davits with their tails floating in the water. He reached up and tried the first one but it broke off in his hands. He swam over to the other line and tried jumping out of the water as high as he could to grab hold of it. When he finally grabbed it … it stuck. *Fantastic*, he thought as he gingerly shimmied his way up the line. Scrambling over the rail he raced to the starboard side and called to Felix and Alex who had returned with the ropes.

"Throw them up here." Gaspar instructed his mates.

Two ropes flew through the air and landed hard on the deck. Gaspar quickly tied them off to the heavy cleats fore and aft, using his father's favorite sailor's knot.

"Okay, guys … now do me a favor … run and find a couple of old tires or something that we can place against the wall of the canal so we don't bump the hell out of *Argente* in case the water gets choppy. Before you go, throw me the rest of the rope, I'll use it to hang the tires from, when they get here."

While waiting for Alex and Felix to return, Gaspar checked on the two pumps. Finding them high and dry, he turned them off and lugged them back on deck. Then he decided to do some housekeeping. Moving the old wicker furniture around the deck where he thought it most likely would have sat in the old days, he found an armchair that, although weather-beaten, felt sturdy and took a sea … waiting for his pals to return.

Gaspar could see Alex and Felix heading his direction, each of them pushing a big rubber white wall tire ahead of them.

His mom was right behind them. "What's going on out here?"

"Look mom ... she floats." Gaspar called out.

"That's nice dear," Elvira was non-commital, "I'm going back in to have some breakfast."

Gaspar couldn't believe how blasé she was, but he also knew his mother well enough not to expect more of a reaction from her.

After he had the tires hanging freely, Gaspar adjusted the ropes around the railing to make sure they hit at just the right spot between the water, the yacht and the top of the coral-stone walls of the canal.

"Okay, you guys, heave ho, and pull *Argente* in as close as possible. Come on you, *filthy-rapscallion-loafers*!" He had to laugh at his attempt at pirate talk. "Heave, that's it, *heave*! Put your backs into it you, *sons-of-subtropical-sea-lice*!"

Once the ship was tied up Gaspar gave more orders. "Felix, I don't want a living sole on board this boat unless I'm also aboard. What I saw down there yesterday makes me think this ship is a *death-trap*."

"Very wise, Señor Gaspar." Felix answered his young master with deference.

Gaspar wasn't surprised. He knew Felix would be the first to concur with him even though what he'd just said about the insurance and the death-trap was utter nonsense.

...

Three days later Gaspar stood on the deck of *Argente*, dreaming of what he might do with her. He'd worked with Alex as his compatriot for three days solid, walking stacks of silver dishes, goblets, candelabra and other decorative articles from the ship's hold, up and out and over, into the Tombs. It was quite a collection of decorative silver table articles.

Looking through the glass doors into the dining saloon, he caught a glimpse of someone moving around the room. Going inside for a closer look, he discovered no less than the best-dressed ghost in town. Why wasn't he surprised. There he was, Uncle Charlie, done up to the nines in a pristine yachting costume, white flannels, blue blazer, and gold buttons emblazoned with anchors and a crest of interlocking gold anchors embroidered over the breast pocket too.

"So you found Gena's silver, and got her to float, all in one day." Uncle Charlie congratulated him. "Very impressive, my boy. But if you think this is an accomplishment, wait until you find *my gold*," he teased Gaspar mercilessly. "Gold and silver have gone sky high since Washington started printing all that paper. I always thought Eugenia was foolish collecting silver decorations, but she proved herself right in the end. You thought she named *Argente* after your great-grandmother, but you're wrong. It was her way of saying, *x marks the spot*. She hid her fortune, her personal collection, in a treasure ship of her own, then sunk it, my clever little girl. To tell you the truth, I never knew she had so much stuff. She was buying all those silver table articles way back, when nobody wanted them, and I wonder how many hundreds of thousands of dollar … maybe millions she must have spent on all that stuff … since I made my departure in 1967? Gaspar, that's a serious haul in silver you've got there!"

"You don't mean to tell me that it's worth a lot of money do you?" Gaspar asked incredulously. "You don't think it could be worth … m-m-m-millions do you?" He stuttered.

"Oh, millions? Well possibly. I really have no idea, but that stuff doesn't come cheap you know, and I can assure you Eugenia was only interested in the bes … you know … museum quality stuff." Uncle Charlie tried using his most casual tone of voice.

"You've got to be joking, real money? What do you suggest I do next Uncle? I'm kind-a stumped," Gaspar admitted.

"If I were you, I'd just keep it all and enjoy it. The last thing you need right now is money, and after you find my treasure, the very last thing you'll ever need is money … so for now … just enjoy the beauty of Gena's collection.

"But it's not enough to just own it, Uncle. I want to know about it, who made it, and for whom." Gaspar interjected.

"That's what I like about you Gasp, your curiosity and inquisitiveness. What you need is a friend in the antiques business. May I suggest a young man I've read about recently, seems pretty bright, works for Beal's in New Orleans. He came out from London with Parque-Bernaise, stayed a spell in New York with Christian's and fell in love with the deep south. Like I say, he's at Beal's in New Orleans. His name is Jason Steinmeyer. Give him a call, invite him out for the weekend. Tell him you live at La Rinconada. If that doesn't get him here, then he's not worth his salt.

# CHAPTER 23

# A TRIP TO CALIFORNIA

G ASPAR AND ALEX WERE SWIMMING IN THE SEA THE
NEXT DAY, WHEN ELVIRA CAME OUT AND INTER-
rupted them.

"Gaspar, we're so happy here, I think I should go back to California, clear out the house and put it on the market now, before school starts. What do you think, honey?

"That makes a lot of sense, Mom," Gaspar really thought it did and couldn't believe Uncle Charlie's powers of persuasion and wondered, *What kind of crazy thoughts Charlie planted in his own mind every night.*

"I really should go with you Mom, but with all the stuff going on here, I wouldn't feel right going away right now."

"I know, dear. I hate to do it without you, but I understand. How about you, Alex? Would you like to come to California with me? You'd be a great help, and I'd pay you to help me with the packing." she promised.

"I don't know, Mrs.," Alex answered shyly, "I'd like to go but I think Gaspar is counting on me here …"

"No, no, Alex. If you want to go to L.A. it would be great. I'd feel so much better knowing you were with my Mom, helping her out. Besides it's only for a couple of weeks." He reminded them both, shaking his head up and down, grinning his approval.

"Well, okay, Señora. I've always wanted to go to California. Let me ask my Mom and Dad."

"I've already spoken with your parents and they said if *you* want to go, *they'd* approve. I'll make the reservations, we'll fly out tomorrow and fly back the minute we're done."

The next morning Felix whisked Alex and Elvira off to the airport, just before a silver BMW convertible pulled through the gates and up to the front steps of La Rinconada. The engine was barely turned off when Jason Steinmeyer jumped out of the car, with a black Gucci briefcase under his arm. He was a young man in his twenties wearing a seersucker suit and round tortoise shell glasses.

Gaspar strode out the front door to greet his guest wearing his usual flowered swim trunks and yellow t-shirt.

"Good morning, I'm Jason Steinmeyer. I have an appointment to meet Mr. Gaspar Brown."

"I'm Gaspar Brown."

"Perhaps your father?"

"Sorry, it's just me. Thanks for coming over, I hope to make this worth your while."

Gaspar ushered Steinmeyer into the house and down the two steps into the sunken living room. He decided to leave his visitor alone so that he could poke around without the owner being present.

"May I offer you some coffee or tea?"

"Tea please, with lemon."

"Look around, Jason. I'll order us some tea and be right back."

Several minutes later, he found Jason staring intently at the large canvas over the sofa.

"Do you like it?" Gaspar asked facetiously.

"It's a Rembrandt!" Jason gasped, swallowing hard."

"It's mate is over there," Gaspar pointed nonchalantly towards the opposite wall.

"Let's move into the library, we'll have tea there.

Walking into the library, something caught Jason's eye. "*The tea set*!" he exclaimed.

"You don't want tea?" Gaspar played dumb.

"Your tea set. If I'm not mistaken, it was made for Catherine the Great, for the Winter Palace. The drawings for it by Cameron are in the National Gallery in London. It's considered a masterpiece of the silversmith's art. It's been lost since before the revolution. How is it that you have it … *here*?" Jason exhaled, wide eyed.

"Oh, we have lots of *old used stuff* around here." was all Gaspar offered not wanting to get the appraiser's hopes up. Uncle Charlie had told him the exact same story about the tea set and Catherine the Great and the Rembrandts, too. *This Steinmeyer, really knew his business*.

"What other *old used stuff*? Can you show me?" Jason begged.

Gaspar feared the young auctioneer might *pee his pants*, so great was his excitement. "Oh paintings and china and silver, some jewelry, easy to move things, like furniture." Gasper wanted to split a gut laughing. But instead he decided to put Steinmeyer out of his misery. "I want to make it clear, I'm not interested in selling anything. Jason, I want you to teach me about the collections I've just inherited. I want to learn about what I have, where it came from and who it may have belonged to and I suppose it wouldn't hurt to know what some of this stuff is worth too. Your knowledge of Rembrandt, and the provenance of this tea set, is remarkable. I only hope you're correct in that they are the genuine article." Gaspar insisted with a wink, Let me show you a small group of silver table ornaments that I've put together for your appraisal. Do you have time?"

"I can stay as long as you'll have me," Jason smiled.

"Fine, stay the weekend or longer if you like ... we have lots of room here ... and my housekeeper Angela is a wonderful cook." Gaspar promised.

Jason drained his tea cup quickly. "I can't wait to see more!"

Gaspar led Jason out onto the garden terrace. "We plan to re-plant this area. We've been here a little over a month now and you can see that the gardens have been extremely neglected, mere shadows of their former glory. My cousin Eugenia died last year. She was ninety-six years old."

They continued walking as the visitor took in the beach, the Gulf, the palm trees and the *Argente*.

"What's that?" Jason exclaimed.

"That's *Argente*, my cousin's yacht. She named it after my great-grandmother. It's about to be restored as a surprise for my mother. Our destination is the Tombs, that's the octagon-shaped building at the end there." He said pointing at the columned pavilion.

Before opening the door, Gaspar made a great show of turning off the newly installed alarm just to make it all seem, too complicated for words.

"I can't wait to hear what you think of this collection." With that Gaspar turned the gold key in the lock and threw open the bronze door.

"Oh, my God!" were the only words Jason Steinmeyer uttered while standing frozen in the doorway.

It seemed to Gaspar that he could barely move, let alone speak. Gaspar did think that the dramatic way he'd stacked all the silver objects up around the magnificent carved onyx sarcophagi made it look just like the treasure hoard from The Pirates of the Caribbean ride at Disneyland.

"So, do you want me to stay while you look it over or should I go?"

"Stick around," Jason whispered opening his briefcase on the tomb of Calico Jack Rackham.

Gaspar closed and locked the door behind them and took a seat at the feet of Anne Bonny. "Take your time Jason. We can work until lunchtime, have a swim, and come back here if you like. There's no rush."

The morning slipped away as Jason reverently picked up each item one by one, studied it, wrote notes on it, photographed it, and put it back. Gaspar was amazed when his new friend exclaimed, "This silver statue of the Virgin is South German, dated 1654. It was made in Augsburg, worth $25,000, any day of the week."

"You've got to be kidding," Gaspar cried jumping down from his perch, "*that much!*"

"It's probably the least valuable of the entire lot but definitely not the least beautiful," Jason proclaimed reaching for one of a pair of covered silver soup tureens. "These are extraordinary, made in Paris around 1804, by Henry Auguste, see his stamp here," he pointed out the hallmarks on the bottom to his young client, "*First Empire*, If you wanted to sell these or buy them they would cost $600,000 for the pair," the appraiser stated with confidence.

Gaspar gulped audibly. He was dumbfounded. He suddenly found a new appreciation for cousin Eugenia's eclectic collecting.

"Don't get excited. It's not all worth that much. Take those two gilded ormolu seven-light candelabras, Louis XVI, around 1770, really very nice but only worth around $600,000 for the pair. If they were *royal* or *signe*, they would be worth more. Don't be disappointed, that's not a bad price for a second tier set of decorative table top articles," Jason informed his wide eyed client in all seriousness.

Gaspar quickly Googled the word *signe* on his cell phone and found out it meant *signed* in French.

By lunchtime Jason had only touched on one eighth of the loot. "Let's eat," Gaspar suggested, getting up and unlocking the door to let in a breath of fresh air.

It took Jason four days to appraise the hoard in the tombs. Four days of breakfast, lunch and dinner, midday swims in the pool or the ocean, visits to the airstrip, a peek inside the saloon and staterooms of *Argente*, and a visit to the abandoned church.

Jason's four day visit extended into two weeks with visits into town to see the Historical Society Museum, lunch at the Grand Hotel Floride and quick visits to Gaspar's two town houses in Calaluna and Llojeta. After their first visit to those two houses so many weeks ago, Gaspar and his mother decided that as getaways, she would get the French town house in Calaluna, and he would have the little Venetian palace in Llojeta. Jason confirmed that Gaspar had, *by far*, made the right decision. "*Party!*" was Jason's one word assessment of the pink and white Venetian confection set amidst flowering tropical gardens in the resort town.

By the time Jason left, he and Gaspar had become fast friends, and a deal was struck between them that Jason would "stay on" as a part time curator of the collections and as Gaspar's tutor in the decorative and fine arts.

Gaspar took Jason over to Peter's office to introduce the appraiser to his lawyer.

"Peter, remember when I told you I was going treasure hunting. Well, I found some treasure, and Jason here tells me it's worth a lot of money." Gaspar broke the news. "I think I've found a way to boost the money we need to get La Rinconada back on track."

"Tell me about it." Peter sat back in his chair to listen.

"Well, when I went diving on *Argente*, I discovered a lot of boxes of silver table decorations down in the holds. They were all sealed in water-tight plastic containers and after I got her to float, I asked Jason to appraise them for me. You're not going to believe this, but cousin Eugenia hid fourteen-million dollars worth of valuable antiques down there!"

"You've gotta be joking. Jason, is this true?" The lawyer was clearly flabbergasted.

"Yes it's true Peter, but there's more." Jason divulged.

"Oh yeah," Gaspar blushed, "I found some of cousin Eugenia's sparklers too."

"We're talking about historic jewels in museum quality settings." Jason explained, "I'd say about fifty-million dollars worth, give or take." He estimated nonchalantly.

"Okay boys, this is information I wasn't prepared to receive. Tell you what Gaspar, let me and Jason figure out how best to dispose of these collections. I would prefer to do so quietly without any publicity. Although we can definitely use the money, the last thing I want to do is incur any more taxes for this estate."

"We're on the same page Peter, I'll leave this between you two businessmen to figure out … in the meantime, I'll just keep my eyes open for more stuff to sell cause I've already figured out where I'd like to spend it." Gaspar grinned.

•••

After Jason went back to New Orleans, Gaspar asked Peter to come over for lunch.

Sitting out by the pool, Gaspar discussed his latest improvement plan. "Peter, after you sell some of my loot, I want to hire a contractor to fix up *Argente*."

"Let me research the best yacht restorers in the country and get back to you?"

"I'll leave the choice up to you Peter, but I'd like to get this started sooner rather than later. By the way, I've decided to turn *my* house in Llojeta into a *playhouse* so I'll need a telephone installed and an alarm system too, the usual stuff, Internet, cable, like we did here. We should probably do the same with Mom's house in Calaluna, don't you think? I know she wants to use it, like I want to use mine, to play in."

"Okay Gaspar. You never fail to amaze me. As always, I'm right behind you on this one. Just keep me posted in case you need any back up."

"You got it, Peter. That's what I like about you, you've always got my back. Speaking of which, let's talk about Unzega?"

"Unzega, what about him?"

"He's been hanging around, making a play for *Mom*. I'm not saying there's anything serious going on there, but he's made it clear that he's not *my* friend, and that he intends to wrest this whole place from me, all 500,000 acres of it."

"You've got to be kidding. Elvira's not falling for that creep … is she?" Peter protested.

"I'm not kidding, Peter. I'm serious when I tell you, I'm scared of that character. Something tells me he's unscrupulous in business and in his personal life too."

"I have to agree with you. I've never had a good feeling about him. He's been hanging around town an awful lot for a foreigner out of season. That big yacht of his with its heliport and motorboats, screams *drug dealer*. I bet he has a full arsenal on board too. I'll do some investigating, look into his background, find out what he's doing here, and get back to you. One thing I do know from the *scuttlebutt* around town … he and Gwendolyn Crump seem to have something *shady* going on. They're inseparable. Get my drift?" Peter summed up his case.

"A marriage made in heaven," was all Gaspar had to say regarding that unholy alliance. "Thanks, Peter. With you on the case, I'm feeling better already about this," Gaspar said sitting back in his seat, relaxing for the first time in days."

"And don't worry about your mother either. You can count on me, Gaspar, I'll make sure she doesn't fall into the wrong arms.

# CHAPTER 24

# THE HUNT CONTINUES

GASPAR SPENT THE NEXT TWO WEEKS, SEARCHING FOR UNCLE CHARLIE'S TREASURE. HE HOPED TO FIND it before his mom and Alex got back. He researched in the library, and hunted under every rock, but always came up short. Every chance he could find he would cajole the old ghost into giving him some kind of a clue, but no help was forthcoming. Uncle Charlie showed his admiration for Gaspar's abilities by heaping praise and compliments on his great nephew, always egging him on, calling Gaspar *a twenty-first century buccaneer*, but what Gaspar wanted was help, not praise.

Elvira and Alex finally returned from California. Their two week trip to L.A. had predictably turned into four. Now Gaspar hoped that he and Alex could have some fun for the last few weeks of vacation before school started up again.

"There was a lot of mail waiting for me in L.A. Gasp, and there was a letter for you too." Elvira informed him, handing over an unopened envelope with no return address.

"Thanks Mom," Gaspar grabbed the envelope, wondering, *Who the heck could be writing to me? I've never received a letter before, not even a valentine.*

Opening it Gaspar couldn't believe what he read. The letter was from Jimmy Larsen, the boy down the block who'd been arrested and sent to Juvenile Hall. It read:

Dear Gaspar,

I just want to tell you that I never meant you any harm. I know you didn't squeal on us to the cops, and I'm glad for your sake that you never got involved with me and the gang.

Hooking up with those guys was the worst mistake of my life, and believe me, from now on, if I ever get out of this place, I'm going straight.

I'm sorry about that beating the guys gave you, I never expected it would go so far, and I just want you to know that all their threats against you and your mother were just a lot of hot air. They were just trying to scare you into keeping quiet.

With Sincere Apologies for any harm I may have caused you.

Have a great Fourth of July.

*Jim Larson*

*What the drivelswiggers?* Gaspar thought to himself. *All that worry and heart ache for nothing. I must have been crazy thinking that some big time mobsters were after me. Damnation! When I think of all those butterflies, cold sweats and sleepless nights.*

Have a great Fourth of July! *This was written two months ago! I really need to curb my imagination. Then on the other hand there were those attempts on my life, and the poison pen letters too. So if wasn't the L.A. gang that was out to get me, then who? The answer's obvious,* he thought with a shudder. Now he'd have to get to the bottom of it. The butterflies were back again as his stomach turned over and a hot flush turned to cold sweat running down his back.

# CHAPTER 25

# GASPAR THE GREAT

T HE NEXT AFTERNOON AFTER ALEX HAD GONE HOME, GASPAR WAITED ON BOARD *ARGENTE* FOR A SHIP builder Peter had contacted to show up. He couldn't wait to hear whether *Argente* was seaworthy or not. From his perch near the rail, he saw a grizzled-looking man walking through the garden, heading towards the yacht.

"Ahoy. Welcome aboard *Argente*." Gaspar began to chuckle at his sailor talk. "Are you Casey Jennings?"

"Ahoy, yourself, *ya son-of-a-hornswagging picaroon*," Casey snarled as he started up the stairs to the deck.

Gaspar was temporarily taken aback before the man started guffawing at his own joke.

"*Enough of this drivelswigger pirate noise*," He cursed as he hit the deck and outstretched his big hand toward Gaspar. "I'm Casey Jennings. Let's look this *rumfustian garbage scow* over, though from what I can see so far I doubt if even I could salvage her."

Although crestfallen with this immediate prognosis, a huge smile crossed Gaspar's face as he led the man over the vessel. *What a riot working with Casey Jennings would have been*, he thought, accepting defeat.

About an hour later they were ready to talk *sea-worthiness*. They moved to the aft deck to sit under the torn canopy.

"Have a seat, Casey. Would you like some lemonade?" Always the host with the most, Gaspar had Angela lay out a pitcher, ice bucket, glasses and dishes, cookies and napkins ... what Uncle Charlie called ... *light refreshments*.

"*Lemonade? LEMONADE!* What kind of *Picaroon's piss* are yer try'n to serve me? Donne-ya-av a real drink? Some rum or ale, arach, or grog, ow-bout a *bumboo beer*, for the love of *salmagundi*." Casey spoke his piece before letting loose with another line of expletives, "*Lily-livered lubberscum ... lemonade!*"

Gaspar got on his phone and called the house. "Two beers please and a bottle of gin, and bring them to the yacht, *rapido!*"

"Gin, who wants gin?" Casey asked all smiles.

"It's for *me*, I always mix it with my lemonade. Keeps it from tasting like *picaroon's piss*," Gaspar lied.

"Ha, ha, ha," Casey guffawed. "Kid, you an me is *gonna* get along *juss* fine. Put it *thar*," he said extending his big paw. "How old are you, eighteen?"

"Almost." Gaspar lied.

"Not old enough to shave and already drinking gin, *juss* like me. I think I started when I was twelve. Believe me, it'll put hair on your chest, kid, *and between you and me, I think you could use some*," the old navy boy confided confidentially, slapping Gaspar hard on the back, nearly knocking him off his chair.

"Now, Casey, let's get down to business." Gaspar got the ball rolling. "Can she be saved, can *Argente* be made seaworthy?" Gaspar asked the million dollar question.

"Yes, yes. She's sea-worthy now. I'll need to beef her up a little, so she can be really strong, and with just a little cosmetic surgery, she can be gorgeous again too. But it's going to take time and worse than that ... *money.*" Casey sang rubbing his thumb and forefinger together.

The tray arrived with the beers and the gin carried by an astonished Angela who made a hasty retreat back to dry land. Casey grabbed a beer, opened it, and started guzzling while Gaspar took the gin bottle and poured a swig into his lemonade. Taking a hearty gulp, he was amused to see the astonished look on his Casey Jennings face.

"Let's not talk about money, I'll leave those details between you and my attorney Mr. Cawthorne. He's the guy who called you.?" Gaspar coughed hoarsely, trying not to gag on his strong concoction while attempting to hold his lemonade-gin-fizz like a man of the world. "What about the decorating." Gaspar was feeling no pain.

"*Zounds ... decorating?* You're talkin' to the wrong guy, buster. You'll need to hire some *dankish, doghearted, dunderheaded decorator* to parley with about futtock shrouds and the like." Casey made it clear he wouldn't be dealing with fabric swatches and tassel trims.

"Hmmm, I think I know a company that could help us," Gaspar muttered out loud.

"What's that," Casey cupped a hand to his big cauliflower ear.

"I'm just thinkin' ... " Gaspar knew it was time to change the subject, "I'll want you to start immediately, but it must be finished by June first of next year. That's when we'll be taking her out for a three month trip, um ... *someplace*. If we start no ... can you get it done in time."

"You drive a hard bargain, matey, but if we get started now, she should be ready to sale by the end of May. I'll be waiting for attorney friend to be calling m ... but in the meantime ... let's drink on it," Casey said, pouring another splash of gin into Gaspar's lemonade before taking a big swig out of the bottle himself. "Here's to *Argente*, queen of the seven seas."

"By the way, Casey. I want to change her name to *Floridablanca*," Gaspar insisted, "that was her name before my cousin re-christened her."

"To *Floridablanca*, the gem of the seven seas," Casey boomed, raising his glass.

Gaspar, clinked Casey's glass, as a toast to their new venture, nearly gagging on the strong new cocktail Casey had spiked for him.

CHAPTER 26

# THINGS ARE LOOKING UP

THAT NIGHT PETER CAWTHORNE CAME OVER FOR DINNER. IT WAS SUCH A PERFECT NIGHT, WITH A BALMY breeze blowing gently off the Gulf, that they all agreed it would be pleasant to have dinner on the terrace. Peter had been coming over a lot lately, and Gaspar realized that it wasn't always just to talk business. He could tell that Peter and his mom were becoming close. Whenever the three of them got together, they always had a lot of fun. Peter fit right in with Gaspar and Elvira's easy-going relationship and never seemed to push his way between them.

"How'd it go today, Gasp?" Peter asked. "Any news for us."

"Well, yes, actually I have a lot of news." Gaspar said between bites of *enchiladas suizas*. "Are you ready? I had a meeting today with Casey Jennings and he says, the yacht is seaworthy. She *will* sail, and she *will* be beautiful again." Gaspar announced with a big smile stretching from ear to ear. "I want you to give him a call in the morning and iron out all the details, Peter!"

"And you're sure you want to do this, Gaspar?" his mother asked.

"As sure as anything you can ever think of." he answered solemnly.

"Well that's good enough for me, and what are we going to do with *Argente* when it's restored?" she asked sweetly.

"First we're going to rename her *Floridablanca*! That was her original name before cousin Eugenia changed it. Then, we're going to take her on a three month cruise ... somewhere. I haven't figured that part out yet."

"What about school?"

"Mom, it'll be part of the contract that the ship will be ready to sail on June 1st of next year just in time for summer vacation. We'll jump on board, you too Peter, and sail away to who knows where."

"Gaspar, you're a marvel," his mother beamed. "Now help me with the dishes, you two, so that we can go and watch TV. My favorite show, *The Walk to Elsie's*, is on tonight!"

They gathered the dirty dishes and carried them into the kitchen, then Gaspar went back to get the rest.

When he pushed the kitchen door open he caught his mother and Peter in a long kiss.

"Oops!" he said.

Elvira and Peter sprang apart. "We were just … um … " she began.

"Oh, Ma, you and Peter don't need my approval. Go, watch TV or whatever. I've got stuff to do in my room." Gaspar said shooing them out of the kitchen.

After he finished the dishes, he went up to the Captain's Cabin by way of the secret passage off the library. He was looking forward to a hot shower after a gritty day on the beach. In the bathroom, he pulled off his shirt and posed in the mirror, flexing his arms over his head. *Hey, I have muscles! When did that happen?* A summer of swimming, and hiking and riding his bike and moving boxes of silver had made a profound difference in his physic. "Looking good," he spoke out loud to his reflection in the mirror.

"Not bad, kid." Uncle Charlie materialized, leaning against the sink, "all that exercise this summer has done you good." As he spoke to Gaspar, he amused himself, watching the diamond studs in his tuxedo shirt sparkle in the mirror.

"Are you going out, Uncle Charlie? Gaspar asked.

"I thought a fling, on the town, would do me good. Maybe a night club in Miami, maybe Nassau, I haven't decided yet."

"Sounds like fun, Uncle," Gaspar smiled. "I think I'm ready for my first night club. May I join you?"

"Listen, kid, before you make plans for going out on the town with me, you're going to need some new clothes. None of your stuff fits you anymore. Haven't you notice … you're growing—look at those muscles, and is that the beginnings of a mustache on your upper lip?"

Gaspar rolled his eyes at Charlie's teasing. "I'll go into town with Al and look around."

"You do that, kid, and while you're at it, get some new duds for Alex too. You've got to show him some style. Besides, since you're gonna have a new yacht, you gotta dress the part."

"Listen, Uncle Charlie, I've gotta shower and get to bed. Alex and I are heading out early tomorrow. Will you be tagging along?"

"No, I'll be keeping my eyes open for you, around here. By the way, I just want you to know, it's great to see the old place looking cared for again."

"Yeah, I've never understood why cousin Eugenia let the place go." Gaspar finally verbalized what had been on his mind since the day he'd arrived.

"I think she was scared that she'd run out of money … and maybe she was a little lonely too. It's hard to decipher. She was beautiful and rich, but without me around, after a while she just gave up. I tried to help her, subconsciously, but she resisted. I'm just glad Cawthorne found you and Elvira to carry on the dream of La Rinconada, because that's what it always was for me, a dream and I hope for you it will be a dream come true."

"I understand, I know exactly what you're talking about," Gaspar assured him.

# CHAPTER 27

# THE END OF SUMMER

THAT LAST MONTH OF SUMMER VACATION FLEW PAST TOO QUICKLY. BETWEEN ALL THE FUN AND EXCITEment, all of a sudden it was almost over. Gaspar hadn't done half the things he wanted to do, but he knew he would have plenty of time to do them after school, between homework and studying. There were the cars in the stables and the Riva motorboat that he wanted to restore and so many other projects that he'd have to put on hold. He knew that any thoughts of owning horses to ride on the beach or flying in his own plane were far fetched for the present. But he reveled in the idea that *Argente*, was on its way to a full restoration, right down to its original name, *Floridablanca*,

Gaspar and Alex rode the yacht all the way to Naples as it was being towed to Casey's shipyard. Together they had the time of their lives pretending they were actually sailing under their own steam, while eating their peanut butter, jelly and bacon sandwiches on deck and generally goofing off, like only teenagers know how.

Gaspar had a limo waiting when they got to Naples so that they could drive back to La Rinconada. When they got home the two boys split up, Alex to see his parents and Gaspar to search out his mom. He found Elvira in the garden room, having cocktails with Peter.

"Welcome home, sailor," Elvira beamed. "How was the trip?"

"Did you see any sea serpents, mermaids or pirates?" Peter asked facetiously.

"Quit kidding, you guys," Gaspar defended himself. "We had a blast. We played pirates all the way to Naples. And we did have a couple of encounters with sea serpents, mermaids and pirates, and I assure you that Alex and I made short shrift of them all, thank you very much."

"Sounds like fun, darling." Elvira said patting the cushion on the sofa next to her, as an invitation for Gaspar to take a load off.

"Tonight should be very interesting." Peter said.

"What's so special about tonight," Gaspar asked.

"Tonight's the night of the big low tide."

"What's that? We have low tide every night."

"Yeah, but here on Perdido Isle, we have a *very* special, *very* low tide once a year, at the time of the full moon, and always during the last week in August. Just wait, tonight the sea will roll out about 300 yards, and you'll see seashells and lots of junk, just lying there in the moonlight. It's an amazing sight. When I was a kid, I never missed going out to search for treasure.

"It sounds amazing," Elvira replied. "Will you take us out to see it, Peter? Who knows, tonight we may actually find pirate's treasure washed up in the shallows."

"Yeah, Peter, I'd love to see it." Gaspar agreed.

"The most important thing is to be careful out there because if you get caught when the tide rolls back in, it could be dangerous. Several people around here have disappeared during this tidal phenomena. You definitely don't want to be out on the beach after midnight, because when the water rolls in, it rolls in fast and furious," Peter warned them.

"When should we go out?" Gaspar asked.

"Right after dinner, I'd say around 8:30 will be the ideal time to watch the tide roll out."

"All right then, I'm gonna go upstairs now and change. Give me a call when dinner's ready and I'll come down."

Back in his room, Gaspar phoned Alex. "Hey man, you want to see the low tide tonight and go beach combing with me?"

"Not tonight dude," Alex responded, "I've got to go into town with my parents to visit some friends of theirs."

"Bummer," was Gaspar's response.

"I'll call you, if I can get out of it." Alex promised. "Don't forget to take a flashlight with you. You'll need it to see all the great stuff that's been lying down there under the water all year."

"Thanks for the tip, buddy, I'll do that."

"GASPAR, DINNER," his mother yelled up the stairs.

"COMING, MOM," Gaspar yelled back. Grabbing two underwater flashlights, he stuffed them into the pockets of his cargo shorts, and headed downstairs.

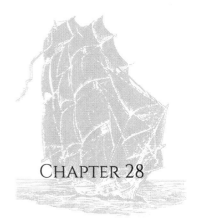

CHAPTER 28

# TRAPPED

E LVIRA HAD MADE HER *SPECIALITÉ DE MAISÓN*, A SEAFOOD AND PASTA CASSEROLE THAT SHE SERVED WITH AN endive salad out on the terrace. Between bites, Gaspar regaled the adults with tales of his tow down to Naples, and the glory of the shipyard and to his mothers horror, he repeated some of the saltiest remarks which he'd taken note of while visiting with the sailors there.

"Listen!" Peter cautioned. "Hear it? The low tide! Come on, let's go see."

Gaspar heard a low gurgling which turned into a loud sucking sound combined with a rattle like marbles hitting each other inside a bag.

They all jumped up from the table and ran to the edge of the terrace. Gaspar watched in awe, as the Gulf rolled back, and back and back ... 300 yards from the shore. Within minutes the sea floor lay exposed before them, glistening in the full moonlight.

"Come on, let's go out there!" Gaspar urged, pushing a flashlight into Peter's palm, then grabbed his mother's hand to drag her down the stairs to the beach.

Together they walked straight out onto the sand, in front of La Rinconada where the Gulf had formerly covered the earth. Their flashlights revealed exotic seashells at their feet, coral rocks and scurrying crabs. Seaweed lay here and there like throw rugs, and odd flotsam and jetsam littered their path. The three adventurers walked 300 yards, right out to the water's edge delighting in their new front yard.

"It's kinda cool to think you own all this land, Gaspar," Peter reminded him extending his arms wide, "as well as everything on top of it and underneath it."

Gaspar took it in and nodded. "*It will do*," he joked, an enormous grin covering his face.

After they had clomped around on the exposed seabed, picking up shells, and oohing and ahhing at all the treasures that the receding gulf had revealed, they started back towards the shore. Having almost reached the beach, Peter suggested they walk further east, in the direction of the landing field, to see what they might find along the way. Figuring that Mom and Peter might like some time alone, Gaspar excused himself and said he was going to walk west, in the direction of the church.

"Be careful!" Mom warned him. "Don't go too far!"

"Okay!" Gaspar called back. As he walked by himself, he passed the house, which loomed gray and mysterious in the moonlight. He could see the wall which retained the garden and the swimming pool. Smack in front of him the seawalls of the grand canal suddenly loomed before him. There they were, jutting straight out from where the *Argente* had been floating only a few days ago. Out here in the gulf, 100 yards from where the yacht usually was moored, the seawalls were more than twenty-feet tall. The two carved alabaster lanterns that were perched at what should have been the opening to the sea, stood another fifteen-feet above that. The lanterns which were perpetually lighted, now cast a soft glow over the still damp sea floor, spread out below them.

Gaspar realized instantly that this was a rare opportunity for him to explore the bottom of the canal and see if any treasure had been purposefully hidden there. Without the slightest trepidation, he stepped between the massive seawalls, and walked right up to the place where the yacht had been scuttled so many years ago. Gaspar figured he was about parallel with the swimming pool, but the walls of the canal were so high, he couldn't see above them.

*I'll just go to the end and walk up the stairs to the tombs*, Gaspar decided. But when he got to the end of the canal where the steps should have been, he discovered that they started ten-feet above his head. Below the now-cantilevered steps was a mess of debris, but no pirate treasure.

Taking a closer look, Gaspar saw something curious which he decided to investigate. Moving a small garbage dump of seaweed and other detritus, he discovered that what had caught his eye was the entrance to an underwater cavern. A large stone, partially covered the opening. It had slipped or moved with the tide, leaving just enough room for Gaspar to squeeze through. Before squeezing inside, he waved his flashlight around and discovered that a staircase carved out of the living coral-stone, led upwards, above where the water line should have been. *It leads right up under the tombs!* Gaspar surmised. Squeezing through the opening, he charged up the stairs, the beam from his flashlight leading the way. His excitement at finding a hidden cave was palpable and his heart was in his throat in hopes that at last he had found the place where Gasparilla had hidden his treasure.

The stairs led directly into a large circular cavern which must have been forty feet in diameter and at least ten feet at its highest point. *A perfect secret place for hiding treasure!* Gaspar thought as his light traced the room only to reveal that the cavern was completely empty. "Aaargh!" he cried loudly, vocalizing his disappointment. For sure he thought, he'd at last found Gaspararilla's secret hiding place. Taking a deep breath, he calmed his nerves and passed his light over the walls one more time revealing drawings of sea creatures, birds, and people made by the ancient cave dwellers who had originally occupied the space. *Cool*, he thought, *the discovery of archaeological and possibly prehistoric treasure would have to suffice for tonight.* It was better than nothing, but he couldn't help feeling dejected not having found Gasparilla's mother lode.

To Gaspar's right a tunnel had been roughly cut into the wall. He started into the narrow passage until he could go no further. A massive bronze door, now blocked his way. Although he pushed against it with all his might, it wouldn't budge. The door had a lock ... and Gaspar had a key. Taking Uncle Charlie's solid gold key from around his neck he tried the lock, and it turned with a sharp, *click*.

Pushing with all his might and using his shoulder as a lever, the door groaned open. Using his flashlight, Gaspar discovered a large rectangular room entirely built of coral-stone blocks. Placed all around the high-ceilinged space were nine stacks of old trunks. Just to his right his flashlight revealed a very convenient, old fashioned switch which Gaspar pushed on, instantly flooding the room with incandescent light. *Was this what he thought it was?*

Reaching the far wall he found something both interesting and distressing. One of the piles of old trunks had tipped over. Probably the box on the bottom had rotted and given way, causing the boxes on top and next to it to topple to the left. The pile of debris was about six feet high, and Gaspar could see that behind it was yet another door, peeking out just above the mess. It was the only other door in the room except for the one he had just entered. Walking over to the mess, Gaspar tried to move one of the boxes out of the way, but he couldn't budge it. When he opened the unlocked box, what he found inside made an electric current run up his leg, through his groin, up his spine and sear through his brain. The chest was filled with Spanish gold escudos, *thousands and thousands of them!*

"Congratulations, Gaspar. You've found the treasure!" was all Uncle Charlie had to say on the subject. He was perched on top of one of the mountains of trunks, dressed in full pirate regalia.

"Uncle Charlie, I can't believe it. All this? Gasparilla and then you … found all this?"

"Yes, it's true, but wait till you look inside some of these other chests! Uncle Charlie exclaimed.

"So what happened, Uncle Charlie? Why this big mess? Gaspar asked pointing towards the tumbled treasure chests.

"Well you can imagine. One of the old rotten trunks on the bottom collapsed, and caused the rest to topple like a house of cards. The unfortunate part is that the collapse caused the door into this place, to be blocked, and my poor Eugenia was barred from entering here, losing her access to the treasure. You see, Gaspar, that door leads right up to the library, through a secret door and up a secret staircase, that not even *you* have discovered yet.

"But I found the secret door to the right side of the fireplace, but that only led to that empty room I found weeks ago." Gaspar argued.

"Yes, that's true, but I couldn't believe your lack of curiosity as to where the other pair of double doors, the ones on the left side of the fireplace went to." Charlie admonished him.

"The left side. I just thought they were dummies." Gaspar could kick himself.

"I told you, the way to the treasure was through the library." Charlie chuckled.

"Oh Uncle Charlie, I'm such a dolt." Gaspar beat himself up.

"Not at all my boy. You found the treasure didn't you? You found it the hard way, but you found it!" Charlie congratulated him.

"I'm so sorry about cousin Eugenia." Gaspar changed the subject, "poor cousin Eugenia, no wonder she started squirreling everything away."

"Yes, it broke my old dead heart, but *she* got along for almost ten years without the treasure. I tried to help her but as I told you before, she wasn't that receptive to my suggestions. I actually think she enjoyed thinking up creative ways of how *not* to spend money when all I ever did was think up creative ways of how *to* spend it.

"So let's talk about you now, Gasp. Let me tell you how I see all this going forward, by bringing you up to par with a little history. First of all, I built the tombs on top of the original cavern with the ancient cave paintings. That domed cavern was the cavern where Gasparilla hid his own and all his buddies' treasure. Until I found it, the treasure was safely hidden there for almost a hundred years. This room is actually part of the basement of the house, but the only entrance, the one leading directly here from the library, has always been a secret. The bronze door you just came through is disguised, look at it. Eugenia never knew there was another way in or out of here, she only knew how to get here from inside the house. These eight piles of boxes," he said waving his hand around the room, "belong to the eight pirates whose effigies I had carved in alabaster, before I moved the treasure out from under the tombs." Charlie said pointing upward with his index finger. The other, *minor investors* of Gasparilla's, are heralded by the banners hanging on the three walls across from the sarcophagi. The loot of those minor investors as well as Gasparilla's own fortune can be found in the ninth pile of treasure, that would be the one that's fallen over. The table in the middle of the room is my desk, and it was also your cousin Eugenia Floride's desk. Now it is *your* desk. The big ledger book on top is a list of the treasure, pirate by pirate, and includes the various markings, initials, coats of arms and devices used to identify each pirate's treasure. The ledger was compiled by Gasparilla himself. You will see that I have annotated next to each item what I have sold or spent or given away, and so did Eugenia, until she was barred from entering here. If you could get through that blocked door," the ghost said pointing at the collapsed mess, "you would enter the secret passage up to the library, and by the way, the empty room you found the other day that you accessed from the library is just on the other side of that wall, in case your wondering where it is in the scheme of things. Anyway, I had that bronze door put in," Uncle Charlie pointed to the big door that Gaspar had unlocked with the gold key, and had the workmen dig a tunnel beyond it ... stopping just short of the domed cavern. I told them it was going to be a wine cellar. After they were gone, I personally excavated the last five feet of the tunnel, connecting this room with the domed cavern. I thought that Gasparilla's secret underwater entrance was too insecure, as the low tide happens once a year, so I moved all the treasure in here myself, little by little, and here it is."

"Uncle Charlie, you're amazing." Gaspar complimented him.

"Yes, but I didn't foresee poor Eugenia being prevented from reaching her source of livelihood because of a collapsing pile of treasure. And as far as that goes, I hadn't counted on you being trapped in here either. Gaspar, it seems you've forgotten the changing tide. If it hasn't already rolled in, it will shortly."

Without a word, Gaspar turned and ran out of the room, through the tunnel and into the domed cavern. Too late, the tide had rolled in and was already lapping over the top of the coral-stone stairs. He ran back into the basement where Uncle Charlie was still sitting, calmly considering the circumstances.

"I'm trapped, Uncle Charlie! How am I going to get out of here. Mom and Peter are going to think I drowned or something. Give me a hand, I need help!".

"Well you're young and strong and can lift things," Uncle Charlie said. "Only one thing for you to do … start moving the *scudi* away from the blocked door, so you can get to bed."

"Uncle Charlie, you've gotta be kidding … all that … by myself?

Well I don't see anyone else trapped in here who's gonna help you move my treasure." Charlie chuckled.

"You mean, *my treasure*," Gaspar reminded him.

"Have it your own way kid. Now move your *blistering-barnacled-butt*, and start hauling this stuff away from the door. I'll meet you later," he laughed, disappearing through the wall.

# CHAPTER 29

# YANKEE GO HOME

T HE MORNING AFTER THE ANNUAL LOW TIDE, GWENDOLYN CRUMP WAS BESIDE HERSELF WITH worry as she arranged her pretty ringlets in front of the mirror of her ruffled pink organdy covered dressing table. She had planned and orchestrated her life for this opportune moment and now she found herself almost defeated.

Her mania for wanting possession of La Rinconada was not without foundation. Her mother had told her on her eighteenth birthday that Harold Crump was not her actual father. In fact, her mother divulged without the slightest embarrassment, that Charles Munoz-Flores y Gaspar was her birth father. The truth, *if it was the truth*, had thrilled her. Years later, on her deathbed, her mother had told Gwendolyn to fight and claim her birthright as the true heiress of Perdido Isle. With the convenient death of old Eugenia Floride, Gwendolyn's time had finally arrived. In her position as the head of the museum and because there were no other heirs, she would successfully control the land and the income and one way or another, siphon all the rich cream off the top for herself. *If it hadn't been for that busybody Cawthorne, finding those phony heirs in California I would have been in clover by now*, she told her reflection in the mirror. She had *much too much pride* as the leader of Calaluna society to ever expose herself as illegitimate, but now she feared that it might be the only way to take over the land legally.

*She* was the brains who'd discovered Unzega and told him about the property and how she could arrange a quick sale to him, as her lifelong dream had been to escape Perdido Isle altogether for a far more glamorous life in New York, Paris, or London, or all three if she could get her hands on her presumed Daddy's fortune. She tied a big pink satin bow in her hair and started working on her make-up.

The minute she'd heard about Elvira and Gaspar Brown, she'd contacted Beverwil, duping the dope into believing that should the Browns accept the inheritance, the Perdido Isle Historical Society Museum would be just that, *history*. She begged the sap to do anything in his power to try and stop them from coming to Florida. Knowing the man's predilection for sending poison pen letters, she hoped he'd be able to scare them off.

Beverwil had told her not to fear, that he would travel to Los Angeles himself to scope out the situation and take care of things personally. Obviously the boob had failed miserably in scaring them off as it looked like the imposters were here to stay. She patted her pink cheeks pitifully with a puff of pink powder.

She was sure that the Browns were plants, paid by Cawthorne to pretend to be kinfolk of Charles Munoz-Flores y Gaspar in return for giving the lawyer a piece of their action. If only she could think of a way to get in on their little game, but without evidence, blackmail seemed out of the question. Her mind reeled with possible scenarios as she painted a slash of bright pink lipstick across her thin lips and smiled at herself in the glass, convincing herself that she didn't look at all grizzly.

She could easily lay claim to the fortune by telling the truth about her birth father, she told herself, but she wasn't at all sure if her mother had been lying about her daughter just to see if she could get old Charles to marry her, out of guilt. Besides, she continued her mental wanderings, she was much too proud to expose the possibility that she, a debutante, who'd come out at the Llojeta Winter Cotillion, was actually the illegitimate spawn of the Calaluna town trollop. Even if her actual father was the richest man in town, her pride just wouldn't allow her to expose herself to that kind of criticism. This was her dilemma. These were the thoughts that consumed her this morning and every morning since the imposters from California had moved in on her territory. She batted her eyes at the mirror thinking herself irresistible before heavily painting their lids with heavy turquoise blue eye shadow.

Before she had time to reflect on any more harrowing thoughts, the doorbell rang. She figured it was only old Norbert the mailman, dropping off the morning mail. At this point Gwendolyn gave thanks for the little things in life that she could depend on and ran downstairs in her favorite pink flowered house coat to open the door.

"Good morning, Miss Crump," the mailman greeted her.

"Good morning, Norbert," she said wearily. "Any excitement today?"

"Here's your mail, Ma'am." The mailman offered her a stack of envelopes, "the usual stuff, lots of bills, and this very special, *fancy envelope*," he said laying a colorful packet on top and handing it to her with a bright smile.

The *fancy envelope* was ominously *collaged* with letters cut out of magazines, it was something too unbearable for her to even touch. Without saying good day, she closed the door quickly and threw the pile of envelopes on the white, marble-topped table in the hall. Gingerly she picked up the offensive packet as if it might bite her and slowly sitting down on the tufted loveseat, (lest the packet explode and knock her flat), she opened it.

Inside was a note, all patched and glued together with cut out letters from newspapers and magazines, similar to those that were glued to the envelope.

The poison pen letter read:

GwenDolyn cRump,
youR SecRET is Not saFE WiTh Me!!!
I knOw WhO youR reAl FaTheR iS ...
AnD iT'S noT wHO yoU ThiNK iT IS oR WaNT it
To bE
i alSo KnOW AbouT The EmBezZelMEnt Too!!!
RUn!!!
Get OuT OF towN Now oR FAcE DisGRAce!!!
ThIS is A WarNIng!!!
TaKE It anD GO!!!
OR else !
mE !!!

Beverwil, the snake, now he was blackmailing her. What could possibly go wrong next? She needed to act fast. What if she wasn't the love child of Charles Munoz-Flores y Gaspar? What if she was Norbert, the mailman's half sister instead! Oh God! Or worse, what if that common waitress, Karen down at the greasy spoon was her kin! She found herself running around in circles, around and around the center table, her hands flying, pulling at her pretty hairdo.

271

"Sweet Jesus, why hast thou forsaken me?" she wailed bitterly at the top of her lungs as she raced upstairs to her sitting room. Grabbing the phone she called the Turners and asked them to come by in an hour, saying that "she had some important business to discuss with them." Her next call was to her stockbroker in New York, telling him to sell her entire portfolio and wire transfer it to the secret account she'd previously set up in Switzerland. She'd initially opened that account with the $500,000.00 advance payment from Unzega, for guaranteeing him La Rinconada. It was a deal which to date, she had hopelessly been unable to deliver on. She had been living in fear of the malicious Mexican for weeks. Unzega had made it clear to her that she didn't want to cross him and reminded her about the fate of the last two men who *had*. Visions of those two helpless businessmen being wrapped in chains and hoisted overboard from Unzega's yacht had haunted her for months. She shuddered at the thought of living with a permanent scar across her pretty pink cheek, and all the other descriptive things Unzega had told her she could expect to experience if she betrayed him.

Next, Gwendolyn frantically called Swiss Air and purchased a one way, non-stop first class seat to Geneva, departing from Mobile the next morning. She then changed into a traveling suit and drove to the bank to withdraw all the funds in her account, *in cash*. The total amount she withdrew was a little under $10,000.00.

Returning home she was just in time to greet the Turners. Without any fanfare she asked them if they'd like to buy the contents of her house, lock stock and barrel. "I know you like to buy beautiful antiques for your furniture stores," she explained, "so I called you first."

"But Gwendolyn darling … we're flattered … but all your pretty things," Gore Turner played hard to get.

"I'm planning to redecorate," she lied. "You know what these priceless antiques are worth." she cooed. "Make me an offer I can't refuse."

The Turners made her a lowball offer based on the word, *priceless* and were amazed when she accepted with alacrity.

"I'll take it in cash," she demanded, "run over to the bank, Gore, while Roberta and I write out a receipt."

Gwendolyn had been correct when she thought the Turners, who owned the furniture store in town and an even bigger one in Chicago, would be her best bet for a quick sale. She'd always suspected that Gore was a fence for stolen antiques and now she was letting him rob her blind … legally. After Gore returned with the promised cash, Gwendolyn gave him the keys to the house telling the couple that she was going out of town for a few days, that they should take what they wanted immediately, so that when she got back she could start her redecorating.

Scared out of her mind, she packed her bags, taking any valuables that she could squeeze into them. Carrying her bulging luggage to the garage, she threw the suitcases into the trunk of her compact car and took off.

•••

What Gwendolyn Crump didn't know as she drove away was that Beverwil had also been busy sending similar letters elsewhere. His interest in getting her out of town was two-fold. He'd made the mistake of deciding to also blackmail Peter Cawthorne, having taken it as gospel that Crump's assumption that Cawthorne had placed the Browns at La Rinconada in order to steal the fortune for himself was the truth. What he'd forgotten was that it was Peter's father, representing Charles Munoz–Flores y Gaspar, over similar poison pen threats, who had discovered the perpetrator, Beverwil, and had successfully stopped the nonsense at least as far as the senior Cawthorne and Charles Munoz were concerned.

After receiving the poison pen letter which could only have come from Beverwil, Peter decided to nip the crazy business in the bud quickly. The lawyer immediately telephoned Chief Morgan at the police station to tell him of his suspicions.

Hanging up the phone, the police made a bee-line for Beverwil's Hardware Store armed with a search warrant. There, they discovered, all the evidence they needed. More importantly, than all the cut out magazines and blackmail paraphernalia, they discovered the additional evidence that Beverwil had purloined, proving that Gwendolyn Crump had been embezzling funds from the museum … for years.

Beverwil was immediately arrested and charged with attempted blackmail, but it wasn't until the next day that the police paid a visit to the Crump residence. When they got there they discovered the Turners hard at work with their moving men, removing every stick of furniture and other decorations from the house, down to the door knobs. After questioning the greedy couple and looking over the receipt they held for the purchase of the contents of the house, the police chief realized that Gwendolyn Crump had decamped, possibly forever.

Having reported the alleged embezzlement from a public institution to the proper authorities, Florida's attorney general along with the IRS joined the search for Crump, putting out an all points bulletin for her. Try as they might to find her, it appeared that the old puss had simply vanished.

CHAPTER 30

# THE SMUGGLERS COVE

Before summer ended, Gaspar and Alex decided to invite their pals to camp out on the beach near the old airstrip. Felix drove the two boys to the campsite and dropped them off along with their tent and sleeping bags, kerosene lanterns, and an ice chest full of provisions which would last Gaspar and his friends the entire weekend. Gaspar had asked Alex to invite Kevin, Sancho, Pat and Mark to join them. The other guys were already pitching their tents, when Gaspar and Alex arrived.

"Hey guys, how do you like the campsite?" Gaspar greeted his pals.

"Cool Gasp, how'd-ya find it?" Kevin asked.

"Al found it and showed it to *me*."

"Can't ya just imagine Spanish galleons bobbing at anchor out there in the bay?" Alex romanced, sweeping his hand towards the glimmering Gulf of Mexico.

"Come on, Al. Stop daydreaming about pirates for a change and help me pitch the tent," Gaspar chided him.

The two boys set up their tent on the sand near to where the jungle growth began. Then they rolled out their sleeping bags and arranged all of the provisions that Felix had left piled in a heap. After they'd made a neat mess out of all the stuff, they emptied their backpacks, which they'd filled with comic books, flashlights, swim trunks and towels, as well as a first aid kit, and plenty of matches. Included in all this, Gaspar had also thrown in Uncle Charlie's fancy old Swiss army knife, which he considered one of his best treasures.

"Lets gather drift wood and make a campfire," Sancho suggested. "Kevin, Pat and I will go down the beach looking for driftwood and you three go up the beach. Let's see which team can gather the most wood."

The two teams of friends took off on the run to scour the shore, dragging back enough gnarled wood, sun-dried to kindling, for ten campfires.

"What next," Kevin asked.

"Let's go swimming." Pat suggested.

"Let's play Marco Polo." Mark urged.

"Last one in's a rotten egg," Gaspar shouted, pulling off his t-shirt and running down to the shore.

The others followed close behind.

"Water war," cried Alex, sending up a huge plume of water toward Gaspar which Gaspar shot right back at him.

"Chicken fight," shouted Pat, climbing up on Kevin's shoulders.

Gaspar climbed up on Alex's shoulders, and Sancho climbed up on Mark's and a mighty battle raged in the shallow waters of the Gulf of Mexico until all three teams tumbled into the surf, roaring with laughter.

Dragging themselves toward the shore, they spread out in the warm water as gentle waves lapped over their tanned bodies.

"There goes that black yacht again," Kevin announced pointing out toward the horizon.

"Pretty cool that it has its own helicopter on board," Mark enthused.

"She's called *Revenge*," Gaspar snarled disparagingly.

"You have a problem with that boat?" Sancho asked.

"It's owned by this guy named Unzega. He's a creep who wants to steal this land away from Gasp and his Mom," Alex let slip.

"Whad-a-ya mean?" Kevin asked. "Gaspar, is this *your* land? Are *you* the kid everyone in town's talking about, *the boy billionaire*?"

Gaspar shrugged, not wanting to make a big deal about it.

"Wow, a billionaire!" Sancho exhaled, "Let me touch you, man."

"Okay, guys. It's true, but it's not what you think. I've inherited a lot of land, and a house and some other stuff, probably worth a lot of money, but I can't get my hands on any cash for at least ten years. It all involves lawyers and taxes and a lot of jealous people who want to take it away from me. Anyway, a few months ago I was living in a little house in North Hollywood. I'm still the same guy you met that first day when we played water polo at the swimming hole."

"Let's go for a hike." Alex suggested, successfully changing the subject.

Donning T-shirts, the six mates walked in a pack into the jungle laughing and joking. Stumbling upon the Crusaders Tower, they raced each other inside and up the stairs. The interior of the tower was in shadows as the sun was setting fast on the horizon. "Let's go up on the roof and watch the sunset," Gaspar suggested as they climbed the stairs. When they reached the big round room, he didn't stop but led them outside and continued up the exterior stairs. Gaspar loved that his pals were all pushing and shoving each other to see who would get up onto the roof first.

Once topside Gaspar thought his friends looked like crusader knights invading a castle-keep as they ran along the ramparts. Suddenly Gaspar stopped short and listened. He distinctly heard the low sound of a helicopter's blades slicing the air, coming ever closer and louder. "Hey you guys," he yelled, "cool it. Come on, *everyone get down*!" As he hit the deck, the others followed suit. In an instant a huge black chopper flew low across the surf and hovered over the landing field, slowly coming to rest on the tarmac, right below where the boys were hiding. Simultaneously, four black SUVs with black-tinted windows broke through the jungle coming to a screeching stop on the broken tarmac of the runway. Alex poked his head up to take a look but Gaspar pulled him down by the shoulder and motioned to the others to stay low. .

By the time the craft had touched down, the sun had set and dusk had fallen on La Rinconada's abandoned airfield. The six boys crouched behind the crenelations of the rampart and watched the action below, in silence. Eight men dressed in black jumped out of the SUVs and ran toward the helicopter as the side door of the chopper slid open and five black clad men jumped out. One by one the men removed large packages wrapped in black plastic from the chopper and placed them into the SUVs. Back and forth, the men lugged the many parcels and piled them into their vehicles.

"Smugglers," Alex whispered tersely.

"I betcha it's drugs, Al," Gaspar assured his friend thinking, *it's like on TV or in a movie, a typical drug run*. Not wasting a second, Gaspar took out his phone and dialed 911. Sergeant O'Malley at the Calaluna precinct answered the call. "Sergeant O'Malley this is Gaspar Brown," he whispered. "I'm at the old Rinconada airstrip with five friends. We're hiding up on the roof of the old tower. We're witnessing what we think is a drug smuggling operation right this minute. There are four black SUVs, and a lot of guys, dressed in black, loading packages from a big black chopper. The chopper looks like the one that usually sits on the poop of that yacht, *Revenge*, he added hopefully.

"Keep low, Gaspar, and don't move from where you are, help is on the way," the sergeant assured him.

"Okay Sarge, we'll lay low," Gaspar promised.

His next call was to the Coast Guard station. When Gaspar got Lieutenant Carl Jacobson on the line, he told the officer the same story he'd told the police, also mentioning that they could see the lights of *Revenge*, twinkling just off shore. Like the sergeant, the lieutenant also told Gaspar to lay low until the coast was clear before signing off.

Gaspar heard a step on the stairs behind him and turned with a start. Five men, dressed in black stood by the rampart, blocking the way down. One of the men was Unzega. Gaspar's blood ran cold at the sight of him. The kingpin's face contorted with rage at the sight of Gaspar and his friends. The crook seethed with fury as Gaspar crouched motionless on the ground staring at him, in wide-eyed disbelief. Before the other boys knew they even had company, Unzega sprang into action.

"Grab that one," Unzega ordered his cohorts, pointing at Gaspar.

"Gaspar attempted to tackle the two men who came at him. It only took a few seconds for one of the henchmen to grab him and lift his ninety-pound frame over his shoulders before carrying the teenager away.

"Get your bony hands off me you *gorbellied gudgeon*." Gaspar cursed while beating his captors back with his fists and kicking the goons ribs with his bare feet.

•••

Alex and the boys couldn't believe what had just happened. Before they could move, Gaspar was gone and so were his abductors.

"I've got to go save him," Alex hollered getting up and starting for the stairs.

"Wait," Kevin insisted grabbing Alex's arm, "Those guys probably have guns. Gaspar's already called the authorities, what we need to do is wait for them to get here and tell them what's happened. We need to let them handle those criminals," Kevin insisted wisely.

Meanwhile the men on the ground had made quick work of their furtive transfer, and jumped back into their vehicles. Within seconds they were speeding back through the jungle towards the highway. At the same instant, the helicopter's rotors started spinning. The boys on the roof watched helplessly as Gaspar, still yelling and thrashing out, was thrown bodily into the chopper. His assailants piled in after him and closed the doors. Slowly the whirly bird lifted off and up, flying away over the waves with Gaspar a prisoner.

Seeing the chopper take off caused Alex and the gang to freak out. "You guys, this is serious," Alex cried. What can we do, what's gonna happen next? We've gotta help Gaspar!" he wailed to no one in particular, completely baffled by the abduction of his friend.

"Let's get out of here," Mark yelped. "*Now*."

"Hold on, guys," Kevin calmed them down. "We better not move. You heard Gaspar call the cops and the Coast Guard. Let's stay put. When the cops show up, we can tell them what's happened. This rooftop is the safest place for us right this minute, and you have to admit, for what it's worth, we do have the best seats in town for this particular show."

"But what about Gaspar?" Sancho fretted helplessly.

As the drone of the chopper's rotors faded away, the boys could hear the beginning of sirens blaring in the distance.

"Listen you guys, do you hear the sirens?" Alex cried hopefully.

"They're coming in from both Calaluna and Llojeta," Pat deduced. "Can you hear them, listen guys, sirens from both directions."

Screeching tires could be heard in the distance as the sound of the sirens grew closer and louder.

"Look over there," Alex yelled excitedly, pointing towards the shore.

In the full moonlight the boys could see a motor boat coming in at top speed, right up onto the sand. Two sailors dressed in black jumped out, and turned the boat around so it was facing out to sea. The sailors just stood waist deep in the water holding the stern steady, while the driver kept the engine revving.

Just then a crashing sound came rumbling out of the jungle as the four SUVs came skidding back across the tarmac, stopping dead in the deep sand beyond the pavement. "*Run*", they heard someone call as eight men tumbled out of the cars, high-tailing-it for the beach. Following in their wake, six black and white squad cars piled onto the airfield and skidded to a stop just short of the sand. Twelve uniformed cops jumped out, pistols drawn and started shooting as they rushed forward onto the beach. Before they could cross the sand, the speed boat, loaded with the fleeing criminals, roared forward and plowed back into the gulf.

"They're getting away!" Mark exhaled.

"What a mess up" Kevin proclaimed. "It's mass confusion down there."

"Look guys, the Coast Guard," Alex enthused, ignoring Kevin's comment and pointing out to sea. "If anyone can rescue Gasp, they can."

From the rooftop the boys watched the huge gray Coast Guard cutter, *Jupiter* slicing through the water with every intention of cutting off the speed boat and its criminal crew.

"Look over there," Alex pointed seaward again. "*Revenge*, it looks like she's running away. She's gonna leave those *scurvy bilge rats* behind to rot in jail, *the miserable pustulant, pox-ridden-flounders*," Alex *Captain Haddocked* just like Gaspar had taught him, then worried anew for his friend's safety.

"Good one Al," Kevin complimented his curses, "Gaspar's taught you well. When the Coast Guard rescues him, you'll need to repeat that one for him."

"Kevin, how can you be so cool, when Gaspar's in such danger?" Mark asked. "Have you no feelings."

"Of course I have feelings. I'm worried sick about Gasp. I guess *joking around* is just my way of dealing with trouble." Kevin shrugged.

"Look," cried Alex again, "that's the cruiser *Orion*. She's been deployed from the Coast Guard station in Llojeta. She's going after *Revenge!*"

"Hold on Gasp," Sancho cried out to their missing friend, "the Marines are on the way! I hope they get there soon guy ... poor Gaspar, I wouldn't want to be in his shoes right now."

"It's a two pronged Coast Guard maneuver," Kevin marveled.

"Brilliant," shouted Alex.

"Fantastic," shouted Kevin

"Bravo," cried Mark

"Altogether, guys," urged Alex. "*Hip, hip, hooray!*" the six friends sang in chorus.

When all the commotion had died down, Alex and the guys called over the parapet to Sergeant O'Malley and his men who had congregated on the airfield with their counterparts from Llojeta to inspect the contents of the SUVs and impound them as evidence.

"Sergeant O'Malley, Gaspar's been abducted. They grabbed him and threw him on the helicopter. He needs help?"

"Come down here boys, the coast is clear now." O'Malley hollered up to them.

The boys scrambled down to the ground and ran up to the police sergeant.

"It looks like you guys are the heroes of the hour," the sergeant told them. "Now what's this about Gaspar, tell me what happened."

"They caught us hiding on the roof," Alex took the lead. "When they saw Gaspar they went straight for him. In fact the tall skinny creep in charge, gave the order. '*Grab that one*,' that's all he said. Gaspar put up a terrific struggle, but he's such a *little-pip-squeak*, they just grabbed him, and carried him off before we even knew what happened." Alex explained, the concern in his voice rising with every word.

"Now don't you worry about your pal," Sergeant O'Malley assured Alex and the others, "Lieutenant Jacobson is on *Orion*. I'll radio him now and tell him that we have a hostage situation here. He'll know exactly what to do." The Sergeant eased their fears, before walking over to one of the cruisers to make the call.

"What did you find?" Kevin asked a policemen who was standing nearby.

"You boys called it. Hundreds of pounds of illegal drugs! Probably worth a couple of hundred million on the streets in Miami. We've had our suspicions about that Unzega fellow for a long time now, but we could never pin anything on him. The Coast Guard searched that yacht when it first arrived here, but couldn't find a thing. Probably had the junk flown on board after the inspection, or had it secreted below decks in some hidden compartment."

"Wow, there's never been this much excitement on Perdido Isle, ever!" Mark exclaimed.

"You've done good work, boys. You're all true citizen patriots," the policeman saluted the boys and his entire team of fellow officers followed suit.

When O'Malley returned after placing his call to *Orion*, he filled the boys in with the latest update. "The cutter's, caught up with the speedboat, which they've intercepted and impounded. They've taken eighteen of the gang into custody and are in pursuit of the yacht along with *Orion* right now."

<br />

CHAPTER 31

# HELD HOSTAGE

WHEN THE GOON WHO HAD GRABBED GASPAR THREW
HIM INTO THE CHOPPER, HE HIT THE DECK HARD
and passed out. That was the last thing Gaspar remem-
bered until waking up on board *Revenge*. Gaspar couldn't
believe his predicament. From the moment they grabbed
him he'd fought like a tiger but he knew his blows were
akin to a kitten pawing at a bear so tiny was his small
frame compared to the muscle bound louts in Unzega's
employ. After the chopper landed on board *Revenge*,
Gaspar was carried down to a room that looked to him
like it must be Unzega's command center. Unzega followed his troop below decks and instructed his henchmen
to tie Gaspar to the big chair behind the desk.

"Bind his bare feet to the chair legs and his torso to
the chair back, and leave his hands free." Unzega barked.

<br />

<br />

<br />

<br />

<br />

<br />

<br />

<br />

<br />

<br />

<br />

289

When they'd done their dirty work, Unzega ordered his thugs out, ordering them to, "lock the door behind you!"

"Alright, you insignificant little sardine. I've finally got you where I want you." Unzega snarled at his captive. "If you ever want to see your mother or any of your friends again, you'll do as I say. There's a document in front of you which I've prepared for your signature and a pen to sign it with. You can read it if you want, or I can tell you what it says because either way I expect you to sign, whether you want to or not. It is a deed, transferring the 500,000 acre land grant of Perdido Isle over to me, Unzega. I'll make this easy for you. If you don't *sign*, I'll *hurt* your mother. If you think I'm bluffing, I can assure you … I'm not. I have her right here … on board. For the moment she's well. The silly woman thinks she's on a midnight pleasure cruise, but I can promise you that once I get through with her, she won't remember tonight with any pleasure. If you don't sign that document, you're both going to regret it." Unzega hissed his final threat at his tightly bound hostage.

"*You vain venomed villainous varlot*, I'll never give you Perdido Isle, *never*! You can threaten me all you want, but I won't change my mind. I don't believe my mother's on this ship. She would never go sailing with you *willingly*. Show her to me, and I might change my mind, but only after I'm assured that she's safe and sound on dry land." Gaspar raged.

"*You brazen spawn of an unmuzzled, sheep-biting rats-bane*. You dare give Unzega, an ultimatum. Have you forgotten who's the prisoner and who's the pirate here."

"Maybe because *he* knows something *you* don't … you *puking knotty-pated malt-worm*!"

Gaspar was speachless hearing the voice of *Uncle Charlie* bellowing from across the room.

"*Carlos Munoz-Flores y Gaspar*," Unzega spat the name, more surprised than pleased to see Uncle Charlie standing in Unzega's command center. Charlie was dressed like a Buccaneer, wearing an embroidered red velvet cape and a huge red velvet hat adorned with white ostrich plumes. "You always did have an overly theatrical way of dressing." Unzega remarked snidely.

"Which is more than I could ever say about you *Moises*. You've *never* had *any style*. Look at you, nothings changed, your just a common drug runner, kidnapper, extortionist and thief."

"Words Señor, you were always so full of *words*." Unzega snarled.

"And *action*," Uncle Charlie insisted. "You haven't forgotten the night I handed you over to Davey Jones. You made a pretty package all tied up with ribbons and a bow as you sank to the ocean floor."

"You filthy crook. That *treasure* was as much mine as yours. I did all the work. I was the lout you ordered around and lorded over. The great nobleman, *Don Carlos*. How I hated you then and how I hate you now, and that

goes double for what's left of your miserable family too."
He snarled, motioning towards Gaspar still helplessly
bound to the chair. "I've come back for revenge, and I
will at last *take* what was always *mine* to begin with!" The
evil man screeched his outrage at Uncle Charlie.

"You'll *never* have Perdido Isle, or the *treasure*,
you *addle-pated lump of anthracitic ectoplasm*," Carlos
Haddocked to Gaspars delight. "And you'll certainly
never occupy La Rinconada. I would see it destroyed
first." Uncle Charlie shouted, then turned around dramatically, making a full circle, his cape flourishing as he
did so and when he was once again facing Unzega, he
magically held a glistening sword with a jeweled hilt in
his elegantly kid gloved hand.

Without another word, but with a flick of his bony
wrist, Unzega produced a similarly menacing rapier as
if by magic and struck a threatening pose.

"*En garde*." He addressed Uncle Charlie.

Gaspar couldn't believe his eyes, he was about to
watch a fight to the finish with swords. His Father had
taken him to several exhibition matches years ago and
he'd written a paper for school about what he'd learned
but he knew that what he had seen in exhibition was
childsplay compared to what he was about to experience
now.

Charlie responded, starting the *attaque* with a
graceful lunge at his enemy, extending his sword arm,
continuously threatening the *unholy spirit*. "Banshee

be gone," Uncle Charlie hollered as he initiated his offensive action.

Gaspar watched in horror as the two combatants dueled. Never was there an *absence de fer*, when their blades didn't touch.

Unzega performed a *balestra* successfully jumping forward, following up with a *fleche* as he lunged towards Uncle Charlie. Fired by rage, they continued their *conversation* with a constant back-and-forth play of their blades in a fencing match composed of *phrases d' armes* punctuated by gaps of no blade action at all as they circled each other threateningly. The two then went at each other, *corps* à *corps*, body-to-body although actual physical contact between the two spectral fencers appeared impossible.

That's when Gaspar realized he wasn't watching two mortal men dueling at all, rather, he was watching two *phantoms* fighting to the finish. Uncle Charlie had called Unzega, Moises. That's when Gaspar realized … *The evil drug dealer was the ghost of Charlie's old servant Moises, the man who had tried to kill Uncle Charlie over 100 years ago.*

The two ghostly enemies, went after each other mercilessly, flying through the air, dodging each others thrusts, and ripping through each others garments. First to go was Uncle Charlie's plumed hat, and then his cape, but Unzega fared no better. His floppy felt hat was off too, and his black shawl now hung in ribbons. Gaspar held his breath as Uncle Charlie commenced *his contre-attaque*. In response to Charlies aggressive moves, Unzega mounted his *contre-temps* in opposition to Charlies *parry of the counter-attack*. Charlie then performed a *contre-dégagement* in the opposite direction, deceiving Unzega into a less advantageous position. Unzega, rejoined with a *coup de taille*, made with a chopping motion of his blade, which landed on Uncle Charlie's shoulder with it's edge.

"You'll have to do better than that, you devilish fiend." Uncle Charlie roared, coming around to the opposite side of Unzega's blade with his counter-parry or *contre-parade*.

Gaspar knew that the moment of truth had arrived. Uncle Charlie saw his opening and quickly made his move.

With a blood-curdling, "*Touche*," Charlie thrust his sword forward, piercing the black-heart of his enemies soul. "*Begone, spawn of Satan*," Uncle Charlie, commanded.

Gaspar watched, wide eyed as Unzega or Moises, or *the son of darkness himself*, disappeared.. evaporate … dematerialize … . "poof."

"Uncle Charlie, are you alright?" Gaspar called from behind the desk where he had witnessed the brutal sword fight, still tied to the chair.

"I'm fine Gasp," said Uncle Charlie, without any sign of fatigue, "Moises was never a very good swordsman."

"Uncle Charlie, is my mom alright?" Gaspar asked anxiously.

"At home and happy, you have nothing to worry about my boy." Charlie assured him.

"Thank God." Gaspar exhaled, "Uncle, get with it, untie me … please!" Gaspar squirmed trying to get free.

"Gaspar, *you* get with it," Uncle Charlie answered facetiously, "haven't you figured out yet that I can't do anything physical. I can't untie those cords, I can't lift the treasure, I can't drive a car, or turn on your bathtub taps for that matter. You've never touched me, but believe me, there's nothing here," the ghost informed him.

"But I saw you drive a car." Gaspar corrected him.

"A fantasy car, a mirage, something I wanted you to see, like my clothes. Look, I can change clothes anytime I want, and I never ever have to close a button or pull up a zipper or tie a shoe lace or a necktie for that matter, watch," and with that, Charlie changed his entire costume and stood in the middle of the room wearing a very theatrical looking admiral's uniform. "Get it? I'm a ghost, not flesh and blood, and Moises or Unzega or whatever he was calling himself was exactly the same. He has all these mortal goons working for him, doing whatever he tells them to. They prepared that paper for you to sign and placed it on the desk. Anything he wanted moved or removed was done for him. That's the power of money here on earth, and he amassed a lot of it … all illegally I can assure you.

"How'd you know where to find me." Gaspar asked relieved that his ordeal was almost over. "Gasp, let's just say I'm your guardian. I'll always have your back.".

"Thanks, Uncle Charlie, you've saved my life." Gaspar smiled. "When the police get here, what shall I tell them about Unzega?" Gaspar wondered.

"How are you supposed to know what happened to that *hell-hated jolthead.* Just tell them that he heard them coming and must have thrown himself overboard rather than be arrested. I'll see you back at the house, Gasp," Uncle Charlie winked as he passed through the door.

Back at the Coast Guard station, Gaspar had a happy reunion with his buddies.

"Looks like that's the last you're ever gonna see of Unzega," Alex exhaled, clapping his best friend on the shoulder.

"And good riddance too," Gaspar spat, a huge smile crossing his face. "Imagine that *mangy cockroach*, thinking that I'd hand over La Rinconada just so he could traffic his drugs undisturbed, the pompous gasbag. That's the last I have to say on the subject of that *bald-headed budgerigar!*" As usual Gaspar always got in the last word, even if he had to borrow it from Captain Haddock himself.

# CHAPTER 32

# TYING UP THE LOOSE ENDS

WHEN GASPAR GOT TO POLICE HEADQUARTERS WITH SERGEANT O'MALLEY, HE FOUND HIS MOTHER AND Peter waiting for him in Captain Morgan's office. After a very teary reunion, with hugs and kisses from Elvira, Gaspar shook hands with Captain Morgan and thanked him for his help.

"Come and sit down Gaspar," the Police Captain motioned to a chair, "that was good work my boy. Let me compliment you on a job well done. You won't believe what Jacobson found on board, *Revenge*. Not only all the evidence that Unzega has been running drugs, but an old friend of yours was also aboard."

"Who?" Gaspar asked confused.

"Miss Gwendolyn Crump. She had also been kidnapped. She was on her way to the airport in Mobile, and says that she was whisked away in a black Olds Cutlass by two men who carjacked her while she was trying to leave the island. The men were operatives working for Unzega who Crump had presumably double-crossed. Anyway, she spilled the beans the minute we picked her up. She and Unzega had well laid plans to get their hands on your property ... I'm talking about, the entire island. Apparently Unzega, with Crump, *she now says that she was just an unwilling accomplice*, made two attempts on your life, once in a Le —"

"The red LeSabre," Gaspar exhaled.

"And twice here on the island." Chief Morgan continued.

"The black Olds Cutlass," Gaspar concluded.

"Precisely, Gaspar and the near miss from the mysterious scuba diver.

"I knew it." Gaspar's ire was up.

"Anyway," Captain Morgan continued, "according to Crump, Unzega wanted your land in the worst possible way for all kinds of nefarious reasons. The FBI has had their eye on him for years and years, but could never pin anything on him. Your tip tonight has brought down the whole consortium, of which Unzega was the king pin."

"What about Gwendolyn Crump?" Elvira asked. "What has she to say for herself?"

"The woman is hysterical," Sergeant O'Malley offered. "She's in the next room now, would you like to listen in."

O'Malley stood up and pulled a curtain on the opposite wall, exposing a two way mirror which looked into the next room. Pushing a button on the wall, he turned on a speaker which allowed his guests to listen to what was being said. Jumping up to join the Sergeant, Gaspar, Elvira and Peter saw *The Crump*, pacing back and forth in front of a prison matron, wringing her hands while crying in a loud pretentious voice.

"… how was *I* to know that monster was a *drug* dealer? Oh that terrible man, and to think that I actually had him to a party in my house. Oh the ignominy, *l'ignominie*" she brought out her best French guns before continuing. "And to think that … *that two-timing tinker* actually tricked me into thinking he was a Spanish aristocrat! You know dear," she sprinkled some sugar in the direction of the matron, "that I, of all the people on this island, would never have invited just a plain old nobody into *my* house. The very thought of me … a Crump … a *social arbiter* of renown, a Llojeta *débutante* no less, inviting a *drug-dealing loser*, to sit at *my* table! Well you can see how this whole situation is just absurd. I'm sure that a jury of *my peers* will understand my predicament entirely, no offense to you, of course, sweetie."

Gaspar and his friends had heard enough and O'Malley pushed the button cutting off the rant from the other side of the glass and closed the curtain.

"With Unzega missing or probably dead and Crump's plans for quick riches dashed, she certainly has changed her tune." Chief Morgan laughed.

"Did she say anything about Unzega?" Gaspar wondered.

"She told us that when she saw him onboard *Revenge*, after he'd abducted her, that he was out of his mind with rage. That he kept mumbling over and over again something about *Moises Revenge, Moises Revenge*. When she asked him what he was talking about, he told her something like, *Charles Munoz-Flores y Gaspar stole the island and the treasure from Moises, then killed him*. He's actually claiming that the island and all of your inheritance rightfully belongs to the Moises person. What do you think he's talking about? Have you ever heard of this Moises character? And what did he mean by, *the treasure*, she says he kept going on and on about *some treasure*?" Chief Morgan shrugged his shoulders at the three friends seated across from him.

"No clue," Gaspar lied.

"Me, neither," confessed Elvira.

"Don't look at me." Peter shook his head.

•••

The only thing people were talking about at Karen's counter the next day, was the big arrest and drug bust.

"Have you heard the news?" Karen asked Gaspar and Alex when they came in to the café for sodas the next afternoon. Not waiting for an answer she launched into her tale of drugs and mayhem. "Beverwil was picked up on some trumped up blackmail charges leveled at him by Gwendolyn Crump, but he was later released for lack of evidence. Meanwhile, he turned O'Malley and Jacobson onto some information they used to tail Crump to a secret rendezvous with Unzega. She was meeting the greaser to buy herself some drugs. While she was there foreign kidnappers captured her and tried to sell her into white slavery, but thanks to Beverwil Chief Morgan was on top of the whole thing and came in a police helicopter and rescued Crump and Unzega and all the Italian Mafia boys who'd been sent to kidnap *Dear Gwennie*. What no one can figure out" she pondered breathlessly, is why they would want Crump in the first place. But crime is *crime*! If it weren't for Beverwil, who was a witness to the entire raid, blood could have been running in the streets and none of us would ever have known about it. He's been interviewed by all the papers, radio and even television too, but I don't think it's for a channel we get down here? Anyway, thank God for Beverwil, *the old sissy*. If it weren't for him, the local cops would probably have bungled the whole thing and then hushed it up like they always do. You boys need to talk with Floyd to get all the facts."

Gaspar and Alex took one look at each other and broke into hysterical laughter. Holding their guts they stumbled out of the café without ordering and fell onto the sidewalk in stitches.

# CHAPTER 33

# THE END OF SUMMER VACATION

THE LAST DAY OF SUMMER VACATION WAS THE SUNDAY BEFORE SCHOOL WAS TO START. GASPAR AND ALEX spent the entire day together, revisiting all the places and recounting all the adventures they'd experienced together during the past three months. Riding their bikes, one of the first sights they visited was the church.

"This church will have to be a project for us Al. It needs a lot of help and a lot of work to bring it back to it's original glory. Wouldn't it be nice if we could turn it over to the diocese as a consecrated place of worship to say Mass in again." Gaspar dreamed.

"I won't be an altar boy!" Alex protested.

"Don't be ridiculous, Al. I don't think either of us are *altar boy material*." Gaspar assured him.

Later they rode over to the tower and the air strip. "I wonder how much it would take to make it amazing again," Gaspar asked Al. Both boys still dreamed of flying but Gaspar knew that the possibility was probably still years away.

They took a swim at Smugglers Cove, the new name that they'd christened the beach where all the action had been, and sat on the beach afterwards discussing the beauty of the setting. "This would be a great site for a beach shack," Alex suggested.

"Yeah, Al. Good idea. Tell you what, you design it, and I'll build it." Gaspar enthused.

Jumping on their bikes they visited Llojeta, and had lunch at the Grand Hotel Floride While in town, they stuck their heads inside The Villa Gaspar, the house in that town that Gaspar wanted to turn into his clubhouse. "Before we build a beach shack, Al, I think we should concentrate on making this a cool clubhouse for our class mates. Wha-da-ya think?" Gaspar asked.

"Good idea, can't wait." Alex was in. "Let's do it first thing, I'm with you all the way."

Heading home, they stopped by the old swimming hole. "You know Al, we should have a water polo team at school. We should start one."

"Good idea Gasp, we could train in the pool at La Rinconada." Alex suggested.

"We've got to fix up the pool first so the guys can come over and practice." Gaspar was impressed at how easily his ideas for creatively spending money materialize right out of the blue lately.

"It will be amazing Gasp, we can compete against all the other schools in Florida and probably win the championship." Alex couldn't wait to get started.

That night before turning in, Gaspar had a long chat with Uncle Charlie, up in the Captain's Cabin, reminiscing and making plans for the future. Gaspar was sitting at the desk in shorts and a t-shirt and Uncle Charlie was perched on the desktop dressed for big game hunting.

"I never would have thought when I first met you Gasp that you would turn out to be such a trooper." Uncle Charlie complimented him. "You not only found Gasparilla's treasure, but you raised the *Argente* too. I'm proud of you boy … the way you take care of your Mom and honor your Dad is commendable and I like how you're so inclusive with all your new friends."

"No one is more surprised than I am, Uncle. I never would have dreamed when I left L.A. that Florida was going to be such an adventure. Every day has brought something new into my life. Some of it was beautiful and some of it was scary, but all of it was life changing. Best of all, I'm not scared anymore, I can tell you that. No more butterflies." He smiled.

"Good for you Gasp. I like the way you meet life head on. That's how people are going to know that you're the boss!" Uncle Charlie assured him. "Listen, I've got a date with a lion-hunting baroness in Mombasa now, so if you'll excuse me, I'll check in with you tomorrow before you head off to school." Charlie chuckled.

"Goodnight Uncle. Have fun. I'll see you in the morning I hope, or at least after school, I'm sure I'll have a lot to tell you." Gaspar yawned.

When Gaspar finally turned out the light next to his bunk, his thoughts turned to starting school in the morning in a new school with a whole new group of friends. He wondered what new adventures the coming days would bring, and where they would take him. Little did he know that, *The Mystery of the Seminole Spring*, would soon pose more danger and bring more excitement to him and his friends.